KING OF THE WEEDS
A MIKE HAMMER NOVEL

MORE MIKE HAMMER
FROM TITAN BOOKS

KING OF THE WEEDS

A MIKE HAMMER NOVEL

MICKEY SPILLANE
and
MAX ALLAN COLLINS

TITANBOOKS

King of the Weeds: A Mike Hammer Novel
Print-edition ISBN: 9780857689788
E-book edition ISBN: 9780857689542

Published by Titan Books
A division of Titan Publishing Group Ltd
144 Southwark St, London SE1 0UP

First mass market edition: November 2015

1 3 5 7 9 10 8 6 4 2

This is a work of fiction. Names, characters, places, and incidents either
are the product of the author's imagination or are used fictitiously, and
any resemblance to actual persons, living or dead, business establishments,
events, or locales is entirely coincidental. The publisher does not have any
control over and does not assume any responsibility for author or third-
party websites or their content.

Mickey Spillane and Max Allan Collins assert the moral right to be identified
as the authors of this work.

A CIP catalogue record for this title is available from the British Library.

Printed and bound in the United States.

In memory of
the screen's first Mike Hammer
**BIFF ELLIOT
(1923-2012)**

CO-AUTHOR'S NOTE

Shortly before his death in 2006, Mickey Spillane told his wife Jane, "When I'm gone, there's going to be a treasure hunt around here. Take everything you find and give it to Max—he'll know what to do."

Half a dozen substantial Mike Hammer manuscripts were found in the "treasure hunt," often accompanied by plot notes, rough outlines and even drafts of final chapters. These lost Hammer novels spanned Mickey's career, from the late '40s through the mid-'60s and on up to *The Goliath Bone*, which he was working on at the time of his passing.

Mickey conceived *King of the Weeds* as the final Mike Hammer, and a sequel to *Black Alley* (1996), the last Hammer published during his lifetime. He set it aside after 9/11 to respond to that attack in *The Goliath Bone* (2008). The time frame here is the late '90s, with Mike in his mid-sixties; realistically, he should be around ten years older, but readers will just have to live with that—Mickey did.

It has been my great honor to complete these six substantial Mike Hammer manuscripts, and my love and thanks go to both Mickey and Jane Spillane. A familiarity with *Black Alley*, incidentally, is not a requirement here.

M.A.C.

CHAPTER ONE

When you suddenly realize you're about to be killed, all your mind does is tell you that you were dumb. You had the experience, you had the physical abilities, you had the animal instincts.

But you were dumb.

Maybe you had played the game too long. Maybe that last round of injuries had left a deeper wound than you thought.

The little man in the tailored navy blue suit, a raincoat draped over his right arm, was waiting on my floor when the elevator opened and I stepped out. He never raised his head to look at me, the brim of his pale blue hat even with my nose. He smelled faintly of too-strong aftershave. I thought nothing of it, but did wonder why that raincoat was dry on a rainy morning like this.

So I got off and began to walk away, knowing—just

a stupid fraction of a second later than I should have—that he was a killer and I was the target, and I jerked my head around to see the face of the bastard who would take me down. He was just inside the elevator, his foot holding the door open while he aimed the silenced gun at me from six feet away, the weapon emerging for a good look at me from under that draped raincoat, and both of us knew there was no hope for me at all, because it was six-thirty in the morning and no one but me would be on the eighth floor this early.

Reflex action worked before thought, and while he fired I was dropping and turning, clawing for a gun that wasn't there any more, but my movement didn't spoil his aim. Both shots pounded into my chest right at the heart region and I hit the carpet with my breath hissing through my teeth as the killer got on the elevator, his back to me, and the door *snicked* shut.

I fought to get air into my lungs, but the double stunning blow was like a paralyzing hand trying to squeeze the life right out of me. I let my torso twist a little and the motion allowed other muscles to take over and I was able to breathe, barely. In ten seconds I tried again and sucked down a bit more air. Rushing things wouldn't help. Nobody was going to see me lumped down on the new carpet. Thirty years ago, hell twenty, I'd have realized his bullets hadn't killed me and sucked up the pain and headed for the stairs to chase him down, my .45 in my fist.

What I did today was stay floored a good ten minutes

until I was breathing almost normally, then somehow got my feet under me and stood unsteadily up.

There were two cigarette-burn holes in my damp trenchcoat as I stumbled to my office and opened the door that read MICHAEL HAMMER INVESTIGATIONS. Only when I had locked it behind me did I reach inside the flap of my coat and yank out the paperback dictionary my secretary Velda had asked me to pick up for her at Coliseum Books. I had stuck it in my inside coat pocket on the elevator when I'd reached in my pants for my keys. Two twenty-two caliber holes were punched into the volume and never wholly penetrated the two and a half inches of paper.

Mister Webster had saved my life, and as I stumbled to a chair, dropping my trenchcoat and suitcoat and unbuttoning my shirt clumsily, I thanked whatever kismet had made Velda dissatisfied with her word processor's dictionary on the new computer that replaced her old typewriter. Still, there was one hell of a black-and-blue blossom blooming on my chest.

Soon I heard Velda's key in the lock, and when she closed the door and turned, her body snapped into momentary rigidity, her eyes wide with the shock of seeing me sitting where I shouldn't be, turned toward her in the visitor's chair at her desk, my shirt wide open, the bruise on my chest like a bull's-eye in a target.

But there were no melodramatics. No wide eyes, no girlish scream. This was a woman, a beautiful woman who could make men decades her junior stop and stare. A woman who was a partner in this business, with her own P.I. ticket and a .22 automatic that had punched other people's tickets, when need be.

She tossed her attaché case on her desk like a bored postman delivering the mail and was out of her poncho in another second, standing there in front of me—statuesque, raven-haired, with a shoulder-brushing page boy that thumbed its nose at changing fashion, and a body that made a silk beige blouse and brown knee-length skirt seem provocative.

On the fourth finger of her left hand was a two-carat emerald-cut diamond set in gold. We'd been unofficially engaged for decades. Officially so for about a year, like the ring said.

Her eyes took me in—she knew something was as wrong as it could be, but there was no blood showing anywhere. I was breathing regularly and didn't seem to be in severe pain.

Her voice was low and throaty, her tone business-like, but the concern was under there. "So what happened this time, Mike?"

"I got shot. Twice." I nodded down at the discoloration on my chest.

Her eyes followed mine, tightening to see if an entry wound was hiding in all that purple, but not finding one. "I don't see any new holes."

I shook my head. "No. No new holes. But it hurt like a son of a bitch. Like Mike Tyson laid a couple on me."

"So did you borrow that fancy lightweight body armor again?" she asked, looming over me.

"No. You were there to save me, kitten."

She blinked. "Remind me."

"I was wearing that dictionary you had me pick up." I pointed to her desktop nearby.

Then she smiled, nodding, getting it. She picked the book up, opened it until she could see the tail of both .22 slugs, then felt the pair of bulges where the noses had come to rest. She folded down the back cover and thumbed some pages away.

"They stopped at page six-nineteen," she said. "If you play the numbers today, make it that one."

I had to grin at her, such a cool cookie, but I wondered how she would have reacted if she had tripped over my body coming out the elevator.

The clock on the far wall said it was five minutes to seven and it wouldn't be long before the photographers from the magazine outfit down the hall would be coming in.

So I said to Velda, "Go out by the elevator and see if you can find any shell casings. Ring the elevator up and look in there too."

She didn't ask questions. The game was on now. The first move had been made, a sudden, decisive and explosive move that was supposed to take out a major player, and it hadn't worked.

But what game were we playing?

Velda came back in three minutes, shaking her head,

hands empty. "Nothing. No brass on the floor at all and the elevator was clean."

"What I expected. He stood just inside the elevator, the rod in his right hand, and it ejected to the right. The casings would have landed on the floor in there, and he retrieved them on the ride down."

"Expecting you'd be dead by then."

"Oh yeah. He was a real pro, all right. He nailed me with two shots an inch apart while I was falling and twisting and if I hadn't had your little book under my coat, those slugs would have torn my heart apart worse than any woman ever did."

Velda ignored that, but her tongue made a nervous pass across her lips and a small shudder touched her shoulders. Then her eyes narrowed in thought. "Your back was to him, wasn't it?"

I nodded.

She stated, "Pro killers who use a .22 go for head shots."

"Generally."

"And you couldn't have been more than three feet away."

I shrugged and it hurt some. "More like six. I came out of the elevator too fast. He had to move back a step and re-position. He was moving when I realized what was going down and started to turn. My heart area was a secondary target, and a better one, and he didn't miss. He saw me hit the deck. Some place he's licking his lips and counting his money."

"Not if he's the pro you think he was."

"Yeah?"

"Mike, think it through. He'd want definite confirmation. So would his contractor."

"So you figure... when he finds out he missed... he may try again."

"He's *going* to try again."

I grinned at her. "Still sure you're up for marrying me?"

She took a deep breath and picked up my trenchcoat where I dumped it on the floor nearby. Her fingers found the twin holes but were too big to go in them.

"I guess so," she said, going over to hang up the coat, "but it would be nice if your hobby wasn't getting shot."

"I'm weaning myself off that, doll."

But just her speaking of it brought on the big ache.

On that cold, cold night, I had come to the piers under West Side Drive to warn Don Lorenzo Ponti that a hit was going down, courtesy of a rival family. I had no great love for the man, in fact had caused him some trouble earlier but thought I might catch the blame if I didn't give him a heads up.

When I pulled in behind the black limo, I saw no sign at all of an ambush. He stepped off that old cargo ship he'd sneaked home on, and I was getting out of my car as the first shots rang out, and then they came rushing out of the woodwork, with military precision, the Gaetano soldiers, guns and breath smoking in the chill. I'd been too late to do my good deed, and with bullets flying in a war I wanted no part of, I made it back for my car...

…but the don's crazy kid Azi saw me, read me as a hostile, and came at me head on, his .357 belching fire and metal and catching me twice in the left side. I went down on my back and half-rolled and then he was on top of me, that big barrel pointing down at my face, but he took a moment to savor the thought of splattering me to hell, and my fist with the .45 swung up and one fat ball-and-cap slug took the top of his head off and ended a nothing life.

So that made me the big winner, only Azi's two bullets had churned into me like torpedoes intent on taking down a sub and then my guts were vomiting blood through two new orifices…

My hand ran down where I had been hit last year. It was healed now, but I'd always know when it was going to rain. I still couldn't quite take the weight of my .45 snugged down under my arm on that side and had gotten so used to it not being there that I rarely carried it any more. No need, right?

Right?

"Mike… Mike! I lost you there for a moment."

"I'm here, kitten."

"Who was it? Who did this to you?"

I described the killer as best I could, but it was pretty sketchy, mostly just the natty blue suit and hat and the slightness of him. I hadn't expected the attack, and his face had been obscured by his hat brim.

"And I saw very damn little when the slugs were pounding into me," I said.

"You're going soft on me."

"One thing—he smelled of aftershave."

"What kind?"

"Beats me. I'm strictly an Old Spice guy. Maybe something foreign. But I'll know it again if I smell it." I tapped my nose. "I didn't make it in this business so long not having a good one of these."

She was frowning in thought—that trick of hers that managed it without wrinkling much of anything. "He was here waiting for you."

"Right."

"Well, how'd your new friend know you'd be here this early?"

"That's no secret. I'm always here early."

"But it's not standard business hours for this or any building," she reminded me. "And our answer machine gives office hours as starting at nine."

We liked having some time to deal with paperwork and ongoing casework before seeing any paying customers.

"So he's been watching us," I said.

"Him or somebody he works with, or for," she said. "Which I don't love."

"I don't love it either, knowing that we've been under somebody's gaze and neither one of us picked up on it."

She nodded, her dark eyes hard. "Us or any of the Hackard Building lobby staffers. They know by now the kind of attention Mike Hammer can attract."

"Well, I don't attract the attention I used to."

She wiggled a finger at the growing bruise, already a rhapsody in sick discoloration. "Really? You'd never guess. What the hell is this about, Mike? What enemies have you… have *we*… made lately?"

"Let me mull that," I said. "Meantime, better call Pat, then make us some coffee."

"Woman's work never being done."

"I'm not chauvinistic, I'm wounded."

"You're a wounded chauvinist."

Velda did all that, giving Pat the basic facts but asking him to come alone. Soon she and I were seated on the couch in the outer office, waiting for Pat, my feet up on a chair, hers nicely crossed, as we sipped coffee— Dunkin' Donuts special blend, the best medicine this side of Four Roses.

"What if this isn't a *new* enemy?" I asked. My shirt was still unbuttoned and I occasionally ran my fingers lightly over the massive bruise.

She arched an eyebrow. "Well, you have your share of old ones. Anyone in particular?"

I shook my head, but then something came to me. Just conversationally, I asked her, "You see that piece in the *News* last week? About the Rudy Olaf case getting a fresh look?"

"Rudy Olaf… why do I know that name? But, no, I didn't see that piece."

I shrugged. "It was a glorified squib. And this goes back to before you were working for me. I'd just gone into business, Pat was walking a beat. This was way, way back, doll. At the beginning."

"Mike, you're talking forty years ago!"

With a nod, I said, "It was the case that made Pat Chambers. Nobody ever became a captain quicker on the NYPD. Of course, nobody has stayed one *longer*…"

She smirked at me. "No captain of homicide ever had a best friend like Mike Hammer as an albatross around his neck, either."

"Kitten, that's unkind. I've helped Pat close out all kinds of cases."

"Yes, but usually with the working end of your .45."

I waved that off. "That was the old days, sugar. But we're talking about the *very* old days with Rudy Olaf. He was a kid, like Pat and me… well, he was a little older maybe. He was a combat veteran, European theater. I was in the Pacific, as was Pat. We both lied about our ages to get in, did you know that?"

"I may have heard that a couple of thousand times. But Rudy Olaf? He may be old news to you, Mike, but he's new news to me."

I stared into nothing in particular. "Like I said, it was the case that made Pat, so it's an embarrassment that it's being re-examined after all this time. Funny thing is, it was just dumb luck. We were sitting in a diner after Pat finished walking his beat, still in his uniform, having coffee… of course, not as good as this, doll."

"Skip the soft soap. What happened?"

"The most wanted suspect in town wandered in. Pat made him from an APB description that had gone around to all the precincts, went over for a friendly chat and the guy saw all that blue coming his way and made a break for it."

"And you didn't just shoot him?"

"No, Pat tackled him out on the sidewalk. My role was strictly to find a call box to phone it in."

"Pat couldn't radio it in?"

"Vel, this was forty years ago. Street cops weren't wired into personal radio communications. Anyway, I made the call and in two minutes a squad car came on the scene and transported the suspect. Pat went with them. I stayed out of it until I was requested to give a statement later."

She cocked her head and one wing of raven hair hung prettily. "What was Olaf wanted for?"

"Multiple murders. Today we'd call him a serial killer. He had knocked off nine guys who had staggered out of saloons, luring them into oddball places, shot and robbed them, all in a two-month period."

"Shot them dead?"

"As hell, kid."

Velda didn't need that new computer—she had a mind that contained computer-like information. I watched her eyes narrow while her sensors searched for answers she had stored away. When the expression on her face unlocked I knew she had finally found it.

"They called it the Bowery Bum slayings," she said.

I nodded. "Today it would be the Homeless Homicides, but a rose by any other."

She was frowning as the vague outlines of a very old,

notorious case took shape in her mind. "He killed his victims. How did they ever get a description for an APB?"

"On the last kill, a kid saw Olaf coming up from the front basement stairs where he'd left his latest victim. Kid recognized Olaf as a guy from a tenement two blocks over."

She squinted at me, trying to pull all this into focus. "What made a random character coming up some basement steps suspicious?"

"The kid heard the gunshot. Oh, he didn't know that's what it was at first—it was just a sound, a very muted *pop*."

A slow nod from her. "So the gun was silenced."

"Yeah. But it was loud enough for the kid to wait till the guy was out of sight and then go down to check things out…"

"And find a fresh body."

"Very damn fresh. The kid walked over to the precinct house and told the story to the desk sergeant. A team hit the suspect's flop, but he wasn't there. A warrant was issued, the cops forced an entry, and inside, neatly arranged on a shelf, were four wallets, each one belonging to one of the dead victims. There was no evidence of a gun or a silencer, no money either, but that was enough for an APB."

She paused to search her memory some more, then said, "And it didn't hit the papers till later, right?"

"Right. Good recall, kitten. Yeah, in those days reporters had some goddamn sense—not that any information was offered to the press. Two days later, Rudy Olaf walks right into Pat's arms with me as a witness to a quick and careful arrest procedure."

The frown creased Velda's forehead again. "Olaf didn't get a death sentence, did he? Despite so many murders. It was life, wasn't it?"

"That's right," I told her. "General feeling was, had the cops located the gun, Olaf would have gotten the hot squat at that big emporium on the Hudson."

She smirked cutely at me. "Mike, you have got to stop talking like that. People are starting to look at you funny."

"Okay, excuse the archaic terminology. Sing Sing."

"No chair there now."

"No. They go the lethal injection route. Progress."

Velda got up, paced thoughtfully a little, then went over to her desk and hiked herself up on the edge of it, her dress inching up her thighs. She knew I was looking and tugged it back in place.

"Don't get any ideas," she said with a soft laugh. "You're wounded, remember."

"Wounded, not dead," I said quietly.

"Such a famous case, and a serial killer…" She shook her head, the dark hair shimmering. "I'm surprised the media hasn't made something out of it being re-opened."

"You know how it is, kitten. Anything not emanating from Washington or a plane blowing apart from a terrorist attack or one of our embassies overseas being hit with a car bomb is hardly news."

I leaned back in my chair and ran my hand over my chest. The bruise mark had spread farther than my stretched palm. Now the black and blue discoloration had streaks of red and purple beginning to show and the ache seemed to come from the ribs, rather than the flesh.

"Hurt, lover?" she asked.

"Stupid question."

"So get back to old Olaf. After forty years, even a mass murderer with a clean nose might have a shot at parole."

"But Olaf doesn't want parole. He was eligible twenty years ago. But he's never copped."

"Never confessed?"

"Nope. Haven't you heard? He's innocent—like everybody else in the slammer."

I didn't have to remind her that in the last few years DNA test results had gotten a lot of wrongly convicted prisoners an overdue walk into the fresh air. The stink from a review of some cases has really made some notables squirm, so when Olaf's came up, it was one of those "Man, let's get him out of our face" jobs.

"But so what, Mike? They had a *witness*…"

"One witness—a kid with a juvie record. About two years later, he gets set up on a robbery beef and shoots his mouth off to another inmate about getting Rudy Olaf nailed for the sheer hell of it. Or almost the sheer hell—Olaf had cussed him out on the street one time."

She gave me a doubtful half-smile. "That doesn't

even make sense. Why go to that trouble over somebody just cursing you out? After what the kid claimed got reported, he got talked to hard, right? To see if his story held?"

I shook my head. "No. The story got reported, but it was strictly hearsay. That young witness against Rudy Olaf died in prison. Shiv in the shower. Same old sweet song."

Her eyebrows shrugged. "Well, some second-hand rumor attributed to a dead con isn't enough to get *anybody* a new trial."

"It didn't stop Olaf's lawyers from trying. And that second-hand statement went on the record book all those years ago... and is still there."

This time her frown was deep enough to risk wrinkles. "Mike... something had to have happened recently to get the case looked at again."

"It has. Somebody out of the past stepped up and confessed."

"After all these years?" Her voice was tinged with amazement.

"Henry Brogan, an old crony of Olaf's who lived down the street came in out of the blue and copped. Said he'd needed the money for medical bills—seems he had a very sick kid. So Brogan started pulling these small robberies and killing his victims to stop eyewitness identification. Then that kid ID'd Olaf, and Brogan seized the opportunity—he beat the cops to Olaf's pad and planted the wallets where they'd be easily found."

"How did he get into Olaf's apartment?"

"Brogan knew where Olaf hid his key. I told you they were cronies. Olaf had nothing worth stealing up there. He only kept the door locked to keep somebody from getting to his wine bottle."

"Prints on the wallets?"

"Brogan was smart enough to wipe his off by smudging them."

Still frowning, she asked, "But couldn't the lab boys find *anything*...?"

"Some things slip by the board, kitten."

"That slip took *forty years* out of Olaf's life."

I gave her a nasty grin. "*If* Brogan is telling the truth."

Her frown vanished. "You doubt him?"

"Why, Velda? Do *you* like Brogan's story? A sick kid—T.B., I think it was—and he decides to pay the medics by pulling a string of petty robberies in the damn Bowery? If you're going to rob and kill, doll, it's only a bus or subway ride to Park Avenue."

"So you don't buy Olaf's innocence?"

I sneered at her. "In a pig's ass I buy it. I feel sorry for Pat having this get stirred up, toward the end of a fine career."

That got a sympathetic series of nods from her. "So what happens now?"

"Waste no tears on Rudy Olaf—he has himself a very high-priced criminal lawyer... Rufus Tomlin."

Her eyes widened for a moment. "Big media ties there!"

"Big mob ties, too."

She just stared at me for a few seconds. "Man of mine, you just got shot. Witnessing an arrest forty years ago doesn't buy you that kind of attention."

"Not unless there's an angle I'm missing."

"Then who shot you, old soldier?"

When my only answer was an eyebrow shrug, she slid off the desk, got behind it, pulled a bottom drawer out, and withdrew a package. Then she looked over at me and smiled a tilted smile and came over and handed the unwrapped box to me. I could hardly move my left arm, so took it with my right.

It was heavy, much heavier than your average gift in a box of medium size, covered in silver-and-white paper, and when she saw me weighing it in my hand, she said, "That was going to be a wedding present, my darling… but I think you might need it more now."

She didn't help me. She let me peel the wrappings off in a clumsy way with my fingertips, slice the taped edges with a thumbnail, then gently lift the lid off to see a beautiful Colt .45 automatic, its blued metal totally non-reflecting as it should be, a little lethal device that came alive solely at the discretion of its handler. It had that faint smell of gun oil, an instrument almost an anachronism among modern-day weapons, but a frightening and frighteningly effective piece of machinery when its mouth was pointed at you.

"You trying to tell me something, kid?"

She smiled with pursed-kiss lips, then nodded. "I don't

want you dead, lover boy. You are in a dangerous business and if any more high-end hitters get paid to burn you, I want you to have a reasonable amount of protection."

"There's nothing wrong with my old piece."

"Yeah? Then why don't you wear it any more?"

"It's just such a big hunk of heavy metal."

"Heavy metal is music, Mike."

I hefted the new gun in my palm. "Music to my ears when I'm firing the damn thing, but—"

"Wear that on your right side for a change." She was not about to let me off the hook.

I said, "I'll take it under advisement… Give me your hand. Left one."

She gave me a puzzled look, but then slipped off the desk, showing off those classic gams again, then wandered over. She held her hand out to me like a princess doing a loyal subject a great honor. I took her fingertips gently.

"I've got a gift for you too, baby," I said, "but now's not the time. I'll just say it's a band of gold with some diamonds and it matches up perfect with this two-karat number. I'm not about to die before I can give it to you."

When she sat in my lap and kissed me, it didn't hurt at all, and I could feel the hunger in her and I wondered how I had let all those years go by before finally making this permanent, and the two of us legal.

She whispered in my ear: "Somebody has a contract out on you, my dear."

Not exactly sweet nothings.

"I know," I said.

"This is no local shooter, either."

"Yeah, and I walked straight into it. Dumb."

She slipped off my lap and sat beside me. "Mike...
he would have expected you to be carrying. You have a
Wyatt Earp reputation and no pro is going to overlook
that. He could expect you to be one heavy target to put
down, so he was ready for anything."

"The guy did his homework, sweetie. He would
have known I was still recovering from being shot."

"Come on, you can still move. Your rep saved you,
Mike—he didn't stick around to confirm the kill,
because if you weren't dead, he would be."

"Once upon a time, maybe."

"No maybe about it. But stop skating on your rep,
Mike. You have a conceal-and-carry permit. Use it."

I got up and started buttoning the shirt. "What gets
me is *why*. What good would I be dead?"

Velda retrieved my tie and slipped it over my head,
tucking it under my collar. "Eighty-nine billion bucks is
a good *why*, Mr. Hammer."

"Eighty-nine billion dollars is a good reason *not* to
kill me, doll."

"Not if somebody *else* knows where that hoard is
stashed, too, my love."

I nodded. In that case, eighty-nine billion dollars
made one hell of a good *why*. Nations would go to war
for that kind of loot, so eliminating one person should
be a simple enough matter.

But who besides Velda and me could know that a certain retirement age P.I. had a stash that size tucked away in a mountainside?

CHAPTER TWO

The $89 billion began for me with an old army buddy, Marcus Dooley. Toward the end of the war, he got Pat Chambers and me into the intelligence end of the military, steering us into police work. Pat and I had gone into the blue uniforms of the NYPD, though I quickly went private when playing by the rules became a problem.

Dooley never made it onto the force. He never bothered trying, not when he'd been mustered out on a Section Eight. He'd gone Asiatic, as we called it in the Pacific, after months of backing Pat and me up during those deadly choruses of singing bullets and blazing shrapnel. Going crazy in the insanity of combat only made sense, but tell that to the peacetime hiring corps. In the years right after the war, Dooley was nothing better than a bum, boozing, womanizing, doing odd jobs to stay afloat, and there had been nothing Pat and I could do to guide him onto a better path.

Finally Dooley fell in with a dipso dame and when a bender almost killed her, the couple staggered into a hospital and took the cure. They straightened each other out for a while, and he was running a fairly successful landscaping business in Brooklyn as recently as twenty years ago. He had a kid, too, named Marvin—well, no kid by now, probably in his forties, anyway—but the wife had died somewhere back in the fuzzy past, that liver she'd ravaged finally catching up with her. Or maybe she fell off the wagon. I don't know.

The truth is, we had lost touch. Pat delivered rumors about Dooley on occasion—the existence of the son, the passing of the wife, the business that fell apart—and the next time I heard about Marcus Dooley, he had been shot in the guts by an intruder in his house in Brooklyn. Pat had told me that, too, but it was no rumor...

We were both wounded warriors, Dooley and me. I'd just spent three months in Florida trying to get over Azi Ponti's .357 kisses in my side. I should have been dead, but it had been cold enough that night, six below, for surface blood to coagulate into cloth and skin, clotting into a kind of makeshift bandage. A washed-up drunk of a doc who happened on the scene decided to make me an experiment in redemption. He dragged me across the rough red-streaked pavement while men screaming made discordant harmony with approaching sirens.

I had not fully recuperated when Pat called me to tell me our old pal Dooley had been murdered. Well, not quite murdered yet—he was in the hospital, holding death back till he could talk to me...

And death was hovering in that hospital all right, waiting its turn with the husk of a once-husky man whose breathing was shallow and whose woozy gaze said narcotics were giving him a brief trip to Happyland before the lights went out all the way.

He'd already told Pat that he hadn't got a good enough look at the shooter to recognize him—just a dark shape in a doorway, an unlocked door shoved open onto Dooley sitting at a little desk, doing his monthly bills, fifteen feet away. Three slugs from a .357—one more than the late unlamented Azi Ponti had given me. But one more was enough to make me a survivor, and Dooley a casualty.

He didn't want to talk about getting shot at all. If I'd thought he'd called Mike Hammer to his bedside to avenge his ass, I'd got it wrong.

Dooley had a story to tell me. A story he felt he just *had* to share before cashing out...

And nobody ever cashed out richer than Marcus Dooley.

Like Congress, mob kingpins don't have term limits—they rule as long as they can last.

So the turnover at the top isn't frequent, unless a

killing war starts. Don Angelo lived to be ninety-something, and that kind of longevity was bad news for the latest generation of the five New York families. Many of them had seen their own fathers confined to minor roles, and the thought of never rising to the top while these retirement-home candidates maintained power was a bitter damn pill the Young Turks were not content to swallow.

They demanded more control, more power. They were a college-educated generation, with technological skills, a computer-savvy crowd that had done much for the Mafia cause by moving into legitimate big business. The days of booze and whores were ancient history; the new mob was high-tech crime and Wall Street finance, with unions and entertainment industry remaining from the old days but contemporized into legality. Yes, drug trafficking continued, but on so large a scale that kilos of H were tonnages now, operations insulated with Russian and Colombian confederates that assured nothing bad could come home to roost.

The dons were grateful to the young pups, paid them well, patted them on the head and back, heard their complaints and suggestions with silent understanding... but ceded no power. The new generation accepted this, perhaps too graciously. So much so that suspicions grew...

The heads of the five families checked the records, computer and otherwise, using top-end independent accountants, who delivered the bad news: the younger generation… the *youngest* generation… was using their combined computer skills to screw their elders, siphoning off income in a cutting-edge variation on the old two-sets-of-books philosophy.

For now, the dons kept this knowledge to themselves, and the capos of all five families convened in Miami to find a remedy, and a bloodbath of their own children and grandchildren was not acceptable. The youngest of the old dons, Don Lorenzo Ponti, suggested a solution so radical, so simple, that it brought immediate smiles and nods.

Cash out.

Empty everything out of banks, both here and abroad, from safe deposit boxes to numbered accounts. Turn as much capital into cash and other paper as possible, and hide it all away from the punks who betrayed them, but who they dared not kill or even replace, needing their expertise and not wanting to slaughter their own. The only thing more unforgiving than a mob boss, after all, was a mob wife-and-mother.

Hell, computer gymnastics could be played by anybody knowledgeable, no matter how old and infirm. Cash flow would be business as usual, from Wall Street to Colombia, and what was emptying out of Switzerland, the Bahamas, and the Cayman Islands could be concealed.

When that process was complete, the capital behind the conglomerated empire that was the five New York

Mafia families would be hidden away till some later date and decision.

Soon cash and valuables were moved by truck to secure warehouses until it was time to transfer everything to a single, even more secure location. That location would have to be immense as well as secret— no small task—because a million in hundreds would fill a carton the size of a clothes dryer.

And a billion meant a thousand such cartons.

Eighty-nine thousand such cartons would together contain, more or less, eighty-nine billion in cash, stocks and bonds.

This was where Marcus Dooley came in.

Dooley was no mob guy. If he'd had his way, he'd have been a cop… once upon a time, anyway. Twenty years ago, he was just a middle-aged guy with a dead wife and a dead business, and when old Don Angelo hired him on, as the handyman and gardener at the apartment house the don owned as well as lived in, getting any kind of gig must have seemed a gift from God. Or, anyway, Godfather.

Of course, Dooley being ex-military intelligence meant that the old don now had a handyman/gardener who could pack a gun and add some security to the mix. Everybody coming up a winner. And after Don Angelo died peacefully in his bed, Dooley was happy to go to work in the same capacity for Don Lorenzo Ponti.

This was a step up—Dooley would not be in charge of an apartment house, but Ponti's Long Island estate, several New Jersey rental properties, and the don's apple farm in the Adirondacks. Dooley could hire and fire additional help, order any supplies he needed, even set his own hours—a trusted employee who Ponti took a real shine to. That was not to say Dooley didn't rake grass, plant shrubs and take out the garbage, and he remained a general handyman. But an inordinately valued one.

In his glorified gardener's role, Dooley made twice Captain Pat Chambers' yearly salary, and bought a house of his own, a nice old fixer-upper in a crummy Brooklyn neighborhood.

No doubt Dooley had been told not to live suspiciously high on the hog—dons like Ponti worked at not showing off their wealth. Mob royalty like Lansky lived peasant-like existences in little houses or apartments, their wives doing the cleaning and cooking; but they had estates in Sicily, and when they traveled, it was first class all the way.

The don's home on Long Island, for example, suited a middle-level exec, and his Adirondacks estate was an unpretentious two-story farmhouse, made to look smaller by the vastness of its yard—a yard maintained by that trusted employee, Marcus Dooley.

Don Ponti found a trusted friend in his hard-working caretaker, a man who seemed not interested in money beyond a fair paycheck generated by steady work. Ponti had on occasion clued Dooley in on quick easy scores, but Dooley showed no interest. This convinced the don that Dooley was the man for a particular job.

On a mountainside near the Ponti estate was a vast cavern, large enough to house those eighty-thousand cartons. Dooley did not share with me the exact details of the transfer of cartoned-up cash, but I gathered that Dooley was at the wheel of the lead vehicle of a caravan of rental trucks driven by lower-echelon mob soldiers.

How long the unloading took, Dooley also did not specify. His deathbed story had understandable gaps. My guess is it took many trips over many weeks, and to preserve the secrecy of the location, Dooley led the city-boy drivers through a circuitous backwoods route to a spot where those drivers would unlikely be able to return on their own. Probably work lights were set up to go through the night, the cave's entrance allowing trucks to be driven in and unloaded, which they were, deep into the cool, dry natural cathedral, and then backed out again.

Finally, when the last boxes had been arranged into a cardboard fortress six cartons high and fifty feet wide, disappearing into darkness like a train into a tunnel, all of the workers were assembled for their reward.

Final reward.

My guess was that Dooley looked on aghast as some other trusted Ponti delegate presented the don's thanks for a job well done, and it wasn't a gold watch— more like a good old-fashioned tommy-gun massacre, creating echoing thunder in that cavern, scaring the bats, spilling shells that would still be there, sharing space with scattered corpses long since turned to skeletons.

It was like old pirate days, when those who buried the treasure were slain without benefit of burial themselves; or back when the Pharaohs paid off their workers in similarly harsh fashion, locking them in a tomb within a pyramid.

Why had Dooley lived as long as he did, with his secret?

Seemed that the ex-military intelligence man had already exercised a precaution—or was it a betrayal?—by switching locations on Ponti. After dummying road signs and covering up paths, and other methods of disguise and deception, Dooley had not led the trucks to the mountain cavern on Ponti's property, but to a similar one a mountain over... a cavern used in Prohibition days by an old pal of Dooley's, the late bootlegger, Slipped Disk Harris.

The five dons likely had a plan for that money—there was talk of trying to buy Cuba back, or some other Caribbean island where they might create a new Havana. It wasn't like them to just let that kind of capital sit—in the old days, it would have gone into business, unions, casinos.

But over the decade that followed, the dons of the five families were busy dying—perishing by natural causes, or causes that were made to look natural. Heart attacks, falls down stairs, preceded a succession of gaudy funerals right out of 1920s gangland days, reminiscent of a criminal life passing into history. What media cameras did not record were the faint smiles on long faces of younger family members who were finally about to come into their own.

My conversation with Marcus Dooley on his deathbed did not fill in every blank. At what point Don Ponti realized he'd been had, I did not know. But apparently about six months before that waterfront war I got caught up in, the Young Turks had put in new upgraded, more sophisticated computers that uncovered the missing $89 billion.

I never did find out exactly why Marcus Dooley, who held such a valuable secret, was murdered even as Don Ponti and his renegade son Ugo were both looking for the mountain hoard, with the U.S. Government clambering right behind. Why kill the man who alone on the planet held the $89 billion secret?

I still didn't know the answer to that. But a clue Dooley left, by putting me in charge of returning his earthly remains to his son, had led Velda and me to that cave, and its secret.

On the urn containing Dooley's ashes was what purported to be his army serial number, but in reality were longitude and latitude indicators. They led us to that cave on Slipped Disk's mountainside, which had been examined by mob guys and government experts alike, but did not give up Marcus Dooley's final secret: that he had used explosives to block off half of the cave, and that eighty-nine thousand cartons of loot were behind what appeared to be a landslide of boulders and rubble fallen from above along a far wall.

Velda and I had rented a backhoe and done the excavation ourselves. I had opened a single carton and removed some walking around money—basically enough to buy Velda her own rock, that fifteen-grand diamond on her left hand, and to generously pay me for a case conducted for no client.

Using some plastic explosive that had been thoughtfully left in my heap a while back to kill my ass when I turned on the ignition, I sealed that damn cave back up. Don Ponti had, at this stage, been killed by his own homicidal son Ugo, whose ass I had delivered to Pat Chambers and a prison cell.

And now, with the exception of a few hundred grand or so, that eighty-nine billion was still back there, hidden away in a mountainside cave, with nobody to look after it but the bones of dead gangsters.

We were back on the couch again, in the outer office, sunshine fingering through window blinds. As we waited for Pat to show, we kicked around the possibility that the $89 billion had somehow sparked this morning's hit attempt.

I said, "Let's suppose the latest revision of the mob scene has the idea I'm sitting on their nest egg. How does killing me lead them to it?"

Velda's forehead creased in a frown. "Maybe they figure if you know the whereabouts of the hoard, so do I. Killing you might shake me up enough to spill."

"Naw, you're just another dumb chick to them. They don't figure a guy lets a dame in on an eighty-nine billion dollar haul."

The frown disappeared and she grinned at me, shaking her head. "Well, maybe they're from a different century than you are, lover. This is the new generation of mob, remember?"

"Let's hope the new bunch has my old-fashioned ideas. I don't want you on the firing line."

"I can take care of myself."

"So can I, and the purple blotch on my chest says how far that takes us. Look, honey, any way you slice it, there's still no reason for the mob trying to knock me off."

"They know *we* know, Mike."

I shook my head. "They only *think* we know." I grinned up at her. "We show any signs of sudden wealth? Las Vegas vacations? Trips to Europe?"

"No."

"We drop any longstanding clients, to lighten the work load? We buy fancy new cars or move to Park Avenue digs?"

"Maybe they've been waiting for you to make a move like that. And now that you haven't, they're trying the direct approach."

I could read her mind. "So you think this shooting was supposed to nudge me into making a move, like grabbing a chunk of the loot and getting out of town?"

She made a wry face. "It's an idea."

"Bullshit, baby. They'll keep an eye on me, but they're not going to cut me down until that mother lode is pinpointed. They won't take chances with that kind of capital."

"Maybe that shooter planned a wounding shot."

I shook my head. "If he figured I was carrying a rod he wouldn't take the chance. No, he had planned for a straight back-of-the-head kill and never expected me to dodge it. He was quick to pick a secondary target and lay down those slugs where they would have counted. No, doll, somebody wanted me dead."

She was nodding. "Okay, then. Not the mob. But, Mike… what about Uncle Sam? You think those spook types you used to run with wouldn't ice a civilian if that's what it took?"

"You're right, the government has had its best teams out to look for that dough. They've had every agency with the greatest technology imaginable scrounging all over the state for the hoard. What have they found? Jack shit. But we're back to the beginning, baby—if they still think I've got a string on it, what good would killing me do?"

She didn't answer me for a full minute. Something was buzzing around in her head and she wasn't liking what her thoughts were chasing.

I said, "What is it, kid?"

"I said it before, Mike, suppose somebody else knows where that money is."

"Like who?"

She stared straight at me a few seconds, then asked, "Could Dooley have had a helper?"

Just the thought of it gave me an eerie feeling. I didn't think Dooley would have entrusted anybody with what he was planning, but it *was* a possibility. I had known my old friend well, during the dark hours of war, but the sleepy hours of slow aging during peacetime was something else again.

No, not peacetime, but a time filled with non-participation in things military, that warm, soft civilian blanket that diffused the memory of bullets whining and the abrupt, terrifying crash of a bomb blast. He'd been a man's man who combat fatigue had sent into the trivial, peaceful occupation of a gardener…

A helper. Somebody who could wield a shovel or hold a light. A close friend. A relative, maybe. Somebody to sit and talk to or have a cold beer with. Somebody like Dooley who didn't care at all about eighty-nine billion dollars in cash.

But somebody who knew where it was.

In that case, I would be better off dead. And they'd take out Velda, too, just to be safe.

It was Pat's day off, but he came directly to my office from his apartment, his expression telling me that a New York City cop is always on duty, but did it have to be so damn early in the morning?

The big rangy Captain of Homicide had the slightly

tired manner of a guy who'd seen everything. This was my oldest friend, a guy closing in on retirement age but still sharp, with street savvy and scientific training second to none.

He nodded to Velda and slipped out of his damp, rumpled raincoat. When he'd hung it and his hat on the coatrack, he went over to the little table and poured himself a cup of coffee and, with his back to me, asked, "Since when do you come in at six a.m., Mike?"

"He's an early riser," Velda told him.

"That one's too easy," Pat snorted, turning toward us. He sent his gray-blue gaze in my direction. "A hit doesn't go down when the sun's coming up."

"Tell that to the shooter," I said.

I was seated by Velda's desk and he came over, pulled up a chair, and joined me. She was sitting behind the desk, arms folded over the generous shelf of her bosom, watching us like a vaguely amused schoolteacher.

I handed him the *New American Webster Handy College Dictionary* that had been my impromptu flak vest and watched while he fished out the .22 slugs and rolled them around in his palm.

"You were lucky, pal," he said. "Let's see your chest."

"Now you're a medic?"

"Nope. Just an interested spectator. Let's see it."

Getting my shirt unbuttoned again wasn't quick or easy, but finally Pat got to see the big purplish splash that flowed around the swelling where the pair of .22s had tagged me.

"That your idea of lucky?" I asked, beginning the slow process of buttoning back up again.

"You'd better believe it," he said gravely. "Those .22 slugs could penetrate four inches of wood, but couldn't go through a paperback book. Know why?"

"Educate me."

"Each page has independent, equal resistance and slowed the velocity of those slugs to the point where they couldn't make full penetration."

"You took the words right out of my mouth."

He smirked at that, letting the slugs bounce in his right palm. "What do you want me to do with these?"

"Let the lab have them. If that gun has been used before, maybe they can match up the rifling marks."

He narrowed his gaze. "With a real pro, he could have changed barrels, if it was an automatic. Some of those heavy hitters get real attached to their tools. Like you and your original .45. You do still have it?"

"Licensed and loaded, pal, but not carrying it right now."

"Maybe you should."

Velda said, "That's what I've been saying."

Pat was watching me with that wry cop look. "I'll send a team out so a report will be on file, but it'll be a short one. No witnesses, no identification, no killing. If you want to show off your bruises, be my guest. You sure won't get much sympathy from these guys. I'll drop the slugs off at ballistics, but don't expect any miracles."

"What, no police guard?"

"Like you'd put up with that," Pat said. He took a little manila envelope from his suitcoat pocket, filled it with the slugs, and dropped it back in. "Twenty-two caliber piece is typical of the breed. And .22s kill just as dead as your .45 but with little recoil to spoil the aim. But one thing doesn't fit."

"Yeah?"

"Assassins usually go for the head."

"That's what he was doing," I said. "But I had a fraction of a second to spoil his shot when I dropped, and he just realigned his sights and went for the heart."

Pat's expression asked me why the shooter had taken his eyes off me in the first place.

"He lost a beat," I explained, "putting his foot in the elevator to stop the door from closing."

Pat let the picture roll around in his mind, then cautioned me, "He may be back, and if not, expect others."

"Where would I be without your experience to fall back on?"

His eyes were moving with thought as he took a few sips of coffee. Then he said in a deceptively calm fashion, "You do realize this could be about that little matter of money you claim not to have found."

I gave him a one-shoulder shrug. "Certainly. Eighty-nine billion is one sweet pile of dough to have squirreled away in a single vault somewhere. Every one of those old dons had their fortunes in that pot."

Pat's eyes tightened. "How do you *know* it's in a single place?"

I shrugged, both shoulders this time. "Dooley wouldn't have had the time to move it to various sites, Pat. This was a studied operation, all right, but it was relatively quick. It had to be."

"Why?"

"The longer it took, the more chance somebody would get wise—like the Young Turks the old dons were scamming. Dooley had a set time frame, the necessary equipment, and the smarts to get it done. The wise guys entrusted him with the mission, but he threw them a curve, and now there's nothing they can do to him because he's dead."

He pointed a finger at me. "Which leaves you up Shit Creek without a paddle, Mike." He shifted that finger to Velda, sitting sphinxlike, listening. "*Both* of you."

Then his attention returned to me. "On his deathbed, Dooley asked for *you*, Mike, and only you, and the reasonable supposition is he spilled his guts. And everybody knows you and Velda are a team. Anything you know, she knows."

"Okay, I'll buy that." I gave him the nasty grin I usually reserved for guys who weren't my best friend. "But you aren't just *my* old bud, you were *Dooley's*, too, going all the way back. Plenty of people would assume anything I got at Dooley's deathbed, I passed along to you."

"Well, you damn well didn't! Since when do you clue me in on anything till it's too late for me to do anything about it!"

That rated a chuckle. "You know that, Pat. And

I know it. But no one else believes it. And that, my friend, leaves you up the same damn creek as Velda and me."

He frowned, shook his head. "Hoods don't go after cops. It isn't healthy."

"Trying to convince me or yourself? Anyway, who wouldn't risk their health a little over a shot at eighty-nine billion bucks?"

Pat stared at me for a long ten seconds, then said, "You want something out of me, don't you?"

"I'm a taxpayer, aren't I?"

"I'll make you a deal. You don't give me the taxpayer speech, and I'll spare you the one where I threaten to toss your ass in the pokey if you take this on by yourself."

I grinned, not so nasty. "Deal."

"So?"

My grin faded. "We've been thinking of Dooley as the sole survivor to the big money move. He claimed Ponti eliminated everybody but him, after the transport. If anybody on the inside knew where Dooley had hidden it, none of this would be an issue."

"Okay," Pat said. "I follow."

"So find out if Dooley had *another* old buddy. Somebody he might have trusted with the big secret. It'd been a long time since we saw him, Pat, and even a loner like Dooley might have made some friend along the way, somebody like himself, someone he might confide in. An outsider like Dooley who didn't give a damn about all that money, but got a charge out of a project, an operation, that size. Maybe another old military guy, out of army intelligence."

Pat was frowning. "Why do you assume Dooley had no interest in money?"

"I don't think it was in his character. He was a messed-up soldier who became a drunken bum, then remade himself into a glorified yard man. He knew where that money was for ten years, but his lifestyle didn't change. If a softer life was his goal, he could have sold the loot's location back to Ponti for a small fortune."

"And get himself wiped out for his trouble." Pat's eyebrows went up. "Hey… maybe he was waiting for Ponti to die. The old boy was in his eighties, even if it did take a bullet to take him out, courtesy of his own kid."

I hadn't considered that. Was it possible Dooley had been playing a waiting game, looking to spend some cushy golden years on a bed of billions?

"And even if you're right about Dooley not caring about that dough," Pat said, "he might have misjudged this pal you're positing he had. Maybe that 'helper' played along with Dooley, figuring to get at that loot himself someday."

Velda leaned forward, placing her hands on the desktop; she was clearly intrigued by Pat's notion.

I said, "Then why hasn't the helper made a move till now?"

"Who knows? Possibly he lost his nerve, considering that he'd be robbing the mob. Or maybe *he* was playing a waiting game. If he even exists."

"Find out for me, Pat."

"Mike, it's just supposition…"

"It's credible enough to check out, but it'll take the kind of legwork that only the police can supply."

"And it has to be done quietly."

"Damn well told."

Thoughts were racing in his eyes again. "There'll have to be inter-departmental cooperation. All the way to the feds, considering Dooley's military intelligence background."

"Sure. Inter-city, too—Dooley worked upstate for Ponti, after all, on that estate in the Adirondacks. No telling just how far it can go."

He shook his head. "Great. Just swell. What did I do to deserve you as a friend?"

"Velda says you'd have been an inspector years ago," I said, "if you had better taste in drinking buddies."

Velda chimed in: "What do you say, Pat? You might as well pitch in. It's too late to go looking for new friends."

He gave her a little smile that carried a hint of the torch he once carried for her, then he said, "I'll think about it."

"You're thinking about it now," I told him.

His eyes looked directly into mine.

Then he took another sip of his coffee. "See a doctor yet?"

"Mine's in the building, but he's not in his office this early."

"But you *will* make an appointment?"

"What, and have my insurance rates go up?"

His smile was as rumpled as his raincoat. "For a guy who knows how to get his hands on eighty-nine billion bucks, you're awfully chintzy."

"I didn't say I could get my hands on it, Pat."

"You don't have to, buddy. Anyway, if I go poking around in Dooley's affairs, you can bet both of us will get back on the IRS radar. And you'll be the bogey blipping there getting the most attention."

I waved that off. "Won't do them much good if all they're working with is speculation."

"Can you prove that?"

"I don't have to, pal."

"Oh you think so? There have been some mighty big Wall Street financiers who thought like you, and wound up in a federal prison."

"Because they committed overt crimes."

"You could end this," he said, sitting forward, expression intense, "by simply telling the feds where that stash of cash is, and then you... and Velda, and maybe me... can find our way to shore off Shit Creek."

"*If* that's what this shooting was about."

"So let's assume it is, unless you have a better one."

"Not yet," I admitted.

"Damnit man, why don't you 'fess up? What the hell would *you* do with eighty-nine billion dollars?"

"I could use a new car." I smiled innocently. "Anyway, I think somebody ought to prove there *is* some money first... don't you?"

Pat's sigh had a laugh in it. "Sure I do, Mike." He turned to Velda with a smile. "Thanks for the coffee."

He got up and was putting on his raincoat when he said casually, "By the way, did you see that piece in the *Times* last week, about this new wave of super-computers? Very informative."

"What about the new computers?" Velda put in.

Before Pat could answer her, I said, "They can work out several billion pieces of data per second."

From over by the door, Pat said, "Funny how that word *billion* keeps popping up."

I gave him half a smile. "But the principle remains the same, buddy."

He answered expressionlessly: "What principle?"

This time Velda saw what I was getting at and beat me to it. "Garbage in garbage out—no matter how 'super,' any computer only knows what's fed into it, Pat."

I filled in the rest. "If… *if* there *is* missing money, it went out of circulation before these new computers came on the general market. If such a mob pot of gold exists, with just about everybody connected with it dead, you could only feed a computer *speculative* information… getting back speculative answers that don't hold up in court."

"You forgot something," Pat said softly.

"Like what?"

"*You're* not dead." He paused and nodded his head sagely. "But they're trying. What makes you think they'll stop?"

That must have been a rhetorical question, because he was out the door before I could answer him.

Not that I had one for him.

CHAPTER THREE

There was a bite in the air that whispered across the new cemetery grounds. Summer wasn't long past and autumn was disappearing quickly, the sky gray but the clouds immobile and the smell of possible rain faint. In the background the concrete spires of the city's skyscrapers made tombstones of their own, adults looking down on their boneyard offspring.

The stillness was a kind only death could engender. It was an eerie quietness as though the small audience was holding its breath and for a while there was no sound of birds or traffic. No plane flew overhead. No insect made a chirp. From twenty feet away you could hear the rustle of the fabric of the flag being folded geometrically until it was completely tucked into a neat unit that would be a family's tangible remembrance of a dedicated policeman.

The rifle volley from the VFW honor league erupted into a farewell salute, the smell of cordite dredging up sudden, wild memories of distant killing fields.

When the lieutenant from the Two One handed the cloth offering to the pretty young woman with the baby in her lap, she took it absently, silent grief making a blank mask of her face, her eyes looking far past the rows of ornamented tombstones, not focusing on anything at all. She held the flag against herself, the baby's tiny hand grasping the corner of it for a moment.

Beside me, I heard Pat let his breath out softly. It was rare that I saw him in his captain's uniform, but although the stamp of the career officer was there in his demeanor, that tight glint in his eyes reflected his hatred for cop killers.

Quietly, I said, "She's awfully young, Pat."

"Twenty-two," he told me. "He was twenty-six."

"Damn."

"Eighth officer lost in two months."

I nodded. It had been another one of those freakish occurrences—a cop on his way home from work caught in the hail of automatic fire from a stolen car in a drive-by shooting that took out three teenagers from the Red Commando gang... and one young off-duty officer.

The drive-by crew had missed a fourth Red Commando hoodlum, who got off two shots from the .38 automatic he carried under his shirt and a lucky hit took out a shooter in the back seat, his buddies dumping him off in an alley to bleed to death.

Just before the ceremony, Pat had been on his cellphone and I knew something had turned up. I half-whispered, "They got a lead on this one yet?"

Muffling his voice, Pat told me, "They pulled in every gangbanger in that car. The one they tossed out fingered them before he died."

"Sometimes justice gets a shabby delivery system."

A day had passed since I'd stepped off an elevator at the Hackard Building into what was damn near my own funeral. Nothing related had happened since, other than Pat reporting that ballistics had run the slugs through the local and federal databases and come up empty. We'd been right that either a new weapon had been used or an old one with the firing pin and barrel switched out.

When we'd spoken on the phone, Pat mentioned this latest officer death and that he was heading out for the funeral. I asked him if he'd like some company and he took me up on it. I'd never met the deceased, but I'd known hundreds of his dedicated kind.

Riding back to the city we didn't say much. I picked up the two New York papers on the seat and checked out the front pages. The big story was the outbreak of police officers' deaths. News was slow enough that the coverage made speculative noises about possible serial killing, but that just didn't seem the case. These appeared purely coincidental, the kind of accidental deaths that could happen to anyone.

The rash of cop fatalities had started with a drunk

running a red light and nailing a pedestrian crossing the street who happened to be a uniformed patrolman an hour from going off duty.

The next death came courtesy of a delivery van blowing a tire and plowing into a squad car, killing the driver and injuring his partner.

Fatality number three was assisting at the scene of a grocery store fire when a gas main blasted a ball of flame onto the street and consumed the cop who had waved civilians back.

Four and five got it when they were responding to a robbery-in-progress call at a liquor store. They were only a block away when the silent alarm touched off by the owner alerted them. They had spotted the pair with drawn guns through the store window, but not the other two waiting across the street in a darkened getaway car. Those two had rifles. Each one got off three shots, dumping both cops dead on the sidewalk. The store was robbed and the four hoods got away, the owner a fatality, too.

Six and seven were having supper together in an old Italian restaurant on Third Avenue. Once upon a time it had been a big favorite with the mob crowd, but for the past thirty years had been respectable enough to get top ratings in the places-to-eat-in-New-York columns. Then, after spending thirty-five years in Sing Sing, a cancer-riddled Monte Massino came in to commit suicide in his favorite old bistro, spotted two cops in uniform and decided to pull a grand slam, shooting them both in the head before blowing his own brains out.

We had just buried the eighth.

"Serial killing by coincidence," I said.

Pat gave an almost imperceptible nod. "Crazy. Do you know what the statistician says the odds are for this many cop fatalities in this short a time?"

"The NYPD has a statistician now?"

"No, but the city does. Anyway, the expert says it's about ten times the likelihood of winning the Irish Sweepstakes."

"People do win that."

"I know you're the rare cop type who believes in coincidence, Mike. But this is way off the charts."

"Anybody looking into it?"

"I've got two teams on it, going over each death like it was a potential homicide, but so far we're treading water." He sighed. "Listen, I'm meeting Tim Darcy for lunch. You want to join us? Something you might want to get in on."

"Why not?" Tim had worked the crime beat at the *News* for going on twenty years and was one of the good guys—for a reporter, anyway.

Pat glanced over at me—odd, and sort of fun, seeing him in NYPD blue, like he'd been when he took down Rudy Olaf way back when.

"We'll stop by my office," he said, "so I can get into civvies."

"Sure."

Uniform or not, Pat had checked out an unmarked

Crown Vic; the trouble with such unmarked cars is that they are as recognizable on the side streets of New York City as a Jaguar D-Type. Every kid with digital dexterity gave us the middle-finger salute with soundless but easily lip-read obscene suggestions as Pat coasted through, breaking up their stickball games while some players rolled out empty garbage cans and ran, waiting for us to play road hockey with the receptacles. Pat had a lot of experience with catching the cans just right and almost nailed a half-hidden perp with a galvanized missile.

"Nice shot," I told him.

"My regular driver would have tagged him," he told me.

"You ever try to make friends with these alley cats?"

Pat gave me a big grin. "What, and spoil all their fun? What do you think I drove up this way for?"

"I figured you took a wrong turn."

"Like hell." His grin got a little bigger. "I thought maybe they'd have added some new twists to the old routine. That's what's wrong with kids today— no imagination."

"I notice they don't toss out any new plastic garbage cans."

"Of course not. Those don't make any racket when you bang 'em."

There was always some logic in Pat's observations. And I was glad to see the street skirmish get him out of his somber mood.

* * *

Tim Darcy met us at The Cavern. It was an old newspaperman's hangout that became one of those showoff places the natives took out-of-towners to, not because it had a forty-foot bar that famous deceased TV newsmen used to frequent, but because you couldn't beat the seafood dishes old Tony G. could dish up. Tony claimed he wasn't sure what the "G" stood for himself anymore, but said it was on his immigration papers if anybody cared to look.

When we'd joined Tim in a back booth, I suggested that he try Tony's Oysters Rockefeller, and the reporter reported that he didn't like the slimy things. Nothing could persuade him otherwise. He ordered the corned beef and cabbage—about what you'd expect from a fortyish heavy-set redheaded character with a florid face and a green sweater vest.

While he buttered his hard roll, Tim alternated his gaze from it to Pat, as he said, "Anything new on the sudden rise in cop fatalities?"

"Mike and I just got back from the latest funeral," Pat said glumly. "Accidents, coincidences, but it just doesn't sit right. After the third one, every death has been investigated by my top two teams. How do you explain bad luck and fate, anyway?"

Tim chewed roll as he said, "Is that what it is?"

I said, "Call it kismet."

"*Kismet* is an old musical, Mike," Tim said. "And I

don't work the Broadway beat."

Pat sighed. "Your paper and the rest of your crowd keep hinting at a possible serial killer... but that's a bunch of garbage. Every one of those cops suffered a terminal case of wrong-time-wrong-place, pure and simple. Hell, there were witnesses on the scene in most instances."

"Well, you can't blame us for speculating," Tim said. "Otherwise, all we'd have is a lousy story."

I said, "Wouldn't want to let the facts get in the way of that."

"Papers don't hold onto their readers," Tim said, "by boring the shit out of them. These are tough times for the Fourth Estate, my friends."

Our food arrived. Tim dug into a slice of corned beef and looked at Pat over his fork. His eyes narrowed, close-set things as green as his vest and as colorful as his blood-shot nose. "When you gonna ask me, Pat?"

"Ask you what?"

A grin twisted Tim's plump lips. He chewed. Swallowed. Eyebrow-shrugged. "Man, for a couple of oldtime wild-ass players, you two don't know much these days, do you? Is the shadow of impending retirement getting to you?"

Normally I wouldn't let a remark like that pass. This time I just looked at these two, wondering what the hell was going on, and ate my oysters.

Pat took a break from his Finnan haddie for a sip of coffee, his eyes never leaving the veteran reporter. "I'm not retiring just yet."

"There've been rumors. And it's mandatory in, what? Five years?"

"A lot can happen in five years," Pat said.

"Like you finally making inspector?" Tim said, with a grin that wasn't exactly nasty. "Don't count on it—not with this Rudy Olaf crap hanging over your head."

"Nothing's hanging over me," Pat said, just shy of testy.

"Sure," Tim said with a full-on shrug. "But even without it, there are some hotshot lads coming up fast who would be glad to have the job you currently hold."

"So that's a newsman's idea of news?"

"Everything old is new again. Like politics, pal."

This time Pat gave him the almost nasty grin back. "I have a union contract. Those 'hotshot lads' of yours, playing politics, can kiss my ass."

"Just looking for a reaction, Pat," Tim said affably. "There may be a story on the horizon. A good one. A *real* one."

"Bullshit," Pat said, pushing aside his half-eaten fish. "You got something else on your mind. Stop farting around and spill it."

Tim's smile was almost impish. He nodded, finished the last of his corned beef, took a gulp of coffee and squinted at the both of us. "Let's talk Rudy Olaf."

For a second Pat turned and glanced at me, the guy who'd been there when he made the now controversial bust. "Must we?"

"If what I have to say isn't worth it to you," Tim said, the blarney making musical tones in his voice, "I'll pick up the tab myself."

I said, "You *must* have something."

"There's a very colorful aspect of the original case that never made it into the media. Forty years ago, some topics were off-limits."

Pat looked at him blankly. "You mean his victims were gay. So what?"

"This killer stalked his victims outside gay bars in a rundown area of the city. He knocked them off with one shot to the head, took their wherewithal and left a corpse."

"Wherewithal," Pat repeated. "Is that your vocabulary word for the day, Tim?"

"Most of his victims were slum-dweller types, and Rudy boy probably got a few bucks for his trouble, and a kick out of who he was killing. But two of them were loaded. And I don't mean drunk."

Pat nodded. "One of his last victims supposedly had over fifteen thousand on his person. The first cops on the scene found an empty money belt. The other flush vic had jewelry taken and a pretty fair roll of maybe five grand, gone—an out-of-towner, with a family who didn't know the head of the house's predilections."

Tim grinned over his coffee. "That must be *your* vocabulary word of the day."

"What's your point, Tim?"

"This is a very famous old case with a background

story that has never been told. That will help it explode all over my paper and everywhere else in the media."

"So?" Pat said.

"Tell him, Mike."

I was stirring a couple of Sweet'n Lows into my second cup of coffee. "The homosexual aspect makes this a modern story. It's what they call a 'hate crime,' and it tips the scale over from homicidal robberies to a kind of serial-killing spree."

Pat winced. "Thanks to the movies, everybody sees serial killers under their bed, these days."

Tim leaned in, his voice more hushed now. "This is a case without a confession, a case built on one eyewitness with a questionable background who died in stir over thirty fucking years ago. To this day, Rudy Olaf claims those victim wallets were *planted* in his apartment."

I said, "Guilty guys claim all kinds of shit, Tim my boy."

"Wallets they found," the reporter reminded us, "but one thing was missing."

"The gun," Pat put in irritably. "They never could find the damn thing."

I said, "That's the only thing that kept Olaf out of the hot squat. Where you going with this, Tim?"

Tim had a mad leprechaun twinkle in his eyes. "It's looking like Brogan really *did* do those killings."

Pat frowned and batted at the air. "Bullshit! I am fairly well-connected in the department, Mr. Darcy, as you damn well know, and what's got back to me is that

Brogan doesn't know anything he couldn't have got from the papers."

I said, "Sounds like another run-of-the-mill Confessin' Sam to me."

The reporter leaned back. "I don't question that you're hooked up well within your own department, Pat. But I've long been owed a big favor by a certain party over at One Police Plaza. And he's paying it off with some pretty sensitive inside information."

Pat was fed up. "You're saying my own department is keeping me out of the loop on this thing?"

Softly, Tim said, "Well, maybe I'm misinformed. Maybe you're so well-connected, Pat, that you already know."

"Know *what*, damnit!"

Tim's eyes narrowed, any amusement in them gone. "The other day, Brogan led some of your fellow cops to the gun. And the slugs matched those in the victims' bodies."

Pat looked like he'd taken a punch. A hard one.

I asked, "The gun wasn't rusted or anything?"

"No. It was wrapped in an oil cloth, shoved into a sheepskin-lined carrying case that was inside a large sealed plastic bag. It had all the earmarks of being kept well-preserved so it could be used again. Brogan's prints were on everything. On top of that, he's been detailing every kill for your NYPD brethren. No two ways about it—old Olaf is going to walk very soon, and New York City will have to come up with a bundle of cash to compensate for bungled police work and forty years worth of false imprisonment."

Pat and I exchanged glances. In this new era, a case like this could be a powder keg that could blow a city apart. If Captain Chambers had sent the wrong man to prison, and left at large a serial killer who had been targeting gays out of hate, a great career would be cut short. Never mind retirement—think resignation. In disgrace.

Pat asked, "Who knows about this?"

"A dozen over at One Police Plaza, including one in ballistics. I know, and now so do you and Mike."

I asked Pat, "Where are they keeping the perp?"

He said, "I don't know. I've been kept away from the case for obvious reasons."

Reasons that were getting more and more obvious.

"Right now," Tim said, "Brogan's at Bellevue in an intensive care unit. The old fart is dying of cancer. They don't give him long."

"Damn," Pat said quietly.

Tim leaned in again. "Come on, Pat, that's why the old boy gave himself up! He said he couldn't die with this on his conscience. He has a couple of grandkids he says he adores, and he wants to go to the grave, clean."

"That doesn't cut it," Pat said, almost petulant, a rarity in him. "Why would he want his grandkids to know Grandpa was a gay-hating serial killer?"

Pat had a point, but so did Tim. If Brogan really was about to buy the farm, maybe he did have his grandkids in mind. Selling his story to the media could make a small fortune, whether he really was the killer or just pulling off a scam.

I said, "Tim, are you going to print all this?"

For ten seconds he stared over my head, as if the wooden booth might provide some advice, then dropped his eyes to mine. "What do you think I called you guys for? I owe you both for more favors than I can remember."

Pat found a small smile. "Thanks, Tim. I guess I do owe you lunch at that."

His shoulders made an almost imperceptible shrug. "Pat, everybody's going to be looking for a scapegoat and it sure as hell seems like you're elected."

"It is looking that way."

"You think they'll come hammering at you, right out of the gate? Hand you off to Internal Affairs and the story to the media?"

Pat shook his head. "I doubt it. This'll stay bottled up until they've looked into every detail. Believe me, this won't get out to the public until the top brass are ready to let it out."

I said, "This one's got you by the short and curlies, doesn't it, Tim?"

Tim grunted. "Are you kidding? I'm sitting on top of the best local crime story in a decade, and instead of running with it, I'm dropping it right in your lap." He sighed, grinned back at me, and said, "Good thing I got a soft spot for you old dinosaurs. My editor would kick my ass if he knew."

"You should be ready," I said, "when it breaks. It's not going to *stay* quiet."

"Don't I know it." Tim looked at Pat nervously. "You think you can keep a lid on this, your end of it, I mean?"

"It's in my best interest to try," Pat said. "I can play it cool and cozy. Check in with ballistics. Say I heard rumors, and work it that way. I can do a lot of things within the confines of regular police work."

Nodding, Tim said, "I get you, but do what you have to do, Pat, just do it fast. It's going to come to a head before you know it."

I spoke for Pat when I said, "You'll get the story, pal. It may not come to you from official sources, but it'll be the straight scoop. There's not much the politicos can hit *me* with, if I leak a few suppositions. Right, Pat?"

"No comment," my buddy said.

"And Tim," I went on, "I may be a little long in the tooth, but it's just possible I can scare up some action that'll give you some nice headlines."

"Related to this story?"

"Maybe. Or maybe something else that hasn't got out yet. Now, don't look at me like that, Tim. I'll clue you in when the time comes."

He laughed. "You *are* a little long in the tooth, Mike, to go on one of your shooting rampages."

I shrugged. "I may not have any rampages left in me. But shooting assholes one or two at a time, that I can still manage."

Pat said, "I didn't hear any of that."

Tim handed each of us a card. "These numbers are

new. My private number and cell, in case you need me...
or have something for me. Now, can we have dessert?"

That afternoon, Pat called at my office to say he'd been
asked to take a meeting in forty-five minutes with a
representative of the District Attorney's office at One
Hogan Place. The subject was the Rudy Olaf case,
and he wanted me along, even though the D.A. hadn't
invited me.

Sounded like fun.

The interview room was a small modern nondescript
yellow-walled windowless affair with a rectangular table
that would seat six. But there were only three of us—no
stenographer. Pat sat opposite me with Assistant D.A.
Mandy Clark at the head of the table.

I'd not met Ms. Clark, a tall, lovely thirty-something
redhead already imprinted with the hard-to-impress legal-
eagle look that playing on the seamy side of New York
streets lays on you. Her severe tweedy dark green suit did
a damn poor job of concealing a compact, shapely frame.
I gave her a friendly smile, but the direct stare she leveled
at me meant she wasn't there to play games.

She spoke to Pat without looking at him, her eyes
on mine. "This man is a well-known and frankly fairly
notorious private investigator, Captain Chambers.
What's he doing here?"

"Why don't you ask him, Ms. Clark? He speaks
English, more or less."

Her eyes held steady on mine. I didn't blink.

"Well?" Her tone was a demand.

I hardly made a movement, but she knew I had shrugged. "I haven't heard a question yet," I said.

Five seconds passed before she asked, "What *are* you doing here?"

So I let another five seconds pass before telling her, "I was with Captain Chambers, forty years ago, when he made the Olaf collar."

A small frown crossed her face and Pat caught it at once. He said sharply, "You haven't gone over the reports yet, have you, Ms. Clark?"

His question threw her *attack mode* button into a fast reverse and she shook her head. A little of her severity melted. "Frankly, Captain, my boss threw this thing at me and told me to get over here and shake it out."

I glanced at Pat. "Shake what out?"

"It's a new expression," he said. "It's like getting rid of a body that won't stay buried."

I grinned at her. "That definition on target, Ms. Clark?"

Mandy Clark gave me another of those several-second pauses before she agreed with, "Relatively speaking."

"Well, Ms. Clark, I may be 'fairly notorious,' but Captain Chambers here is among the most decorated police officers in NYPD history. He deserves more than a hasty interview from an unprepared pup."

Her eyes, which were light blue, flashed; I bet there were cute freckles under that face powder. "*Mister*

Hammer," she began, "may I suggest we not get off on the wrong foot. I could have you ejected right now."

"Then you'd just have to call me and ask nicely for me to return. Because if you had taken the time… or giving you the benefit, had you been *allowed* the time to read the proper materials… you would know why Captain Chambers brought me along. And it was not to hold his goddamn hand."

Her nostrils flared and she looked around as if wishing there were a judge she could make an objection to.

Pat said, "In Ms. Clark's defense, Mike, the original documents have to be pretty well buried under the paperwork of a lot of decades. This goes back way before departmental computers, and the transfer of materials from paper to electronic form is a long, ongoing process."

"So?" I asked him.

He flashed her a polite smile, then said to me, "So let's cut Ms. Clark some slack. This case is so damn explosive I can understand that they have to get it taken care of fast. Real fast."

I kept looking steadily back at Ms. Clark. Then, just when my eyes were about to start watering, I relaxed in my hard chair and finally blinked. "Be nice, Ms. Clark," I said. "It's an election year."

Finally, she let a smile touch her lightly glossed lips. "I heard you were a smart-ass, Mr. Hammer," she said quietly. "You live up to that much of your reputation, anyway."

"All part and parcel of being fairly notorious."

Her chin crinkled a little as she suppressed a real smile. "If you're going to be part of this conversation…"

Pat said, "He is."

She nodded. "Then I'll need some background from you first, Mr. Hammer. But keep in mind this is just an informal interview."

"Is that why we're in a room rigged for the kind of recording that picks up ice melting? Slowly?"

"Why, do you object to being recorded, Mr. Hammer?"

"No."

"Do you, Captain Chambers?"

"No."

She took my P.I. license number, rolled her pretty eyes hearing the year of my first licensing, had a look at my permit to carry a concealed weapon and my driver's license. That was when Pat called a halt.

I complained to him, "She didn't get to the good parts yet."

"You can bet they've got all the 'good parts' on file here, Mike," he said. "They may even have taken the time to transfer your history to computer."

I grinned at her again. "That right, Ms. Clark?"

"I wouldn't know," she said.

"But then none of us are under oath here, are we?"

She ignored that and said, "Captain Chambers… at the time *Officer* Chambers… was off-duty when Rudolph Olaf entered the Star Diner."

"That's right," I said.

"Was Mr. Olaf sober?"

"Yes, I thought so."

"Thought?"

"He looked like he might *want* a drink. He was living on the Bowery, Ms. Clark. A skid row area. And he was what we used to call a 'denizen' of the slums."

"What would make you classify him as such?"

"I've seen enough of that type."

"More specific please."

"His shabby clothing, his poor grooming."

"Are you a professional in making such judgments?"

"I've been a professional investigator for forty years, Ms. Clark."

"You were new on the job, though, at the time, Mr. Hammer. Like Captain Chambers."

"He was walking a beat, I had just opened my P.I. office. We'd just finished fighting the war to preserve your freedoms."

"Well, thank you both."

"Anyway, I guarantee a jury would take my word about Olaf's social status at the time of his arrest. You could smell who he was."

"You mean there was an odor about him?"

"He had an odor, all right."

"In what way?"

"A wino smell. Don't ask me the brand name. That much an expert I'm not."

She let that go. "Was he belligerent?"

"No. He just spotted Officer Chambers in that blue

uniform, coming at him, and got the hell out of there. Officer Chambers ran after him, tackled him half a block down."

"There was violence?"

"Not beyond what I just said."

"What was Mr. Olaf's manner at this point?"

"When Officer Chambers helped him to his feet?"

"Yes."

"Well, he was pretty meek, I'd say. Resigned to the situation. There were two of us, remember. I'd come up behind Pat. He may have assumed I was a plainclothes officer."

"Did you represent yourself as such?"

"No. Olaf saw two big guys, one a uniformed cop, and he just... acquiesced... quietly."

"Were you armed?"

"Yes. I was already licensed to carry."

"Did Mr. Olaf see your weapon?"

"No. There was no need to display it. Officer Chambers did all the work. It was a very clean arrest. Identification was immediate. All the proper procedures were observed."

"Did Officer Chambers read him the Miranda warning?"

"No."

"Why not?"

"Ms. Clark, this was *before* the Miranda warning."

She flushed in embarrassment, just a little.

I went on, "Officer Chambers gave Olaf the

then standard anything-you-say-can-be-used-against-you caution."

"Were there other witnesses to the arrest?"

"There might have been, but nobody intervened. When you *do* get the proper papers dug out of storage, I don't believe you'll find any other witnesses listed."

Across from me, Pat nodded at that.

She asked me, "Did you stay with the suspect while Officer Chambers called for back up?"

"No. The opposite. Officer Chambers gave me his call box key and I went to the nearest one and phoned the incident in. In a few minutes a squad car arrived and the prisoner was transported."

"Did Officer Chambers institute a search of Mr. Olaf's person?"

"Just a quick frisk for weaponry, not what I'd call a full-on search. Didn't have him empty his pockets, for example. The routine was very proper."

She nodded. "Is there anything further that you can recall?"

"No. It was quick, cut and dried, in the best sense."

She gave me a crisp professional smile. We were almost friends now. "Thank you, Mr. Hammer. That was helpful. My apologies for doubting the appropriateness of your accompanying Captain Chambers here this afternoon."

"No problem, Ms. Clark."

Pat asked her, "Can you tell me anything about this Brogan character who's come forward?"

She considered that, then said, "I suppose I could give you a quick rundown."

"Please."

Mandy Clark reached down and withdrew a single page of typewritten script from her briefcase. She spread it before her and referred to it as she spoke: "They were neighbors of a sort. Henry Brogan lived two tenements down from Olaf. They used to play chess together, mostly in a public park. When they had money, they drank at the same saloons."

I asked, "Real tight, these two?"

"More like birds of a feather. Nobody else wanted anything much to do with them."

Pat asked, "How'd they support themselves?"

"Welfare."

I grunted. "Well, one of 'em supported himself by robbing and killing homosexuals. The question is, which?"

She didn't bother to answer. What the hell—it was rhetorical. She put the single sheet back in her briefcase, then gave me a cool, professional smile.

"If you could wait outside in the hall, Mr. Hammer, I would like to go over a few things with Captain Chambers without any further input from you, however expert and/or colorful it might be. Meaning no offense."

I glanced at Pat, who nodded his approval, and I said, "No problem."

She was an efficient young lawyer, I'll give her that. Pat was only in there for ten more minutes. While I waited, though, I had that funny itch I got whenever I had to cool my heels like this. I had quit smoking a good long time ago, twenty years anyway. But certain situations gave me a vague hankering for a cigarette even after all this time. Not when or where you'd expect, like after a meal or a smoky bar, no. But in waiting areas at police stations or hospitals, the old nicotine craving kicked back in.

When they had emerged from the room, I exchanged nods with Ms. Clark as she clip-clopped off in her heels. She had a nice rear-end motion under that mannish executive suit.

"Mike," Pat said disapprovingly, "you're old enough to be her father."

"At least. But I'm *not* her father."

"You're engaged, remember."

"Hey, I'm perfectly satisfied with the meal I've been served. But that doesn't mean I can't glance in a bakery window... What's the D.A.'s office up to, buddy, do you think?"

We were walking down the corridor now, taking our time heading to the exit.

"I'm not sure they know exactly. Just that they're being extra careful. And I mean extra. The public's view of the police is lousy right now, and the media is ready to tackle anything that will throw dirt on the department."

"Typical," I said.

"Mike, they have a right, even a responsibility, to explore subject matter like the over-reaction at Waco or the assault on Rodney King. It doesn't help when a bunch of bad apples in Brooklyn haul in the wrong man and give him a broom-handle ass-raping."

"That does make for lousy public relations."

He almost shuddered. "Imagine what the media could make out of some poor slob who spends forty years of his life in prison on a bum rap."

Behind us more clip-clops of high heels were coming our way, and when we turned, it was Mandy Clark again, working to catch up with us.

"Glad I caught you, Captain," she said.

He gave her half a smile. "Not always comforting words to hear from a district attorney."

She did not smile at that. "I just spoke briefly to the D.A."

Pat's eyes half-closed as he regarded her. "What's your boss got on his mind, Mandy?"

"He'd like you to interview Rudolph Olaf before they release him, Captain Chambers. That means… tomorrow at the latest."

Pat did not hide his surprise or his displeasure. "For God's sake, what for?"

Very deliberately, the lovely Assistant District Attorney said, "For one thing, to get your read on the man. For another, maybe you can determine why, forty years ago, Mr. Olaf let himself be convicted without putting up any kind of reasonable defense."

"Maybe he had a lousy lawyer," Pat said brusquely.

Mandy nodded. "Well, he doesn't this time."

"Rufus Tomlin," I said.

They both looked at me like I knew more than I should—I'd had that look plenty of times from cops and D.A.s.

"That's right, Mr. Hammer," she said. "The celebrated Rufus Tomlin, 'Champion of the Underdog,' has a reported multi-million dollar lawsuit ready to drop on New York City on behalf of the much-inconvenienced Rudy Olaf."

And on behalf of the celebrated Rufus Tomlin too, I thought.

CHAPTER FOUR

Nothing but faces had changed at the prison. No one had to be told what it was, this dismal walled-in series of buildings filled with society's refuse, its ancient marble formed of local stone by long dead prisoners forced to build their own rooms in hell.

The foreboding fifty-acre sprawl on the east bank of the Hudson was the original "up the river" destination for everybody from Lucky Luciano and the Rosenbergs to the Lonely Hearts Killers and Albert Fish—all but Lucky rode Old Sparky, the facility's famed electric chair.

Today the quietness was eerie and the only movement was the figure of a guard surveying the area from a medieval turret silhouetted against the gray sky. For a second you could see the rifle he cradled in his arms.

Pat left his Crown Vic in a visitor's slot in the hillside

parking lot. "Been a long time since I've been here," he said.

"Have any trouble clearing me for this visit?"

"No problem getting you inside," Pat said, flashing a smile. "Let's see if they let you back out."

Two uniformed guards were walking toward us, neatly in step.

I asked Pat, "Why do we rate such first-class treatment?"

"They just want to make sure there aren't any reporters with us."

That seemed a reasonable precaution. I figured attorney Rufus Tomlin only put up with this interview with his client for PR purposes, and was surprised a press phalanx wasn't waiting.

I asked, "Wouldn't the Champion of the Underdog like it better if this meeting were made public?"

"Apparently not," Pat said. "He's holding onto the bad publicity card to help him get a fatter out-of-court settlement."

We had our IDs ready and Pat handed over a letter of authorization from the District Attorney's office. Everything was handed back so we could display it all again to other uniformed personnel inside. Pat checked his weapon—I wasn't carrying—and we both went through the metal detectors and followed a guard to the warden's office.

You might expect to meet a big hardcase of a guy, chisel-faced, tight, nasty lines etched along the corners of his mouth to match a bulldog demeanor; callused hands, maybe, from beating on things or people. What you wouldn't expect was a small, thin man who looked like an accountant, wearing a trimly tailored suit and smiling gently when he got up to shake your hand in the introductory ritual. Even his voice was thin. I had a teacher like that in the fourth grade, and he'd been tougher than he looked.

But even my tough fourth-grade teacher didn't own the kind of eyes Warden Percy V. Ladd turned loose on you. They were a strange color with a dark ring around the irises and no matter what his smile said or his small, near-limp handshake indicated, this guy was a bulldog, all right, but with the stealth and striking power of a scorpion.

The media had always treated Warden Ladd well. Maybe the reporters hadn't noticed those eyes. Word was, the inmates were scared to death of him. They *had* noticed.

Percy V. Ladd had earned the moniker Vlad the Impaler, courtesy of some literary-minded con who knew his *Dracula*. At least that's what the cons called him when he couldn't hear them.

Pat and I were seated across from the warden, separated by a large, dark oak desk with piles and piles of papers arranged in as orderly a manner as the prisoners on their cell blocks.

Warden Ladd said, "Rudy Olaf will be in an interview room in ten minutes. We'll be recording video with an audio tape back up, and we'll provide copies. Two guards will be at your disposal, both of whom can stay inside with you if you wish."

"I prefer they stay outside," Pat told him. "I don't want anything to distract your inmate."

"Oh, he'll be no problem, Captain."

"Never had any trouble with him?"

"Never. You know, Olaf's been here almost twice as long as I have... and I've been behind this desk for twenty-one years. He was already a trustee working in the library. One of the best-behaved and most trusted prisoners in the history of this facility."

I said, "Is he still working in the library?"

"Yes. We have a civilian employee who is technically head librarian, but the truth is, Rudolph Olaf has been running the library for decades." An embarrassed smile flickered. "This may sound strange, but... we're going to hate to lose him."

Pat said, "We understand Olaf was inside at the time that Dennis Reist was here—the witness whose testimony put him behind bars. That means Olaf was inside when Reist was knifed and killed in a shower."

But the little warden was already shaking his head. "That was before my time, but I can assure you that the two prisoners were kept quite apart. They were not on the same cell block, and Olaf was in the library when Reist was killed."

I said, "You don't know this from experience, but from the records."

"The records can be trusted, Mr. Hammer."

"Could Olaf have engineered the killing?"

The warden paused, and his answer ducked the question: "He has demonstrated no signs of violence in forty years. If it's true that he was wrongly convicted, I'd have to say that society has been denied an individual who might have made a positive contribution. Did you know he has an IQ over 180, Captain Chambers?"

"I didn't," Pat admitted.

"Don't take that to mean that I assume Olaf is innocent. These confessors come out of the woodwork, don't they, from time to time. And there are individuals who fit in well within the regimented lifestyle of a prison but who cannot function properly on the outside."

I said, "So model prisoner or not, Olaf might be guilty in your view?"

"Mr. Hammer, Rudy Olaf is a very clever man. You asked if he might have… engineered the death of that witness against him. It seems far-fetched, but here's a fact that you may find suggestive—for the last thirty years, Olaf has been the president of the prison chess club. He has taught many, many of his fellow prisoners how to play that demanding game."

I nodded. "You're implying that a man that smart might find a pawn to shiv somebody in the shower."

"I said nothing of the kind. But you are free to form your own conclusion."

Pat asked, "How about visitors?"

The warden had a folder ready for him with two typed sheets in it. "Rudy Olaf had one guest, never anyone else. This visitor came once a week, the maximum allowed number of visits, and on holidays. Speaking of chess, they invariably played the game while they spoke." He handed the sheets across to Pat. "That visitor's name was Henry Brogan, as you can see."

I asked, "Another pawn?"

The warden smiled the thin smile again and shrugged.

Pat, sitting forward, asked, "You ever monitor their conversations, Warden?"

"On occasions. Sort of a random screening. We don't see the necessity for doing it more often, and even if we did, we lack the manpower."

I said, "Well, these days you could monitor every one of these conversations electronically, and check the tapes later."

"We have seventeen-hundred prisoners, Mr. Hammer, and they have tens of thousands of visitors a year. That would be a lot of tapes to go through, wouldn't you agree?"

Pat asked, "What about gifts?"

The warden bobbed his head and folded his arms across his chest. "Always the same—Brogan brought along two cartons of cigarettes each visit. Olaf is a chain smoker and every cent he's earned in the library here goes for butts."

I asked, "Does Olaf earn enough here to support a habit like that?"

"Undoubtedly. There was nothing else he wanted. He isn't into drugs or booze like a lot of the other lifers."

Pat asked, "How available *is* that kind of contraband, Warden?"

I watched the warden's eyes. They didn't waver from Pat's and without any hesitation or embarrassment he said, "In any prison this size, Captain, there are guards who profit from running black-market operations. Some cons can get their hands on money and buy whatever they want."

"Not unusual."

The warden's eyebrows went up and down. "They even have businesses of their own on the premises, peddling dope and booze. I let it ride to keep down the violence, but let it get out of hand and I will crack down like a shark on bloody bait. There will be no insurrections in this prison as long as I'm here and they damn well know it."

Neither of us bothered to belabor the point.

I asked, "Has there been any change in the prisoner's status in the last year or so?"

"How do you mean?"

"Health problems, maybe. A drop-off in the quality of his library work. Or maybe a new cellmate."

The warden narrowed his eyes. "That's impressive, Mr. Hammer. Olaf lost his longtime cellmate just last year. As a trustee, he's now in a smaller cell, but by himself—it's a rare privilege."

I followed up: "When you say 'lost' his cellmate, do

you mean the guy was released?"

"No. Olaf's cellmate died of a heart attack, a lifer who'd been inside for thirty-some years—killed two men." The warden hesitated, then went ahead: "Specifically, the cellmate was in for killing his lover and another man."

I frowned. "Did I hear that right?"

"Yes, the cellmate was a homosexual who had killed his boyfriend and his boyfriend's, uh…"

"New boyfriend," I said. "How long did Olaf and this guy share a cell?"

"Twenty-seven years. He and Olaf were… a couple."

So a little booze and dope action wasn't all the tough warden put up with to keep the lid on the prison.

"Cellmates is right," Pat said.

The warden's chuckle had little humor in it. "Yes, an old married couple, really. Olaf was very depressed about the death, at first. But he sprang back eventually… maybe six months ago."

Pat and I exchanged troubled glances. That Olaf had been in a homosexual relationship with his cellmate was an indication that he indeed may have been innocent, considering the Bowery Bum slayer targeted gays.

The warden asked, "Anything else I can tell you, gentlemen?"

"No, thank you, Warden," Pat said.

"Then let me ask a question," Ladd said, directly to Pat.

"What's that?"

"How the hell did you get Mike Hammer cleared to be part of an official D.A.'s office investigation?"

I grinned enough so he could see the edges of my teeth. The muscles in my jaw had tightened and I met the challenge in his eyes, and then he backed down.

"Sorry," he said. "None of my business."

"That's all right, Warden."

Pat began, "Mike…"

"The D.A. requested that I be here. Interesting touch, don't you think? Maybe it's because I put as many sons of bitches inside these walls as any five NYPD cops combined."

The warden raised a conciliatory palm and said, "Perhaps I owe you a debt of thanks, Mr. Hammer, for helping keep us in business."

"No problem."

But those eyes were watching me, his gaze like soft tendrils reaching out, looking for an opening that could be used later to inject a venomous needle.

"Funny, though," he said, his tone suspiciously light, "how many times I've heard from law enforcement and prisoners alike that someday I might find you within these walls. Just not as a *temporary* guest."

Then Vlad the Impaler looked up at the guard at the door and said, "We'll escort you to the interrogation room now."

We both said thanks and followed our chaperone out; Pat and I exchanged amused smiles once our backs were to him. Behind us, though, I knew the warden was smiling a shrewd smile of his own, and not bothering to hide it at all.

Rudy Olaf, in prison green, was sitting very primly in the highly polished antique wooden chair, a tall, almost skeletal figure with a gray pallor and eyes of a washed-out light blue, like the knees of worn-out jeans. His face was a narrow oval with deep lines on either side of his mouth, his forehead well-grooved, his gray hair longish for an inmate. Trustees did have privileges, after all.

A half-empty pack of cigarettes and a Zippo lighter were under his fingers and when we sat down opposite him, he said, "You guys haven't changed much in forty years. Chambers, you're still a handsome man. Hammer, you're still ugly as hell. What's new?"

"I made captain," Pat said.

"I heard. That was a long time ago, wasn't it? How about you, Hammer?"

"I'm getting married."

"Well, it only took you forty years to find a woman. Well, good for the both of you." His smile looked like a rip in the gray mask of his face. "What can I do for you fellas?"

Pat said, "Tell us about your pal—Henry Brogan."

Olaf's fingers found his deck of cigarettes and he shook one out, stuck it in his mouth, and then offered us one. We both waved him off.

He flicked the lighter, took in a big drag, held it in his lungs a long time, then let the smoke seep out like gray fog. "My only vice," he said.

"That shit'll kill you," I told him.

"At my age, what's to lose?"

Pat said, "Maybe that big settlement your lawyer's trying for."

"Trying hell. He'll get it. You fellas screwed up. Sometimes a mistake takes a while to catch up with a guy. But this one finally caught you two in the tail."

Pat ventured a smile and said, "Not if your buddy changes his story."

"Why should he do that?"

"Because it's not true. You killed those people."

"Captain Chambers, believe that if it helps you sleep at night. At this stage, what difference is it, what really happened? If I did it, I've served my time. I could've got out on parole years ago if I'd just copped to the killings... but I didn't, because I'm innocent. And as an innocent man, what can I do to get those forty years back? Not a damn thing. But I can milk the city for enough to make my retirement years a hell of a lot more pleasant than living 'em out in Sing Sing."

I said, "You're trying to say, 'no hard feelings'?"

"You might say that, Hammer. Oh, I'm human. I suppose I'll take *some* pleasure in seeing Captain Chambers here denied his inspectorship after all this time. For him to have to put up with a little disgrace for a while... But it's better than being tagged a serial killer for forty years, hey, Captain?"

Pat asked, "You want me to believe Brogan is telling the truth?"

"So what if he isn't? Ol' Brogan hasn't got long before he kicks off, anyway. Maybe he's decided to do his old buddy a favor."

"Is *that* what he's up to?"

His laugh was a smoker's cough. "You wish! The bitter reality, Captain Chambers, is that *finally* Henry Brogan got bothered by what he pulled and what he put his pal through and he decided he had to repent somehow. He tells me what he did and begs me to forgive him. So I forgive him. Why not?"

I echoed him, astounded: "*Why not?*"

"Hammer, this place is home to me. I have spent most of my life here. You forget I was living on the Bowery. Here, I get three hots and a cot, like the man says... so I keep my nose clean and land a cushy job in the library, which means plenty to read and plenty of time to do it in. They got movie night weekly and TV in the commons, man—hell, it's not so bad. You two should try it."

"I'll pass," I said.

Skeletal shoulders shrugged. "But I'm also fine with moving up to a whole new class of goodies. Walk right into a restaurant and order a meal, imagine that. That's one thing I miss—deli food. You know, Brogan really deserves a cut of the pie New York City is gonna dish out to me."

"From what I understand," Pat said to him, "he won't have much time to use it."

"Well, remind me to cry my eyes over that, will you?" The words had a sneer in them.

I asked, "You ever suspect Brogan of setting you up?"

"Never occurred to me. He didn't seem that smart."

"Yet you expect us to buy that he was smart enough to pull it off."

"Well… he was… shrewd. Yeah, that's the word for it. Back then, he saw a way he could get himself off the hook, let somebody else take the fall, and then he stopped killing, which made it seem all the more credible."

Pat said, "And all these years he's visited you."

"Yes. Isn't that something? I thought it was friendship, and here it was guilt."

I said, "You played chess with him. So he was smart enough to do that."

"Ah, but ask him how many times he *won*."

Pat shook his head. "No hard feelings for Brogan, either, huh? You expect us to believe a lot, Rudy."

"Too late for hard feelings. I'm an old man, and he's an old man—*dying* old man. Hey, at least he kept coming up here to see me." He blew out more gray smoke. "Kept bringing me my butts, bless him."

I asked, "Why isn't your lawyer sitting in with us today? Where's the Champion of the Underdog?"

"What's for him to hear? What's for him to say?

Brogan came forward and got it all off his chest. He produced the gun for them, and what else is there? Except, 'Goodbye, Sing Sing, it's been nice to know you.' Funny, once his confession was on the table, everything made sense, even his coming up here to visit. He was trying to make up for what he did to me. Little pieces of redemption, one visit at a time, and then one final pay-off."

"No bitterness," Pat said, "about the system? About me and other cops?"

This time Olaf let out a harsh smoky laugh and shook his head. "Captain Chambers, I won't lie to you—I got no love for cops. I never did have. I don't love dentists or lawyers either, but sometimes a guy needs a tooth pulled… or somebody to sue the city for you. Captain, if you want to know how I feel about you? It's nothing. Hell, I don't waste my time worrying about what's happened. The joint's not so bad when you get used to it. In fact, I'm going to miss a lot of things about it… but I'll be glad to go home again."

I asked, "Where's home after all this time, Olaf?"

"Damn, that's a funny one. Till the settlement comes through, I'm staying at Henry Brogan's place. It's empty 'cause he's in the hospital, and he invited me. Isn't that the craziest damn thing you ever heard?"

Soft, Pat said, "The whole world's crazy."

For maybe ten seconds there was a quiet spell with Olaf just looking at us blankly. Then he frowned again and reached for his cigarettes. He stuck one in his mouth and thumbed the wheel on his lighter. He flicked it four times, but nothing came up but sparks.

"You're out of fluid," I said.

"One of you guys help me out with a light?"

"I don't smoke anymore," Pat told him.

I shook my head. "I quit years ago."

"Nobody quits smoking," he rasped. "You think you have, but one day that old urge'll rear up and kick you in the slats. Don't you worry about me, fellas. I'll get a light from one of these screws. They love me in here. But they're gonna just have to learn to get along without me."

When we got in the car, Pat asked me, "What do you make of old Rudy?"

"I'm not a psychologist, pal."

"Sure you are. All cops are."

"Then you go first."

He waited till we were out of the prison lot and on our way back for the thirty-mile ride to the city.

"That Olaf has one strange reaction to all this," Pat said. "He takes it like it's just another day in the life. He's not mad, he's not grateful, he couldn't care less. All the money that could come his way from the city makes no real impression on him. He's looking forward to eating at restaurants."

"Like the local deli," I said with a smirk. "Pat, if Olaf and his cellmate were shacked up for decades, how does that tally with him as a killer targeting gays?"

Pat gave a one-shoulder shrug. "That was just the part of town he was working, Gay Bar Row. Anyway, plenty of guys in stir are just having the kind of sex that's available."

"Yeah, but maybe Rudy was a self-loathing gay. Maybe he was killing *himself* each time he killed a victim. Maybe he lured guys into the alley for a brick-wall fling, then killed and robbed them, hating himself all the way."

Pat smiled a little. "Mike, you *are* a psychologist. But it's all just theory, and forty years ago, there was damn little exploration of the gay angle in our case, and what little there was got kept out of the media."

I chuckled without much humor. "Mandy Clark isn't going to like our report very much, buddy."

He gave me one of his noncommittal grunts. "I don't think she expected very much either. The big deal here is keeping this played down in the press."

I grunted back. "Olaf doesn't seem revenge-oriented. If he gets his payday with no questions asked, maybe he won't go to the media."

"Any negative blowback will put a hell of a dent in the D.A.'s election plans."

"Come on, Pat. Aside from a minor human interest story, what can the media make of it? There's a big Wall Street trial starting today that'll grab all the news flashes. Everything else will go on the back page."

"You think so?"

I felt a smile tugging at my mouth. "You're wondering

where Rufus Tomlin fits into this, aren't you?"

"Well, we know Rufus loves the spotlight, and if this goes all the way, he'll be in the middle of a big one. Doesn't seem likely there's a mob tie-in, though."

I nodded. "Agreed. Have you asked yourself why the D.A. chose *you*, the guy who supposedly screwed the case up forty years ago, to interview Rudy Olaf?"

Pat let out a short laugh. "To keep me nice and snug in the pasty seat, right?"

"As rain, old buddy. You're big enough to keep the heat off the politicos, but small enough not to cause a ruckus if a fall guy is needed."

"Grim damn evaluation, Mike."

"But that's the way you size it up, too, isn't it?"

That didn't require an answer. Conversation fell off, Pat staring out the windshield, eyes tight with thought.

Ten minutes passed before I finally said, "Spill it, buddy. What's on your mind?"

"Name Roger Buckley ring a bell?"

"Should it?"

"Old holdover from two administrations ago. Very sharp operator. Got into law enforcement right out of college, then into government as a specialist in nailing syndicate money deals. Broke up a money-laundering scheme that went from the U.S. through South America and into the Orient."

"So I'm impressed. So what?"

"So word is that your eighty-nine billion bucks has caught his attention."

"Who says it's mine? Just a rumor, buddy."

"Mike, Buckley starts with rumors until he tracks down the facts behind them."

"And rumor says I'm the guy who knows where the big bucks are."

"Right."

I grinned at him. "Buddy, not long ago we had a president who was predicting a one-hundred-eighty-seven trillion dollar surplus. *Surplus*, man! That makes eighty-nine billion look like small pickings, doesn't it?"

"Why, you got change for a billion on you?" Pat wasn't grinning back.

"Okay," I said. "What's the largest denomination note you can get from a bank these days?"

"Five hundred."

"Right. And till thirty years ago, you could still get thousand-dollar bills. Now, do you think these mobsters would storehouse five, tens and twenties when they could lay their cash up in five-hundred and thousand-dollar bills?"

"Of course not."

"But," I went on, "walk into a bank now with a bundle of thousand-dollar bills, you better have a verifiable story of how your old grandfather left them to you in an attic trunk."

"Nevertheless," Pat said, "those bills still have face value."

My grin grew bigger now. "And you think I'm smart enough to figure out how to cash them in?"

"You'd sure figure *something* out."

I didn't want to disappoint him. "Probably."

"Those old bills were larger, too," he mused, "if they go back that far. But still backed by the U.S. Government."

"I'll bet the bulk would be in five-C notes."

"You speaking from experience, Mike?"

"What am I, a suspect you're trying to trick a confession out of?"

Pat and I had been friends for a long time. We were tight enough that we didn't infringe on each other's affairs and knew where the lines were drawn, but both knew there were times when the door had been left open just enough to take a peek inside a forbidden room.

Quietly, he said, "If I asked you to confirm that eighty-nine billion, would you?"

"Sure. On my deathbed."

Pat nodded silently. He took that as the implied yes that it was.

"Let me tell you about Buckley," he said. "He and his office don't like the common man thumbing his nose at the idiots in Washington."

"I like to think of myself as an uncommon man."

"Mike, Buckley's here in New York, and you're the target. He's got financing and power to back up his actions."

"Big fucking deal."

"You're not bothered by it?"

"Been tried before, pal."

Pat glanced over gravely. "These aren't the old days, Mike. Our political system has updated its technology. And I don't just mean computers. Federal agents carry guns that have eighteen rounds." He turned his head and looked at me slyly. "And we both know what *you* carry."

A little shrug touched my shoulders. "My good old Army Issue Colt .45 with six in the clip. I could slam in seven, but I don't want to put too much pressure on the spring."

"Just six?"

"Yeah. But there's always one in the chamber in case the action goes down fast."

"You think that's safe?"

"Nope," I told him. "Just practical."

"Then why aren't you carrying the thing? Or has that blossom on your chest already faded?"

"Maybe a man of my advanced years is scared of loaded guns."

Pat just shook his head and pulled into a parking lot close to Bellevue Hospital.

Henry Brogan was a shriveled-up old guy who still looked like he could survive a New York winter the hard way—cooped up in a cardboard box with newspapers for blankets, living off garbage-can buffets and never catching cold or getting a bellyache. Somebody who wasn't very good at it had given him a haircut and shave.

Had he been able to get out of that hospital bed, and remove the tubes in his arms, he'd have been maybe five-six. Scrawny. Nothing impressive about him.

With one exception—those rat eyes. So many survivors out on the street had such eyes, dark, steady, merciless. Such eyes could see everything without moving at all. He saw us and he knew us even though we'd never met. He nodded to Pat and to me. We both nodded back as we took our place at his bedside in the small single room.

The plainclothes cop near the door said, "You want me to wait outside, Captain?"

"Stick around in case the witness gets tough."

Brogan coughed up a phlegmy laugh. "Hell, I'm a dying man down to a hundred-ten. Couldn't hurt you if I had a tommy gun."

Pat said, "You know, you don't have to talk to me at all without your lawyer present."

"Sure, I know that," Brogan agreed. "You're not even assigned to this case, are you?"

"No."

"Didn't figure you to be. You're the cop who took Rudy down, aren't ya?"

Pat just nodded.

"Captain Patrick Chambers. Natural for you to have an interest. Potentially embarrassing, me comin' forward."

Pat said nothing.

"And you're Hammer," Brogan said to me. "You were there when Rudy was arrested. And then you got famous. Whatever happened to you, anyway? Not much in the papers for years."

"I died," I told him.

That stopped him. Then his colorless face came up with a ghastly yellow-toothed smile. "I musta missed that edition. You know, back when the Bowery Bum kills were the big thing, I saved *all* the newspapers. Kept them for years. Lot of pictures of you, Captain Chambers, when you was a rookie cop. Hell, you haven't changed much, considering."

If Henry Brogan thought Pat was smiling, he was dead wrong. "But you have, Henry," he said.

"How's that, Captain?"

I had seen Pat with that placid grin before. "I'm sorry you're dying," he told him, "only because it's too easy a way out for you."

"So you believe I did those killings?"

"If you did them, you're getting off easy. Decades of freedom followed by a few weeks of dying. If you didn't do the crimes, you're letting a serial killer loose, and that makes you an accomplice. So I'm fine with you being dead."

"Expect me to be offended, Captain? Or maybe bust out crying?"

I said, "Getting good drugs there, Henry? Feeling no pain?"

"It's morphine. It's the best."

To Pat, I said, "Means I might have to put some muscle in it, to loosen him up. But we should try. Why don't we let this nice officer here step outside for a while, Pat, and take a break while we... *interrogate* the suspect?"

Brogan gave me a sudden, sharp stare.

I went on: "We can break some fingers and maybe an elbow and he'll hurt like hell, morphine or not, and it will look like he fell out of bed. Oh, he'll still be able to talk, when he's not screaming."

Suddenly the chatty Brogan couldn't think of a thing to say as the uniformed cop got up out of his seat and started for the door, doing a damn fine job of hiding his grin.

Then Brogan got his voice back and yelled, "Don't you go, officer! Don't you go, you hear!"

The officer stepped out into the hall, closing the door behind him.

I took Brogan by the wrist; it was thin and brittle. "Your heart is beating like a bunny rabbit's, buddy. Breathe in, breathe out, nice and steady."

"Hammer, you're as crazy as they say you are!"

"Did you do those crimes, Henry? Or are you taking the rap for your old buddy Olaf, now that you're about to buy it anyway? Has he promised you a prize chunk of his settlement?"

"If he did, what *good* would that do, you crazy asshole!"

I said to Pat, "Watch the door, would you, Captain?"

Pat nodded, went to the door, turned his back to us.

I grinned at Brogan. "Maybe he said he'd look out for your precious grandkids, after you're gone. Lot of money'll be coming in. But how can you be sure you can trust him?"

"I'm an old man! I'm a sick old man!"

"I'm an old man, too. We're about the same age. How about that?"

"You're sick!"

"Yeah, but I'm not dying, Henry. And if you're the serial killer you claim, why should I show you any mercy? Maybe I have a client who was the brother of one of your victims, and he sent me here to get even. To make sure you die long and hard and nasty. *Did* you kill those men?"

"I did. I did. Fuck you, Hammer, I did. Kill me if you want. If you want the goddamn truth, that's it."

"*Why* did you kill them?"

"I had a sick daughter. She needed medicine, expensive care. She pulled through, too. I'd do it again! I'd do it again!"

"Why gays, Henry? Why were they your targets?"

"Uh… 'cause I *hate* them fags! Always have! Stinking queers."

I let go of his wrist. Patted him on the shoulder, smiled down at him. "Take two aspirin and call me in the morning, Henry."

"*Fuck you, Hammer! Fuck you!*"

A white-frocked doctor burst through the door, his face pale with concern. Pat, with a very studied gesture, lifted his badge from his pocket and flipped the leather flap up and let the doctor see the gold.

In a hushed voice Pat said, "Appears the patient's too disturbed to be interviewed right now."

The doctor nodded, and Pat moved past the medic and I followed.

When we got out of the elevator, Pat said, "You haven't lost your bedside manner, Mike. What do you think?"

"Pat, you're not going to like my diagnosis. I think the odds are strong he did do those killings."

"That bit about hating homosexuals sounded forced, though. Something about it was off."

"I'd agree. Maybe *he* was the self-hating gay luring victims into alleys. But I'm starting to think he did those kills, and tried to make it up to his old pal by regular visits and cartons of weed. Now he's taking one last shot at redemption. And Rudy Olaf, though he doesn't seem to give a shit, will be out breathing fresh air again."

"What, in New York?" Pat grabbed my arm as he spoke and I saw what he was looking at.

Somebody had left a late edition of the paper on a chair and there was a picture of two pedestrians and a paramedic standing beside a crumpled body on the sidewalk. The body was in shorts and a dark T-shirt and the small caption stated, *Police Officer Dies While Jogging*.

Pat said very softly, "Damn—another one!"

CHAPTER FIVE

It had been a long time since I had packed the Colt .45 on me. I took it out of the zippered sleeve and hefted it—clean and oiled with that good gun smell, and when I put the empty clip in, the action was still mechanically beautiful. For now, its brand-new brother—Velda's early wedding present—would stay here at home in my hidden gun locker, from which I'd retrieved the older gun and its shoulder holster. Like me, this baby had a lot of miles on it, but neither of us was ready to get off the road just yet.

I thumbed the button, popped the clip out and fingered in a full load of fresh G.I.-style cap-and-ball ammunition. With a weapon like that, you don't need fancy loads. A graze will spin you around like a top and any kind of a hit at all is a stopping one. Hell, you don't even have to *shoot* it to make your point. The thing looks downright intimidating just hanging loose in your hand.

The shoulder holster was still quiet and limber, no squeaking leather, and the encased spring was still tensed to the degree I liked. I slipped the harness on, adjusted it to the proper snugness and dropped the .45 into its own little hiding place where it nestled like a cat behind its favorite cushion.

There was no encumbering weight at all. No over-balancing, so there wasn't any strain on the scar tissue where I took those slugs last year. The bruised area on my chest felt the weight a little, but no big deal. I slipped my jacket on and looked in the mirror. The tailor had done his job again. No bulges. You couldn't tell I was wearing the rig at all, a real trick with a weapon this size.

And so we were together again. Maybe I didn't like it the way I used to like it, but it was a necessity once more. Very casually I'd open my coat somewhere and eyes would see the butt end of the gun and the word would go out so that anybody coming for me would be put off stride just enough for the older, slower me to take evasive action and get into my own attack mode. Maybe.

I'd lived a long time, a lot longer than I thought I would, and a hell of a lot longer than most people figured. That cop yesterday had been twenty-eight, putting in four years on the force, with several citations for valor, a non-drinker who didn't smoke. He had been active in youth groups and was a great role model for kids. His latest physical exam showed him to be in top physical shape. By all rights, he should have lived a lot longer than me, even though like me, he carried a gun in his work.

But a gun didn't kill him.

He had an unexpected heart attack and was dead before he hit the ground.

It was fifteen minutes after five and the sun hadn't come up yet. The streets were empty and a cruising cab saw me wave and stopped outside the apartment house doors. After I gave the driver my office address, I sat back and thought about how the hitman in the pale blue hat and the tailored navy blue suit would have carried out his assignment.

Until six a.m., everybody at the Hackard Building had to sign in, showing identification to the wary ex-cop at the security desk. He was armed and ready, his hand always near an alarm button that alerted mobile backup. The man in the pale blue hat would have known this if he was any good at all.

But promptly at six the guard went off duty and the doorman and other lobby personnel came on. The early birds would start coming in at odd intervals, the photographers on my floor, the commercial artists who did their own freelance work before teaching classes later, the group who did telephone solicitations until they were relieved at three in the afternoon.

I had gotten in just before six-thirty, so the shooter

had plenty of time to make his under-the-radar entry. He would have been too ordinary-looking for anyone to have taken special notice of him. On my floor, the eighth, simply by standing near the elevator, he could easily assume the look of someone taking leave after an early morning meeting. If anyone noticed him particularly, he could simply check his watch and act as though he were waiting for someone to join him.

At five-thirty I paid off the cabbie and stepped out onto the nearly deserted street. The inactivity at this early hour was always a little startling. New York was awake, but like many an early riser, it hadn't started to really move yet. The people of this city were mostly clawing at sleep-caked eyes or showering or having a buttered hard roll and coffee. It would be another hour before the collective entity that was New York City would be ready to face the competition. Which had made this a great time of day for the man in the pale blue hat to case the workings of an office building.

Now it was my turn.

The avenues at each end of the street had a steady but intermittent flow of traffic. Two cars turned toward me but passed by, and I started walking east against the one-way occasional traffic. Half-way up I turned around, crossed the street and headed back to the Hackard Building.

Right ahead of me, a janitor came out of the dark front of a store, dragging two huge plastic bags of garbage. Fortyish, black, with solid shoulders and a modest paunch, he set them on the curb, made sure they were steady, and brushed his hands off on his pant legs.

I went up to him and said, "How early do the trucks come to pick up your stuff?"

He looked at me like I had straw sticking out of my ears. "Man, those guys are done before dawn shows off her crack. You see any garbage out now?"

"Just yours."

He squinted up at me, a quick but careful inspection—the suit and tie, the hat worn only by old hardcore types. "You some kind of official, mister?"

"Naw. Just a curious neighbor."

This time he nodded sagely. "Yeah, I shoulda knowed that. Officials don't get up that early in this city." He paused and let a grin spread across his face. "You know what's in them bags?"

I shook my head. "They didn't look too heavy."

"Paper," he told me. "All the ends off the spools in the store. They got maybe thirty feet on each roller and when they get low, my cousin picks 'em up, takes a load to Jersey, and we each make a hundred extra bucks a week."

"Do the owners know what they're giving away?"

"They don't give a shit. They're glad to get rid of it."

Across the street an old shopping cart gal pushed her load of odd bits and pieces of city flotsam along on wiggly wheels. The janitor saw me watching her and said, "That's Alma. Sure looks like an old bag lady, don't she?"

"Yeah, I've seen her around. Why, *isn't* she an old bag lady?"

He yelled out, "Hey Alma, what's happening?"

She yelled back, "I've been invited to breakfast at the Waldorf to discuss eliminating the capital gains tax!"

I laughed. *"That's* bag lady talk?"

"Ah, don't mind Alma," he said, laughing too. "She's got a wacky streak."

"She sure doesn't talk like some old bag."

"You'd better believe it." He leaned in. "Tell you a secret. She ain't what she seems."

"No?"

"She's great with stage make-up and if she's talkin' to somebody she don't really know, she sounds like she's got a mouth full of wood chips."

"What is she, some Broadway type researching a part?"

This time he let out a soft chuckle. "Man, have you got that wrong. You must be new in this neighborhood."

I shrugged. If thinking that about me kept him talkative, that was just fine.

"Well, this is New York City, friend. The *real* New York. That gal over there? A lady cop. Nice broad, too. Decent-looking cleaned up, but even then? Real fuckin' tough. Took down two pushers who were all set to get into a knife fight last week. Clubbed them out with some little gimmick she swung."

"What the hell could that have been?" *A hand sap.*

"Who knows? And I ain't askin' her." He gave me

that squint again. "Where you from, mister?"

I didn't really lie to him. It had been many months since I had been a temporary resident there, but I said, "Florida. Down in the Keys."

"But you sound like New York, when I listen close."

"I was from here originally. But the Keys has fewer knife fights and the bag ladies aren't dangerous unless one bites you."

He laughed a little, then his eyes got distant. "I should go there someday. The Keys."

Somewhere a garbage truck screamed.

"Just be sure it's the off-season," I advised him.

He started to ask me why, but I had turned and was following Alma down the street, crossing over to catch up to her a hundred feet from the corner.

She had heard me coming, even though I hardly made any sound in my crepe-rubber-soled shoes. Her subtle turn seemed almost harmless until you noticed that it was a spring coiling, ready to do a deadly unwind in one second.

I said, "Hiya, Rita."

She played it straight and grimaced at me. In that dull light she looked a good seventy years old. "Who you think I am, chump?"

"I know you're Rita Callaghan," I told her. "You gave a great talk at the academy five years ago."

She only half-sounded like an old gal when she asked, "You a cop?"

My answer went around her question. "We didn't

meet, Rita—I was there with Captain Chambers on another matter. He recruited a couple of your attendees for that campus shakedown that spring."

Callaghan played it straight right to the end. She held onto the handle of the shopping cart, turned slightly, but deliberately and out of nowhere a pencil light flashed in her hand. The sun was barely up and we were in a concrete canyon and she could use the help. The little beam ran over my face a couple of times, then snapped off.

It took a moment to get set in her mind, then she said in a much younger, almost melodic voice, "Well, I'll be damned. You're Mike Hammer."

"Everybody's gotta be somebody," I said.

"You're somebody all right."

I nodded. "Where did 'Alma' come from?"

There was a lovely dark-haired brunette in her late thirties buried under that get-up and stagecraft.

"That's my street name," she said. "Like it?"

"I like Rita better."

"Didn't you used to be heavier?"

"Yeah. And younger."

Her eyes looked me up and down like a lecher taking in a bathing beauty. "Walkin' around naked now, are you?"

I shook my head, opened my trenchcoat and unbuttoned my suitcoat to let her see the big gun in the rig, its butt poking out insolently at her from under my left arm.

She whistled. "Some damn tailor you got."

"You don't want to know what this suit cost me."

"What're you doing around here?"

"Working."

"I thought you retired after that shoot-out on the waterfront."

"Maybe I should have."

"Why do you say that, Mike?"

"Because somebody is shooting at me again."

"Damn. You're walking around. They must have missed."

"No, this guy's aim was pretty good. I caught two twenty-two slugs in the heart area."

"Ah. You wear a vest."

"No. A dictionary."

"Huh?"

"A nice thick paperback in my raincoat pocket. Stopped those babies on the last few pages."

Rita was a streetwise cop, all right. I didn't have to draw her any diagrams. She was nodding, asking, "What can I do for you?"

"My office is down the street." I pointed.

"The Hackard Building, right?"

"Right. Somebody has been casing it for at least a week, most likely between five-thirty and six in the morning. There's a possibility that somebody spotted him. I'd like a description."

"He know you're still alive?"

"Maybe. It happened two days ago."

"And you're just looking into it now."

"I got distracted. Some crazy shit going down lately, Rita. I may be old, but I'm still interesting."

"I just bet you are."

I described the man in the pale blue hat to her the best I could. "The time delay's no problem. If he goes true to form, he's got to make contact with whoever hired him, and that's probably through a middle man. He'll be looking for his payoff."

"Which he will not get."

I grinned. "And that will piss him off no end."

"So you figure he'll make a second trip back, to do the job right this time."

"You got it."

"Well, Mike. I'm a cop, and I know what your reputation is."

"Oh, I'll be a good citizen and turn him over to the police."

"Dead or alive?"

Another grin twisted my mouth and I said, "Such details will depend on the circumstances."

"Then probably dead."

"Probably dead."

"Man, you're just like they said you were."

"No, I'm mellow now. And the younger me would have got your phone number." I handed her my card. "Here's mine. If you see or hear anything, call me, okay?"

Her eyes were steady on mine and I answered her unspoken question. "I'm not asking you to go out on a limb for me. Check in with Pat Chambers and get clearance on this. I'd hate to see you have to turn into a *real* bag lady."

"You don't think I have other skills?" she asked, the prettiness under there making itself apparent, though the fake gunk on her teeth took the edge off.

We exchanged nods and grins and she and her cart rolled off.

There was one more contact I wanted to make, and my watch said the squad car would be coming down this street within the next five minutes, if it hadn't been routed onto a call somewhere else.

A touch of gray in the sky to the east said the night had given up the fight and almost as if a warning bell had gone off, the day's public parade began its dreamlike emergence. I didn't bother to study it because then the familiar blue-and-white from the local precinct was coming toward me and slowed when I waved it down from the curb.

The driver, Patrolman Steve Gonzales, gave me a grin the way Rita had, once she knew who I was, but this guy already did. He turned his head for a glance at his younger partner.

"We got ourselves a celebrity, Chuck. Probably on his way home from drinking a bunch of young dudes under the table."

Chuck's smile had some smirk in it as we exchanged nods.

My pal at the wheel wasn't through building me up:

"This is the guy who whacked out the Bonetti bunch all by himself."

I said, "That's just a rumor, Steve."

"Is it a rumor you blew out Azi Ponti's brains in that waterfront fracas?"

"More like an urban legend."

Steve stuck his hand out the window for a shake. "How you doin', Mike? Pat told me to be on the lookout for you. I hear you're popular again."

"If you mean somebody wants me dead, yeah. Tell me something—you been covering this area about the same time the past week?"

He let out a grunt. "For the past six months is more like it. We're winding down the shift right now. Why? What is it you need?"

I gave them a description of my assailant, but both were quick to say they hadn't noticed anybody fitting that description, or for that matter anything unusual on the Hackard Building's block. They did admit that they might not have been quite so sharp at the end of their tour, which wound up in this section. And the past week had been a pretty busy time. But they'd ask around and if anything turned up, they'd pass it on to Pat.

"Or me directly," I said, and knowing a card from a P.I. was nothing a cop wanted on him, added: "I'm in the book. You never know when a client wants to get in touch."

"Yeah," Steve said, "or some asshole with a gun."

When they pulled away I went back to the Hackard

Building and waited till Bill Raabe, the night security guard, came up from the basement locker room. He was in slacks and a sports jacket with a raincoat slung over his shoulder; like a lot of retired cops, he still wore an out-of-sight gun in a belt holster.

He knew that I had spotted the bulge and said, "Mike, it's a habit I can't seem to break."

"Yeah, I know," I told him, and gave him a quick peek at the .45 under my left arm.

"If that baby could talk," he said, shaking his head and smiling.

"If it could, my friend," I said, "I would be in stir."

He laughed at that, then moved his head to see behind me, making sure nobody was in earshot. "What went on upstairs, Mike? Two uniforms came around, kids I broke in on the street ten years ago, and took statements from me. Not that I could tell 'em anything."

"Somebody tried to knock me off. Couple days ago. Shot me twice."

Nothing fazed this guy. Without a change of expression, he asked me the same body armor question Rita had.

When I told him about the dictionary, he said, "Well, I'd trade Mr. Webster in on some real armor if I were you, Mike. If some bastard is out for you. You wouldn't believe the bullet-proof gear they got today."

"Actually I would. I've used it."

He frowned. "Well, use it again."

I was privy to an experimental lightweight vest courtesy

of an inventor pal of mine who developed high-tech gear for law enforcement, both local and federal.

But when I didn't share that info with him, Bill just said, "What are you after, Mike? Clue me in."

"You had much foot traffic through here at night lately?"

"For the past month, it's been only the same six tenants. Five males and one female. They've been in this building since I been here. Two are with an insurance outfit, the other three, which includes the woman, is a lawyer's office. These six do a lot of night work."

"And how do you pass the time?"

"Sit and read, mostly. If I get antsy, I get up and go look out the window. Hardly anybody out there at night, no drunks, no hookers, in this section… It's a real quiet street."

"You said 'hardly.'"

His mouth worked itself into a very faint smile. "Sometimes I forget what business you're in."

I waited.

He said, "About four days ago, I saw the same guy go past here three different times."

"So?"

"Where's there to go around here? There's two office buildings, one small apartment house that's empty 'cause of refurbishing, and all the rest is closed stores. Closest diner or coffee shop is two blocks."

I described my assailant as best I could.

Bill nodded. "That could be him. Small guy, natty but

not flashy. I was close to the window the last time he went by, and he turned his head as if he had seen somebody on the other side of the street, which maybe was him not wanting me to get a better fix on him. I glanced over where he was looking and nobody was there."

"You think he could have been casing this building for anything?"

"Why? It's not like we're the diamond district. I suppose the computers in these offices might be worth a…" He stopped abruptly and frowned. "Jesus, I'm slow on the uptake today. I blew that guy off because… Mike, damnit, I'm sorry. A hit never occurred to me." He wet his lips with his tongue. "Nobody in this place is worth hitting except you."

"Don't I count, Bill?"

"Yeah, but… you don't run in the kind of circles you used to. Everybody says… nothing."

"What, Bill?"

"I mean no offense, Mike, but after you got shot up on the waterfront, and fell off the grid, well… since you came back, everybody talks like you're just another…"

"Old fart?"

"I didn't say that. I feel like a fool, a goddamn idiot, not alerting you to this guy. I mean, a lot of people could have grudges against you. I remember you knocking off some real hard-cases back in the old days. They could have relatives."

"That's not what this is about."

"What *is* it about, Mike?"

"If I knew," I said, "I wouldn't be out asking questions."

He looked past me, as a couple walked toward the elevator. "Married," he said. "They run that photography studio. Not the commercial, the studio."

"Yeah."

Then, very casually, and softer than before, he said, "Back before the holidays, I heard a rumor that you had come into some real dough. That true, Mike?"

"Do I look like I'm carrying a bankroll?"

"Well, that might explain somebody popping you. Maybe you're carrying around a wad, and this was just a kind of mugging."

"Not what it was. Where did you hear this, me coming into money?"

"Ah, I'm just passing on a rumor."

"Where'd you hear it?"

"In a bar." He leaned in. "Remember Teddy Baer?"

"Sure. Killed breaking into an electronics store. Didn't know the owner slept there. How would *he* get a story like that?"

"Teddy told a friend of mine. Said that's what one of Ponti's guys had heard." He saw my face tighten at that. "Fatso Berg told Teddy. Fatso ate like a horse but was skinny as a rail, which is why they called him Fatso. It's ironic."

"Is that what it is. Where's Fatso now?"

"A cemetery. He got hit by a bakery truck and killed not long after."

Now *that* was ironic.

I said, "Hell, a small-fry like Fatso wouldn't have the skinny. He was no made man."

"Come on, Mike, he had ears. Even those fringe mob guys pick up on things."

"You tell all this to the cops who came around the other day?"

"They didn't ask me the same questions as you, Mike. Since I didn't know what was going on, I never gave it much thought."

I let out a sigh. "Okay, Bill. Keep your eyes open, will you? If you see pale-hat boy again, let me know."

He patted his jacket over the belted .38. "Want me to take him?"

"No! Don't get ambitious. Just call me. I'm more anxious to talk to him than kill him. You know—first things first."

"You want who hired him."

"I want his employer, yes." I reached in my pocket and took out some bills.

Bill caught my wrist. "Mike… cut the comedy. Not necessary."

"I'm always glad to help a guy out who helps *me* out."

He grinned, shook his head. "In thirty years with the department, I got to know some high-rollers on Wall Street. Over time, I made a bundle. Now I'm retired and nobody's shooting at me."

"Then why the hell are you working nights in this place, Bill?"

"A guy's got to get out of the house," he said. "I have breakfast with the guys from the precinct, then go home and sleep all day, so I don't have to listen my wife ranting and raving."

"Personal problems, Bill?"

"Oh yeah." His eyes widened. "She's a Democrat."

When I got on the elevator, I had that funny feeling in the pit of my stomach and I automatically opened my jacket to make it easier to get to my .45. I went up and the elevator door slid open, but nobody was there. From down the hall came the muted voices of the commercial photographers having a final coffee before getting to their assignments.

I stepped out, saw nobody, and walked to the office. I unlocked the door and went in, Velda not in yet. I shrugged out of my trenchcoat and hung it up, feeling that small ache in my side and the tightness of my bruised chest. I started the coffee, then went into my inner office, took the clip out of the automatic, and laid it on my desk. My watch said it wasn't seven yet and for some stupid reason I felt like I had already done a hard day's work.

The window behind me as I sat at the desk revealed a day that couldn't quite stop being night, overcast and threatening rain. Suddenly every ache in me decided to throb and I had that fox-hole feeling where everything seemed to be closing in on me.

There was a time when waiting for school to let out for the summer, the days dragged by as if they were hauling a load of rocks. Time moved slow when you were a kid, and summer lasted forever but not long enough. Summer for me as a kid was the beach. But now hot days and warm ocean water seemed a lifetime away. No, not summer, but Florida was calling me back, to spend whatever time Velda and I had left far away from bullet alley, where the sand was warm and the pace was slow. This was the city, where everything was greased and slippery; time was on a fast roll, rocket-driven, and all you could see was an indefinable blur that was your life passing by and it hardly made any sense at all.

How long ago was Marcus Dooley killed? Not much more than a year, that's all. How long had it taken him to bury eighty-nine billion dollars? He had all the time he needed and the equipment to do it with, and a bunch of doomed workers, and nobody to oversee him because Don Lorenzo Ponti made sure he was a world away when the big haul went down. It was all done so silently and quickly. Nobody would notice bulldozers working if that's where they were supposed to be. Nobody would pay attention to trucks if they were supposed to be there. And who would care if they saw nothing accomplished after all that work? They'd probably just figure it to be some government project.

So how long ago was it that the fertile minds of shrewd old men decided to harvest all their vast wealth into a single touchy-feely pile, dollars in denominations that could still be cashed? Ten years ago, minimum.

Their offspring couldn't be trusted. The new generation would kill their fathers as fast as their enemies. The spawn knew the old guard had given them a royal screwing but they didn't know how.

What they did know was that eighty-nine billion dollars in unmarked, used currency represented one vast accumulation of wealth that just didn't turn into dust and blow into the wind.

No, that was wrong. They *didn't* know. There was no proof. *But they suspected with near absolute certainty that the rumor was true.*

And that was enough to kill for.

To send an assassin in a pale blue hat to take me out.

So I would deal with the prick. Fine by me. That was the price of doing business when you were Mike Hammer.

But why now?

No money ever surfaced. Any wise guy would have to assume that if somebody had tapped into that pile of dough, a lead to that somebody would have surfaced by now. The Ponti affair was ancient news. The government had turned its best people loose to find that rumored cache. They had probed and dug and searched and come up with only a rumor.

The legal minds in the mob must have done some heavy thinking, trying to weave me into that caper. All they could come up with was an old-time shot-up private dick who'd rushed to the bedside of a dying war buddy. A dinosaur with no smarts, not when he shows himself back in New York where Don Lorenzo

Ponti would surely want vengeance on the man who killed Azi, his beloved son, his heir apparent.

But it hadn't worked out that way. Azi and his brother Ugo had turned on Don Ponti, and now Azi and the don were dead, and Ugo was buried deep in federal custody. The Pontis were ancient history. And, in a way, so was I.

But if somebody in what remained of the Ponti camp had figured out that I was the key to all that hidden loot, why in hell would they want me dead?

The outer door opened and shut and I heard Velda cross the room. Her purse thudded on the desk, and when she opened the door to the inner office, her lovely dark eyes read my mind as easily as if were they were the front page over her morning coffee.

Speaking of coffee, she brought two cups as she asked, "Any news on various fronts?" She was in a gold silk blouse and a darker gold skirt, and looked like a million.

Make that billion.

I said, "What happened to 'good morning'?"

She grinned and came over and leaned across the desk and kissed me. It was a soft, warm, light kiss that shouldn't have done much, but still drew my stomach in with an erotic tickle.

"Is *that* good morning enough, Mike?"

"You're lucky you're on that side of the desk," I told her.

She glanced at the unloaded weapon on my desk. "What's with the gun, Mike?"

"It's a heavy piece, kitten. Rubs where I hurt." She didn't say anything, so I added, "The butt's pointing my way and it's well within reach."

"It's unloaded."

"There's one in the chamber."

She gave her head a little shake and all that raven hair bounced beautifully. "You never change."

"Neither do you, and I like it that way. You're packing the .32 in your pocketbook again."

"How do you know that?"

"I heard it hit the desk."

"One would almost think the man's a detective."

She walked around the corner of my typewriter—no computer for me—and settled her sweet rump on my desk and took my hand in hers, then made me feel where she kept her hidden .25 automatic. I took my hand away and said, "Keep that up and I'll have you go lock the office door."

She sat in my lap and put her arms around me, her head back, studying me for clues. "Why don't we get out of this town, Mike? Find a beach and a cottage where we can make love all day."

"And not the night?"

"The nighttime, too." She gave me another light kiss, then got up and went around to the client's chair, settling in and having a sip of coffee. "How long are we going to wait till things 'settle down' before we can get married?"

"Baby, before taking that step, I insist on finding out

who wants a piece of me besides you."

For a second her eyes went troubled. "You think the hit is tied to the money issue."

Now I sipped coffee. "I do. After talking to both Olaf and Brogan, I admit to not knowing which of them was the Bowery Bum slayer, but I can't see any way either of them could tie in with some sophisticated hitman making a try on me. I asked around the neighborhood, doll—this guy was good. The only person who spotted him was Bill Raabe. And Bill says the guy definitely was casing the building."

"A pro."

"A high-end pro."

"So it's got to be the money."

"Well, it *could* be some revenge angle from the past, but I don't buy it."

She shrugged and her breasts fought the silk blouse like puppies under a blanket. "You've killed more than your share of high-up mob types."

"Yes, but any new regime that comes in doesn't give a shit. Hell, I helped them! No, it's not mob. Not unless they have somehow figured out where the stash of cash is, and want me out of the picture."

An eyebrow arched. "That *is* possible, Mike. Is anything *else* possible?"

I nodded. "The mysterious helper. If Dooley brought along a buddy to help him out, that means another person knows about the mountain cave and its secret."

Her frown was thoughtful. "So how do we track that? Pat's tracking the military intelligence side, but what can we do? Dooley is dead, his wife, too, and his employer, and... but not his *son*!"

I grinned and nodded. "That's right. His son Marvin is alive. He and his father weren't all that tight in recent years, but Marvin may know if there were any friends of his dad's, maybe drinking buddies from the old days, who Dooley might have turned to."

She was already on her feet, heading back to her desk. "We have a phone number on him. I don't think he's employed, so we may catch him. I'll call." She paused at the connecting door and glanced back prettily. "Finish your coffee."

"Why, you think I need the caffeine?"

"You never know. And load that gun."

But I already had.

Marvin Dooley was willing to see us. He lived in New Brunswick, New Jersey, and that was a forty-five-minute drive this time of day. If the rain ever happened, that might slow us, but this seemed a worthwhile day trip.

Velda locked up the office and we took the elevator down to the building's basement parking garage. My heap, as I affectionately called my nondescript black Ford, was parked in its designated slot between a pillar and an empty space.

We were in the car, and I was about to turn the key

in the ignition when Velda gripped my arm. *"Mike!...* This is too familiar..."

For a long time Velda had bugged me about what a slob I was, getting my car washed every decade or so. But a while back she had finally figured out the method in my madness—that the dirty vehicle left telltale signs of tampering. She had learned this last year, when my gaze down the hood line had stopped me and I had pointed where somebody had left a smeared-clean patch, having squeezed in between the car and the wall to open the hood.

That had hardly been the first time my car had been rigged to explode upon ignition—back when the Evello mob was after me, they'd left me a sweet new ride, with a very special set of accessories, starting with dynamite sticks rigged with the starter, easy to spot, and a second more sophisticated kicker prepped to go off when I hit a higher speed.

But last year's package had been more sophisticated in one sense—a foil-wrapped plastics explosive charge, one inch by four inches—but less so in that the bundle simply used the ignition as a power source.

And now, as I paused with my hand on the key, looking toward the hood where Velda pointed, I again saw a clean area where it had been lifted.

"Doll," I said quietly, "get out and stand back around the corner."

She shook her head firmly, black arcs of hair swinging.

"Walk away, Mike. We'll call Pat and he can get his bomb squad experts over."

"Don't be a backseat driver. I'm dealing with this."

"Mike, don't be a macho idiot. Let me call Pat."

"Okay, honey. Go ahead. I'll stand watch here."

She nodded and got out, then walked quickly toward the elevator and once she had stepped in and disappeared behind its sliding door, I unlocked the hood latch from inside the car. From the glove compartment I got a small flashlight, then went around to the front of the vehicle. The nose of the heap hadn't been so close to the wall that there wasn't room for me to do my work, and I lifted the hood a little, slid the lever over, and pushed the lid up.

That was when I smelled it.

Not gas or oil, no—an aftershave, vaguely foreign, and very damn familiar.

When I dropped to the floor, the bullets carved into the concrete wall above me, sending cement shrapnel flying, the .22 shots echoing in the chamber that was the parking garage. I had perceived him only as a dark blur, stepping from behind the nearby pillar, catching that glimpse as I dropped on my side and I would have screamed, landing on the old tender waterfront wound as I did, but I was too busy hurling the metal flashlight at him.

The little projectile hit him on the left shoulder, knocking him back a bit, and the small man in the tailored navy suit lost his pale blue hat, revealing a head every bit as bald as an egg, and a skull eerily apparent under the skin, dark eyes almost glowing as despite the inconvenience of getting knocked back a shade by that flash, he pushed forward and aimed down, the narrow nose of the .22 preparing to spit fire and death.

But my .45 was out from under my arm and as much as I wanted to talk to this son of a bitch, as much as I needed him alive, there was that .22 to contend with, and a guy like this doesn't miss the second time, so I couldn't.

I fired off three rounds so fast they made one massive recoil, and each one made purchase with that round hairless orb that split into bloody ragged chunks like a target-range melon. Bone and blood and brain sprayed and splattered, mostly on the pillar and the nearby wall, but also on me and the Ford and even his fallen blue hat. He staggered, but he wasn't feeling anything, and then he went down all at once, like a sheet that lost its ghost.

I got to my feet and looked down at him sprawled on his back, arms and legs going every which way, as what was left of his head drained what used to be a brain onto the dirty concrete floor of the parking garage.

"*That's* how it's fucking done," I told him.

CHAPTER SIX

Having a captain of Homicide for a best friend can come in handy. Pat Chambers came straight over from his One Police Plaza office and had a look at the crime scene before the lab boys even showed.

I recounted the clever ruse used by the dead hitter to distract me—there of course was no explosive rigged to my starter at all—and commented on his poor judgment in aftershave choice. As Pat took this all in, Velda looked on with narrowed eyes and folded arms, her body language stating she was pissed at me for sending her off on an errand that had left me alone and to my own devices.

"Honey," I said, in a peace-keeping manner, "you better call Dooley's kid and set up a new time for the meet."

"This is a for *real* call?" she asked, arching an eyebrow.

"Calling Pat was for real," I said defensively.

Pat was amused. "You usually wait till *after* you've killed somebody before calling me, Mike."

"Go on, doll," I told her. "Set it up for this afternoon or this evening."

She turned to go, walking quickly, which always made for a nice view, and Pat put in, "Why don't you two get cellphones and join the twenty-first century?"

Dark hair bouncing, Velda glanced over her shoulder. "Are you kidding? He won't even go for beepers."

Then she was gone.

"Buddy," I said to Pat, "it isn't the twenty-first century yet. Let me enjoy my Luddite ways, will you?"

He was over having a look at the corpse in the natty blue suit. "This is nobody I know," he said. "How about you?"

"Just that it's the guy from the other day. My elevator man."

He knelt and checked for I.D. "His name is Ronald Johnson and he has a New York State driver's license. But nothing else. No credit cards, no Social Security card, nothing."

I wandered over. "Just enough I.D. to show a cop or anybody else official who might ask."

Pat rose, nodding. "We'll run his prints and let you know what we find. You know, even with me here streamlining things, this'll take a while. Always a headache, dealing with a crime scene in a parking garage."

I shrugged. "It's a slow time of day. You won't need

to bring in many uniforms to deal with cars pulling in and out."

"I'll need your .45 till after the inquest."

I handed it over and he slipped it in his trenchcoat pocket, for the forensics bunch to bag.

"Hate to think you're walking around naked, Mike."

"I may find something else to wear."

He nodded again, then gave me the squint that meant he was trying to pull me into focus. "What's this about Dooley's kid?"

"Just checking in with him, to see how he's doing. You know, following through for our late buddy."

"Well, that 'kid' is in his forties, right?"

"Pat, it's just a social call. You're getting suspicious in your old age."

"I'm suspicious at any age. This is about the billions his old man hid, isn't it?"

"He doesn't know anything about that."

Then Pat was looking past me. "Here come the forensics boys… Why don't you go back to your office? I'll come up and get a statement from you after we wrap up here."

I patted his shoulder. "Thanks, buddy."

He checked his watch. "We'll catch some lunch, after. Chinese okay?"

"Sure, as long as they don't require chopsticks."

"We'll make it Suzie's in the Village. Anyway, there's someplace I want to drop by down there, if your afternoon's clear."

"Sure."

"Okay. Have fun."

"Doing what?"

His smile was damn near impish. "Getting torn a new one by your fiancée."

But Pat was wrong. Velda was over her snit by the time I strolled in. She was getting herself some coffee and asked if I wanted one myself. I said yes.

She sat behind her desk and I sat on the edge of it, half-turned to her, sipping from my Styrofoam cup.

"I re-scheduled the meeting with Marvin Dooley for this evening," she said. "Eight o'clock."

"Good."

"Any idea who you killed downstairs?"

"A pro."

"Does that mean mob?"

"Probably."

Her forehead got thoughtful. "Then why bother trying to track down this accomplice of Dooley's? Any old rummy pal of his wouldn't have the means to hire a hitman. That puts the kill attempt in the mob column."

"I don't like that word 'accomplice.'"

She looked up at me, patience and irritation fighting a battle. Maybe she wasn't over the snit after all.

I sipped coffee. "What is it, baby?"

"Why do you assume your pal Dooley wasn't after that money himself?"

"Just wasn't like him."

She wasn't buying it. "Then why did he go to the trouble of changing road signs, covering up paths... why did he *steal* it in the first place?"

"He *didn't* steal it. He hid it away."

She rolled her eyes. "Mike, listen to yourself."

"Doll, Dooley didn't steal that money, he just took it out of circulation. Put it where nobody could get their hands on it, not the mob, not the government. He was having a big horse-laugh at a world gone to pot after he had fought a damn war to save it."

Her smile was thin, her eyes hooded. "I heard you say this before, Mike. That your old pal was making a statement."

"That's how I see it."

"It's how you *want* to see it. What did he ask you to do with the money? What were his instructions, Mike?"

"Well... you know he died before he could—"

"How much *did* he get out?"

I shrugged. "He said I'd be able to find it."

"And he left you his ashes, to return to his son in an urn that had longitude and latitude on it, disguised as an army serial number."

"Right."

"So did it ever occur to you that maybe... *maybe* he wanted his *son* to have the buried treasure?"

Was she right?

Had I read Dooley wrong? I kept thinking of him as my old pal in army intel in the war, but decades had gone by without much contact. People change. He'd gone to work for the mob, hadn't he? But as a goddamn gardener, not a soldier!

Not a soldier...

She put her hand on mine, looked up at me with kindness and patience. "Mike, I've been thinking about this a long time. Maybe Dooley *did* steal that money, intending to either sell it back to Don Lorenzo Ponti, or just wait until the old man died. Lorenzo was the last of the Old School capos, wasn't he?"

They'd all died of "natural causes," the rest of the Five Family capos who had backed the scheme of cashing everything in on paper, and hoarding it away. Some were murdered by their kids, under the guise of medically induced heart attacks and falls from high places, and sometimes time had simply caught up with them. Only Don Ponti, well into his eighties, had been left.

Had Dooley been waiting the old don out, till he could "inherit" the loot? Waiting for the black-robed guy with the scythe to take Lorenzo Ponti down to the Hell he so richly deserved?

"You might be right, doll," I admitted. "But we don't dare level with Marvin Dooley."

"Why not?"

"With the kind players in on this thing, he'd be dead in a day."

She was quietly contemplating that as I headed into my inner office.

Fifteen minutes later, the intercom on my desk let out a short blip and Velda told me I had a visitor. No details, just a tone of voice that said I'd want to see this unscheduled caller. I said send him in.

And when he came in, he needed no introduction—I had never seen him before, but knew exactly who he was.

Something odd happens to people who work in Washington, D.C., in those great buildings they like to say belong to the American public. Their clothes change for the better, their expressions change for the worse, their whole demeanor transmogrifies as they become important persons who hold power in either hand.

Flippantly, I said, "Mr. Buckley. What took you?"

A momentary furrow streaked between his eyes as he recalled that Velda hadn't mentioned his name over the intercom and that there had been no appointment.

Then he smiled and said, "I was advised not to underestimate your deductive skills, Mr. Hammer." He held up an opened wallet so I could see his credentials—Roger Buckley, United States Department of the Treasury.

I just nodded and waved to a chair. "Have a seat, Mr. Buckley. Always pleased to be a good citizen when the government comes calling."

He slid into the client chair and crossed his legs, gazing at me with gray eyes that went well with his prematurely gray hair and a three-piece suit just a shade darker. His face had a chiseled look, but a certain pouchiness touched his features, and even that tailored suit couldn't hide a growing paunch. He was dining well on the taxpayers.

"It's interesting that you're not surprised to see

me, Mr. Hammer. Usually the mere fact that I am a Treasury agent is enough to… unnerve a person."

"As long as you're not Internal Revenue Service," I said with a shrug, "there's no sweat."

"Tax problems, Mr. Hammer?"

"No, just a bad joke. Even if the IRS dropped around, it wouldn't be a pain—my taxes are all paid up. So, what can I do for you, Mr. Buckley?"

His smile was a twitch that left a frown. "My office is trying to put a closure on what is a fascinating story, but most likely a fictitious one… and your name has appeared on eleven different reports that have crossed my desk."

Why fence with the guy?

I said, "You're still looking for those eighty-nine billion dollars, aren't you?"

A few seconds passed before he answered, "That's a concern. Yes."

"What happened to Homer Watson? He was the last fed who came sniffing around."

"I've taken over the case."

"Is it? A *case*? I thought you said it was a fascinating story that was probably fictitious."

"It probably is, but nonetheless investigation is required. As I said, we'd like to close the matter."

"Why all this bother?"

"Eighty-nine billion dollars is a considerable sum, Mr. Hammer."

"It's less than ninety."

He shifted in his seat, and his twitch of a smile lingered a tad longer. "Mr. Hammer, I'm sure you realize you just can't march into a bank and deposit this sum. Pull up in a Brinks-type truck at the head of a fleet of such trucks, and cart in box upon box for deposit. If the story of this fortune's existence is true, the denomination of those bills would be of no practical use, would they?"

I said, "If another *government* had them, they could be put to good use, couldn't they?"

Buckley nodded, the gray eyes half-lidded now.

I went on: "Of course, there would be one hell of a lot of trouble arranging for delivery between here and overseas."

He drew in a breath, then let it out. Was he going to engage me in this conversation?

Yes he was: "Not for experts, Mr. Hammer. They move tons of illegal drugs and forbidden imports around the globe."

"Hardly my line, Mr. Buckley."

The Treasury agent leaned forward a little. "It doesn't *have* to be your line, Mr. Hammer. All you would need do is provide the location of that hoard and it would all be taken care of."

"Including me," I offered.

"Do you really think your government would—"

I raised a hand. "It's buried in my official history, and perhaps still confidential, but I was briefly associated with an agency that operated in the shadow world between the F.B.I. and C.I.A. An agency that took care of liquidations whenever they were deemed necessary."

Finally, he seemed a little shaken. A little.

Then the twitch of a smile again: "Mr. Hammer, at this stage of your storied existence, you would frankly be too little to bother with. Your reward would be beyond your wildest dreams, yet a mere business item to the others. Your personal safety would be secure, since you would have no direct dealing with anyone other than myself… You wouldn't have to leave that comfortable desk chair."

That rated a laugh. "You have an oversized supposition going for you, Agent Buckley. How the hell would a private investigator at this stage of my, what was it? Storied existence? How exactly would a guy my age walk into an eighty-nine billion caper? How could I hide that kind of dough, assuming it existed? *Where* could I hide it? Damn, man, a dozen government agencies have been on my back since the Ponti crowd went down. It would take one hell of an organization to pull off a job like that, and all I am is one man."

Buckley smiled, not a twitch this time. "Hitler was just one man," he reminded me.

"So was Patton," I said, and gave him the nasty grin.

This time he reminded me: "I hear Patton's dead."

"I heard the same about Hitler," I told him. "But last time I looked, I was still alive."

Buckley's smile was anything but friendly. "For how long, Hammer, how long?"

"That's always the question, isn't it? Someone tried to kill me just this morning."

That got his attention. He blinked and sat forward. Way forward. "What's that you say, Hammer?"

No *Mister*…

"Somebody in a suit every bit as nice as yours, Agent Buckley, tried to kill me in the parking garage of this building, oh…" I checked my watch. "…an hour and ten minutes ago, give or take. You needn't be concerned. I killed him."

Buckley gave me a strange look as if he were trying to put me into some definite category. His head made a brief, puzzled movement and he said, "I just can't see how a person in your… modest circumstances can suddenly become a major cog in an international financial scandal."

I shrugged. "What scandal is that, pal? You're all running around like chickens who just got acquainted with an axe, looking for money you aren't even sure exists. Your computers came up with a number. So what? You're running down rumors and nothing sticks, does it? Just answer one question for me, will you?"

His eyebrows raised.

I said, "What would I do with that kind of dough, anyway?"

The smile twitched again. "You make an interesting point, Mr. Hammer. But first let me assure you that this morning's attempt on your life was not the doing of your government."

"It's not really my government. I haven't voted since Dewey and Truman."

He ignored that as he got to his feet. "I mentioned a reward earlier. Might I be more specific?"

"Be my guest."

"The Treasury Department would offer you a ten percent finder's fee on this eighty-nine billion... should it in fact be real. In fact, we would round it off to a billion. Couldn't you make do with that, Mr. Hammer, to supplement your retirement years?"

That made a good exit line. Anyway, I couldn't think of a better one.

When he'd left, I hit the intercom button and it took about thirty seconds for Velda to join me. She wore a pleased expression as she laid a miniaturized tape spool on my desk. Buckley probably had been wired too, but at least our visit was on record now.

She sat where Buckley had, but when she crossed her legs, the view was much better. "You sure get some high priority types for visitors, Mike."

"He was just putting me on notice, doll."

"Oh?"

"From now on we're going to have Big Brother's top-of-the-line surveillance teams covering every move we make. Their top guns, their best equipment... the works."

She cocked her head, unsure. "Mr. Buckley seemed to have trouble considering you a real threat... at least till you mentioned our deceased parking-garage visitor. So now you're comparing yourself to Patton, huh?"

"Better than Hitler."

She was amused. "You don't need to be Patton or Hitler. You're Mike Hammer, and that's plenty."

"In this thing, I'm just an accidental participant, due to my long-ago association with Marcus Dooley. But an accidental participant can really screw up the best laid plans of mice and men."

Velda shook her head and jerked a thumb over her shoulder. "So is that guy Buckley a mouse or a man, Mike?"

"Not just sure yet," I admitted.

She got up. "Pat stuck his head in fifteen minutes ago and I told him you were in with a visitor. He said he'd meet you for a late lunch at Suzie's, and then drive you over to his office for your statement."

This lunch date meant Pat had something to tell me he didn't want someone else listening to. Which was odd for Pat. He was a real by-the-book type and didn't like to jump off the rules.

As I was heading out, Velda was back at her desk, musing, "A billion-dollar finder's fee, Mike. Think of it."

"Yeah, doll," I said, getting into my trenchcoat, "but after taxes, we'd only have half of that."

We had one of Suzie's special dinners, eaten American style with a fork. The soft hum of voices was easy to blend into and there were no faces there we recognized. Nor any that paid any attention to us, either. Fragrances of steaming food on its way to tables tickled my nose like friendly phantoms.

Between bites, I asked, "What's going on, Pat?"

"This is the computer age, buddy."

"Stop the presses."

"I'm just saying," he said, with a shrug, "the New York Police Department works on a very sophisticated level these days."

"Good for them."

"In the last five years some incredible talent has come out of the academy. They have university educations, they've specialized in law enforcement, and on top of that, they are top-flight computer experts. Hell, even the F.B.I. would like to go head-hunting among our personnel… but our guys are strictly New York City types who have no love for the Fibbies."

"You *are* working toward some kind of a point here, aren't you, Pat?"

His eyebrows rose and he smiled, just a little. "One of our boys has come up with some interesting and… *offbeat* information."

My forkful of food and I waited.

Pat said, "Do I have to tell you organized crime has reached new heights, too?"

"So the rackets are still flourishing. So what?"

"So they will continue to flourish, but in a much revised fashion. The mob organizations still in operation exercise considerable influence in public affairs. They are more and more in legitimate business, leaving the illegal stuff to affiliates from overseas—

Asians, Russians, South Americans."

"With layers of insulation and money-laundering to protect them," I said, impatiently. "What's with the Mafia 101 routine?"

"Four of the five families are in the hands of that young, better-educated generation, the computer generation the old dons distrusted so much. But since Don Ponti bought it, the Ponti family is in flux. They are in a... crisis of leadership. They may be dying out, Mike. Somebody like the Gaetano bunch may swallow them up."

"Am I supposed to bust out crying?"

"I'm just suggesting... what would a massive infusion of cash do for the Pontis about now?"

"Not much, since the Pontis are pretty much all in the ground."

He was enjoying this. "But if a *new* leader steps in... with all that money... then what?"

"I guess they're back strong as ever. What do I care?"

Pat ate a few bites, and we sat in silence, as if the conversation was over. Then Pat touched his lips with a napkin and said through a small smile, "Your dead friend in the garage. We already have a match, Mike. We already know who he is."

I pushed aside my half-eaten plate. "Hell, that was fast."

"I told you it was the computer age, pal."

"Spill it."

"Well, he isn't Ronald Johnson. Elias Cardi. Corsican.

Freelance assassin with mostly French connections, if you'll forgive the joke."

"So he's mob. Big surprise."

"No, he's somebody the mob *uses*. Used. A high-end hitter who is about as out-of-town as talent gets. Mike, this guy was suspected in some major political hits."

"Which means that there is likely a mob contract out on me. Well, we suspected as much."

"Oh, but there's more, Mike. Our computer experts have zeroed in on some highly sensitive transmissions. They've uncovered coded communications out of the mob groups that read like a World War Two spy network in operation."

"What the hell are you—"

"If you're wondering why I'm laying this on you, it's because your name has come up enough times in these transmissions to make you a subject worthy of investigation."

I grunted a laugh. "So we're back to the eighty-nine billion dollar missing hoard of mob loot again, huh?"

"There's more to it than the money," Pat said.

I didn't try to hide my surprise. "What do your computer cops think is more important than eighty-nine *billion*? Hell, Pat... you could finance a small war with that!"

For a few seconds, Pat sat quietly. If he were a smoker he'd be lighting up a butt, but a long time ago he had quit like I had, so he simply shifted in his chair before he said, "*Something* in that treasure trove the old dons left was a lot more important than the money."

"Like what?"

"Beats me," Pat said with a shrug. "Nobody alive has ever seen that money. Nobody except maybe…"

"Don't say it, Pat."

"…you."

"I'm not on my deathbed yet, buddy."

"I'm not asking you to tell me, Mike. If you're keeping it to yourself, I guess you've got your reasons."

"Then what the hell are we talking about?"

The check came. He cracked open his fortune cookie, glanced at the little slip of paper, made a face and tossed it away. I broke open mine and ate it without reading the fortune. I'll make my own future, thanks.

He said quietly, "You're walking around like a guy without a care in the world while federal agencies are keeping a constant check on you, and the new crime outfits have you listed under a code name in their computers, while unanswered suppositions fly around like bees on a summer hive."

I let out a snort of a laugh. "Nobody's going to knock me off if they think I'm the only one who knows where that loot is buried."

Something grave came into his tone. "Mike, you're about to get married. You think I'm the only one who knows how close you and Velda are? She's been used as leverage to get at you before."

"She can take care of herself," I said.

But he was right. If this was just me, I'd say fuck it and take what came at me. But if anything happened to Velda, when we were finally heading into the sunset together...

"People close to you, Mike," he said, "make a bad habit of dying."

"You're doing all right, Pat."

"Who knows? Maybe I'll be the next cop to go down in this unlucky streak."

This morning, two cops in a squad car had interrupted a burglary in progress, engaging the perps in a gun battle, capturing both, but one uniformed cop was seriously injured with a gunshot wound to his chest. He was hospitalized and currently in critical condition.

On our way to One Police Plaza, Pat took a detour to a place that time had worn out and tried to throw away but couldn't quite shake off its hand, as if static electricity or stickiness prevented it.

The famous bums of the Bowery had become an endangered species lately, the city trying to shoo the homeless out as part of the general revival of the Lower East Side. The restaurant supply places hadn't been chased, and neither had the lamp shops. But the high crime rate of Skid Row days would soon be replaced by high-rise condos. Yet even now there were flophouses and tenements, blocks where the tide of gentrification had not yet swept through in its wave of cleansing cruelty.

There was room to park because nobody who lived

on this block owned a car, and those on other blocks wouldn't want to. Kids didn't play here because kids didn't live here. Old stores were empty and if their windows weren't broken, it was because they had been boarded up.

Pat parked in front of the ratty old four-story tenement where Brogan had lived for many decades and cut the engine.

"I did a little digging," he said, before we got out, "and came up with something interesting."

"I'll bite."

"Brogan purchased this building not long after Olaf was sent up."

"Where did Brogan get the dough?"

"Presumably from the robbery-murders he pulled off. It's one of the most convincing aspects of his story. The rent here has been his income ever since. His only job was playing super, which in a rat-trap like this didn't amount to much."

Up the steps and at the front door, I asked Pat if we had a warrant to search the place.

He shook his head. "We're checking the roof is all. We don't need a warrant."

"Checking the roof why?"

"You'll see."

Not having to trip over garbage or drunks on the stairs was a little unexpected. A smell of musty emptiness permeated the building, no odor of cooking, though the bouquet of a stuffed-up toilet hung on like a bad memory. At the top of the stairs the roof door was open an inch and had to be forced to swing back all the way.

"Nice view," Pat remarked.

Across the rooftop were the similar clusters of tenements, old wire clothes-dryer racks sagging between their T-bar uprights. One roof held the remnants of a TV antenna, a bent aluminum relic with a pair of crossbars still attached.

Pat motioned with his head for me to follow him and we picked our way through the accumulated clutter and across two retaining walls until Pat pointed one building over and said, "That's where Olaf originally lived."

"Why'd we come up through the other way?"

"Because we'd still be climbing through the garbage, that's why. Besides, right here is where Brogan led our boys to the murder gun."

I didn't say anything. This was Pat's day, a lot of years after that first day when we took Rudy Olaf down. He walked to the chimney, a weather-eroded old redbrick affair. On the north side a pair of iron pipes jutted up out of the wrinkled tar surface. The debris that had been caught between them had been pushed away. The masonry between the bricks had been removed and wooden wedges kept them in their proper positions.

Pat yanked the wedges out, tugged at the bricks until they came loose and the carefully constructed hiding place for Rudy Olaf's gun became evident.

"The wrapped-up weapon was in a galvanized can," Pat said, "painted with several coats of black waterproof material. Of course that, and the sealed plastic bag that had been inside, is now in an evidence locker."

Traffic sounds seemed oddly muted, a world away, not mere blocks.

I said, "Pat, why the hell did you drag me all the way up here to see this?"

"Because you were there at the beginning, kiddo. I want you to be right there at the end."

"Why?"

"You tell me, Mike."

I thought for a few seconds, then said, "Because something is seriously fucked-up about this."

"You got it. Figured out what yet?"

A siren screamed a few blocks away.

"Maybe," I said. "But for sure I know it smells worse than anything else in this neighborhood, which is saying something."

"Damn right." Pat pointed. "What was the purpose of this hidey hole? I mean, initially—going way back?"

"To stow the rod between jobs. The wallets that were found just hadn't been dumped yet, but the Bowery Bum slayer would always take the time to hide the murder weapon."

"A weapon bagged protectively for its next use."

I nodded. "So say Brogan is the killer. All those years ago, he lucks into having Olaf get wrongly tagged for the crimes. Now he has a free pass. He's had a couple of big scores, so cuts out the robberies and the kills that go with 'em. He buys his building and lives off the rent money, happily ever after."

"Right."

"But Pat—*why would he hold onto the piece?*"

"Maybe to have something to hang over Olaf's head."

"Naw, that stinks, Pat. Olaf was already in stir for the long haul. Look, we didn't have professional mob types here. We have two old slobs with nothing on their minds, just plodding along like Old Man River... only then one of them suddenly learns he's got the Big C. He has skyrocketing hospital bills and a couple of grandkids he cares about, and maybe, just maybe, he sees a way to lay one hell of a debt load on the city."

"So Brogan initiated the plan?"

I thought about it a while.

Then I shook my head and said, "I don't think so. I think this is Rudy baby all the way. Brogan came on his regular visits, and Olaf—hearing his old pal was dying—came up with the big scheme."

Pat was nodding slowly. "Olaf tells him where to find the gun. Brogan takes the rap. That simple."

"That simple, but..."

"But what, Mike?"

"Something still smells. If Brogan wasn't the killer, why those visits?"

"They were pals."

"Pretty damn good ones for Brogan to come around once a week for forty years bringing smokes and playing chess. Maybe it was Olaf who had something hanging over *Brogan's* head."

"What are you saying?"

My grin was suitably nasty. "What key group of people didn't testify at Olaf's trial, Pat?"

"Well… the victims, of course. They were dead to a man."

"Right. So maybe Olaf and Brogan were a team. Maybe they were in on this together from day one. Two muggers can take a guy down easier than one."

Pat snapped his fingers. "Shit! That makes perfect sense. Cut to the present day, and Brogan is dying. Olaf suggests his old pal step up and take the whole rap, and make his release possible so he can look out for the terminal Brogan's precious grandkids—thanks to the settlement the city will make for forty years of false imprisonment."

"Irony is," I said, looking across the ragged desolate landscape of rooftops, "when gentrification gets to this block, this old building will be a valuable property. There are probably speculators even now who would give a half-way decent price."

Pat punched a palm. "Brogan doesn't have the time to wait for this property to accumulate worth. And why settle for a speculator's low-ball offer when you can take the whole damn town for a bundle?"

I nodded. "*And* have the pleasure of damaging Captain Patrick Chambers' rep, right around retirement time, as a cherry on the sundae."

He thought about that, paced a small area of the

rough rooftop. Then he said, "How do we *prove* this? My God, these are forty-year-old murders!"

"*We* can't," I said, "but you *could*. Go back to the original files. Put some grunts on the detail and get them digging."

"For what?"

"For similar way-back-when incidents on Skid Row's gay-bar row. There may have been unsuccessful attempts, where a victim wriggled away. And/or robberies without killings that preceded the spree, as Olaf and Brogan warmed up. Hell, maybe Olaf had problems handling victims one-on-one and brought Brogan in as back up. Or vice versa."

His brow was furrowed; he looked worried. "That's thin, Mike. Any victims would be reluctant, particularly back then, to come forward, because of the homosexual aspect."

"It's worth checking, Pat. You may find old police reports that will lead you to surviving witnesses. Yes, it was forty years ago, but guys in their twenties or thirties hanging out in Bowery gay bars may well still be around today. And with changing times, may be more forthcoming."

"Does sound worth a try." Pat shook his head. "I would hate for these old bastards to get away with it."

I grinned at him. "You mean, get away with murder? Or tarnishing your golden reputation?"

"Screw you, buddy," he said.

But he was grinning, too.

* * *

At five o'clock that evening, when the late papers were already on the stands, Rudy Olaf was released from Sing Sing. The six o'clock TV news shows made mention of the incident, and radio stations carried brief bites about it, but the original crimes all happened so long ago, and involved such long-dead inconsequential people, that there was little news value. Nothing was said about the cash settlement Rudy Olaf was to receive.

Pat's rep took no hit at all—that the well-known captain of Homicide had made the initial arrest didn't rate a word. Apparently lawyer Rufus Tomlin had agreed to avoid publicity, if the price was right, and Pat got a free ride in public.

But at One Police Plaza, and at City Hall, powerful people would consider Pat a loser. He would likely be pressured to take early retirement, blotting out any possibility that he'd conclude his NYPD service as an inspector.

That wouldn't sit well with Pat.

And it sure as hell didn't sit right with me.

CHAPTER SEVEN

At precisely four forty-five p.m., Velda buzzed me on the intercom and said, "There's a call you're going to want to take."

I was swiveled toward the window where a gray afternoon was contemplating a shift into a gray evening. "That so?"

"That's so—an attorney whose name will be familiar to you."

I swiveled back around. "You don't mean Rufus Tomlin, Champion of the Underdog?"

"My man's a detective."

"Put him on," I told her.

There was a click and I said, "Michael Hammer here. What can I do for you, Mr. Tomlin?"

The voice was liquid with the Southern accent he had brought up with him from South Carolina many decades ago, a molasses drawl with a soothing pleasantness that had lulled many a juror.

"Mah apologies, Mr. Hammer, for callin' so late in the day. Unlikely as it seems, we have never met, but ah believe we both know of each other by deed and reputation."

"I believe we do, Mr. Tomlin."

"As you know, I'm the attorney for Rudolph Olaf, and you might assume that's my principal reason for callin'. But you would be wrong, Mr. Hammer. Ah am callin' in reference to another client of mine, a gentleman who desires certain information and thinks that you might be able to supply same. Might we meet and talk?"

"I'm free right now."

I was about to tell him to come to my office, but he anticipated that and said, "It's toward the end of your business day. Might I make up for my abrupt insertion of myself into your schedule by offerin' to buy you a meal over which we might talk a little business?"

"I could do that."

"At some neutral meeting place, if you please. Mah client prefers anonymity as much as possible. Of course, he will pay for your time."

Ordinarily, I wouldn't walk into a deal like that, but I'd figured something like this was going to happen. And a public place would make it safe enough.

I said, "I don't charge for a first conferral, but I will let you pick up the check."

"Agreeable, sir."

"You have any place in mind?"

"Ah believe there's a deli restaurant a few blocks from your office, is there not?"

"Charlie's you mean?"

"The very one, Mr. Hammer."

"You close by?"

"Ah can meet you there in ten."

"On my way, Mr. Tomlin."

I told Velda where I was headed and was half-way out when she called, "Don't forget we have an eight o'clock meeting with Marvin Dooley in New Brunswick."

"I won't be that long. This'll be supper—what can I bring you?"

"Just a salad with Italian."

That was part of how she beat back the clock. That and no smoking, moderate drinking, and every-other-day at the gym. I kept a similar regimen, but salad for supper wasn't part of it.

Charlie's Deli was a lively place with artifacts from the fifties. You could slip coins into a Wurlitzer and watch it spin 45 RPM platters still playing the best of Elvis or eye the gum-snapping waitresses in their short-skirted uniforms or be dazzled by the authentic signs, gas pumps and fixtures of an America that seemed more a figment of the imagination than a memory.

I took the side way in and spotted the big man in the small booth immediately—he wore a yellow corduroy jacket with a string tie and suspenders, his white-ish hair a mop on loan from Clarence Darrow. The booth was a good choice, with a commanding view of the dining area.

He had a finger hooked in a cup of coffee and pretended he hadn't noticed me until I slid in across from him and said, "Good afternoon, Mr. Tomlin."

He had the kind of light blue eyes usually reserved for movie stars. The pleasant face on the bucket head was tanned from trips home, as well-worn and grooved with use as a Yankee catcher's mitt. We were both seated as we shook hands.

"Please take no offense, Mr. Hammer, but ah'm afraid ah must ask—are you electronically compromised?"

"I'm not wired. Are you?"

Shaggy black caterpillar eyebrows rose and fell and the blue eyes twinkled. "Ah am not, sir. But meaning no offense again, ah'm afraid ah'm unable to settle for your assurance. Might we repair to the men's room?"

I shrugged. "Since you asked nicely."

In the smallish john, he reached in the old briefcase that he'd set on the sink and took out something in a paper bag. He ran the electronic scanner over my body. I held my hand out with my keys, change and a penknife, and let him see Velda's forty-five-caliber early wedding present under my arm, which got a non-twinkly look out of the blue eyes.

When he packed the device away, he said, "Ah'm afraid mah client insisted." The eyes held mine, waiting for several seconds, but I didn't ask him who his client was.

Then he graciously gestured for me to go first and we returned to our booth, which the waitress had held for us, getting rewarded with a ten-dollar Tomlin tip.

As we both settled back in, he said, "Ah'm pleased that your friend Captain Chambers won't be subjected to public humiliation due to the release of mah client."

"I admit I was surprised by that. Pat, too. Of course, as you know, counselor, the captain and I visited Rudy Olaf in prison, and the old boy didn't express any particular bitterness toward either of us."

"No. He's an interesting fellah, my client. He made the best out of his years of incarceration. And now he's ready to enjoy a new life, a... richer one."

"I don't suppose you'd care to say just how much richer."

His smile was a charming rumpled fold in that well-worn face. "No, Mr. Hammer, ah would not. Couldn't if ah wanted to—client confidentiality, y'know, as well as the terms of the agreement. Suffice to say, Mr. Olaf's final years will indeed be golden."

"But that's not why we're here."

"No, sir. It is not. Shall we order?"

We did. I ordered a corned beef and Swiss on rye with potato salad on the side, while Tomlin was on the same health kick as Velda: salad with Italian dressing, though the attorney added in a broiled chicken breast.

Conversationally, he said, "Say, the press surely made quite the hullabaloo out of that Ponti affair."

"Not an 'affair,' really. More a series of interwoven events."

"Concluding with the murder of Don Lorenzo by his son Ugo, and the latter's capture by yourself, Mr. Hammer. It's a particularly barbaric act, even in a world as cruel as ours, a son killing a father. A tragedy of Shakespearean proportions."

"Fuckin' A."

My calculated crudity amused him, momentarily. "This Ugo Ponti... he killed your *friend*, too, didn't he?"

He meant Marcus Dooley. This was a sideways method of introducing the real subject of this meeting.

"Ugo admitted it to me," I said. "He wasn't tried for the murder, though. They had him cold on his old man's killing."

The attorney shook his head and the mop of white hair seemed to pulse. "It was as if the entire eastern-seaboard of that, uh, *fraternity* was havin' itself a nervous breakdown." He pointed at me with his fork. "Your sudden exit from the scene, after that waterfront fracas, followed by... some months later... your unannounced entry back to the land of the living, Mr. Hammer, well... that was perfect theatrics."

"Mr. Tomlin, there was nothing staged about it. I was in the wrong place at the wrong time and got shot up pretty damn badly."

"Everyone thought you were dead. Even the press speculated as much."

"You know what they say about not believing everything you read in the papers."

Our food arrived. I gave the waitress Velda's to-go order. The Champion of the Underdog ate a few bites of salad while I starting working my way through my thick sandwich.

Then he said, "Now that the elder Mr. Ponti and many of his staff are dead or in prison, those still standing can only wonder just what the fuss was all about."

Elvis was singing "Jailhouse Rock."

I gave Tomlin a quick grin and said, "Somebody ought to make a movie. Sell billions of tickets."

"Is that right, Mr. Hammer? *Billions?*"

His eyes were like probing laser beams, but I was as good at this game as he was. Then he pushed the barely touched salad aside to say, "We are both busy individuals, Mr. Hammer. Might we please cut through the bullshit?"

"Do they let you talk that way in court, Mr. Tomlin? But be my guest—cut away."

"Ah will do just that, but… delicately. Ah have a responsibility to keep my client out of the limelight. Mah client, and *his* client. Understood?"

"Clearly."

"You do know the *real* subject at hand, here today… don't you, Mr. Hammer?"

"Money," I said. "Everything's about money."

He nodded sagely. "From the price of this meal, to the vast quantities of the stuff that it takes to run major corporate enterprises."

"Like the capital behind the late Don Ponti's corporate enterprises?" I chuckled. "Isn't it funny how death seems to exaggerate a person's wealth? How in death *rumored* wealth seems to get bigger, grander…?"

"Ah thought we were about to set *aside* the bullshit, Mr. Hammer."

"Then get to the point," I told him through a rudely chewed bite of sandwich.

Patiently he said, "Great organizations have modern technology at their literal fingertips. They hire persons with mind-bogglin' expertise to search out what they want to know. Once they obtain that information, Mr. Hammer, they can squeeze *very* hard." He paused, locking eyes with mine. "You do understand my meanin', sir?"

"Cash doesn't leave a paper trail, Mr. Tomlin, and the paper it's printed on doesn't hold fingerprints."

"Perhaps I don't understand *your* meanin'…?"

"The kind of money that 'great organization' you represent is looking for wasn't recorded in ledgers and, as far as tax records go, never existed."

"But it not only exists, Mr. Hammer—somebody *stole* it."

"Don't look at me, Mr. Tomlin." I was chewing again. "I'm just a two-bit NYC P.I. driving a Ford."

The black caterpillar eyebrows twitched, as if anxious to become butterflies. "Nonetheless, sir, there's some who would say *you* know where all that money is."

"You believe that, Mr. Tomlin? Is street talk enough to sway a man of your expertise?"

Tomlin's blue eyes narrowed somewhat. "Why, you're a rather interestin' character, aren't you, Mr. Hammer?"

"Don't pretend like you're taking a crash course." I leaned across the table. "You didn't come at me cold, counselor. You researched me first. You should have a damn good read on me by now."

Tomlin's eyes were so hard they might have been glass. "You could say that ah have, Mr. Hammer, yes."

"Then maybe you can tell me something. Where could *I* hide eighty-nine billion dollars? And if I had all that money, how would I spend it?"

A touch of wry humor seeped into his expression. "Strange as it is," he said, "there are some people who have little consideration for money at all. Are you one of that rare breed, Mr. Hammer?"

"Maybe."

"What do you suppose makes that kind of person tick, sir?"

I shrugged. "Imagine you suddenly had ten million bucks dropped in your lap. That may be small change to a successful Champion of the Underdog like yourself, but if that happened, who in your circle would be the happiest? You? Your wife? Your kids? *Who*, Mr. Tomlin?"

"Ah would imagine *ah* would be the happiest in mah circle, Mr. Hammer."

"Not you, pal. Your banker. You'd dump all your new loot across his desk and he'd rub his hands and be giddy as hell because now he has ten million more bucks to play with. And what do you get in return? A deposit slip with numbers on it."

His half a smile was wider than most normal ones. "Well, now, Mr. Hammer, that may be the most outrageous, out-sized over-simplification I ever heard."

"It's not an over-simplification at all. Tell me, Mr. Tomlin, what I could buy with eighty-nine billion dollars?"

"Well, obviously, anything you might wish."

"Suppose I have a pretty good list of things and stuff I'd like to have. Now suppose I've bought them all. A penthouse on Park Avenue, mansions in the Bahamas and Hawaii and France. Three or four garages, full of cars, classic and contemporary. Small fleet of boats. Closet after closet of Brooks Brothers numbers. How much of that eighty-nine billion would be left?"

"Most of it," he admitted. "And ah think ah can speak to that very point."

Tomlin rested his hands on the table and sat forward. His voice was low and friendly, but his smile was the one little girls see when a guy in a van offers them candy.

"Mah client," he confided, "wants you to know that he is in a position to offer you a substantial sum, sir, enough to make you a very rich man for the rest of your life. In return, he can assure you and your lady friend absolute, complete safety, no matter where on the face of this earth you might choose to reside—with absolutely no recrimination from any of the organizations with whom my client associates. If you would require further inducements, he is prepared to consider whatever... *sweeteners* you might desire."

"Maybe you could be more specific about those 'sweeteners.'"

His smile turned sly. "How about keepin' the gov'ment off your tail? We have surprisin' influence in those quarters. Left to their own devices, the federal folks don't take too kindly to the notion of a private citizen holdin' onto these kind of unrecorded funds."

"Your client seems to have a lot of clout."

"Oh my, yes."

"But what makes you think Uncle Sam would hold still for that kind of pressure?"

"Eighty-nine billion dollars is a whole hell of a lot of capital, Mr. Hammer. An off-the-books arrangement to share in the wealth could make everybody happy... and not just your hypothetical banker."

I grunted a laugh. "Know what else is hypothetical, Mr. Tomlin? Your eighty-nine billion dollars. You have any idea how big a pile that would make? Where the hell could I keep it without an army to back me up? But all right—let's say those billions *aren't* hypothetical."

His eyes twinkled again, cornpone Santa Claus that he was. "All right, Mr. Hammer—let's *do* that little thing."

"Fine. And as soon as I give that information to your client, or to Uncle Sam for that matter, I'll get a couple of slugs in the head and a grave in concrete."

He frowned, pretending to be offended. "This isn't Chicago in the '20s, Mr. Hammer. Nor is it Nazi Germany."

"Come off it, Rufus. Remember Waco? Wounded Knee ring a bell?"

"Nothing has happened to *you*, Mr. Hammer."

The muscles across my shoulders started to bunch up and get jumpy and I snarled, "Like you said earlier, let's cut the bullshit. Two days ago, I was shot twice outside my office. A pair of twenty-two slugs slammed right into the heart. A top notch pro did that, a studied hit with my moves researched and an aim worthy of a Desert Storm gunnery ship."

His change of expression was so subtle I almost missed it. "You are decidedly still alive, Mr. Hammer."

"Yeah, thanks to a pocket dictionary in an inside coat pocket. It decelerated the bullets and stopped them short of penetrating me. Hurt like hell. Still aches like a son of a bitch."

We might have been discussing the weather. "You know who did it?"

"Yes."

"You could identify him?"

"I don't need to. I killed him this morning."

If he was shocked, he didn't show it, and he asked for no details. "You don't seem terribly concerned, Mr. Hammer."

"Whoever sent him will probably send somebody else, and I'll send that somebody back the same way—dead as hell. And in the meantime my focus is on finding out who sent him. Any questions?"

"If the implication is that my *client* sent him, Mr. Hammer, I assure you that—"

"If your client sent him, he wouldn't have told you about it, would he?"

The attorney said nothing. Then he leaned back in his seat, as if putting as much distance between us as possible. "Mr. Hammer, my client would appreciate a response from you, as to whether you might be amenable to negotiating a…"

"Finder's fee?"

The attorney gave me a slow nod.

Our waitress brought me a paper bag with Velda's to-go order in it and put down the check. Connie Francis was singing "Who's Sorry Now."

I slid out of the booth. "Tell your client I appreciate his offer, Mr. Tomlin, but if I did know where that kind of loot was stashed, I'd probably just let it stay there."

"Why on earth would you do such a fool thing, man?"

"I don't have any love for the mob or the federal government. Why help either one out? Hey, but it's a real ego boost to think somebody would give me credit for sitting on a pile of cash that size." I grinned at him again. "What's *your* opinion, Tomlin? Unlikely reality or urban myth?"

"Well, you were right about one thing," he told me.

"Oh? What's that?"

"I did do a good deal of research on you, Mr. Hammer, and I do know the outlandish things of which you're capable."

He collected the check, but he and his shabby old briefcase remained in the booth as I headed for that side door.

I knew he wouldn't leave until I was out of sight.

As for me, I was wondering less about who his client was than who his *client's* client was.

Traffic on the Jersey Turnpike damn near made us late, but my lovely navigator got us to the New Brunswick address a couple minutes before eight.

The gray sky wasn't keeping its vague promise of rain, and the night had an almost sultry breeze, odd for this time of year. I left my trenchcoat in the car when we parked just down the block from the decrepit old apartment building in this rundown neighborhood on the city's outskirts. In this shambling structure, a haven for unfortunates surviving on welfare checks and food stamps, lived the son of a father who had been worth eighty-nine billion bucks.

A single bulb, its yellowish glow giving us immediate jaundice, hung high in a common vestibule where all but one of the mailboxes had slots with a scrawled identifier. The blank one was Marvin's and that was the button I pushed. We went through the door and up a creaking wooden staircase into a world of ethnic cooking smells and the muffled behind-closed-door sounds of rock radio, squalling babies, and screaming domestic quarrels.

I knocked at Marvin's paint-blistered door and waited while he checked the peephole that was as upscale an extra as this dump provided.

Then he opened the door and gave us each a nod by way of greeting, offering me no hand to shake.

In his late forties, Marvin Dooley had his father's rugged build but his mother's dark blond hair and dark blue eyes. His expression was one of weariness and barely withheld irritation. He wore a light blue polo shirt with a frayed collar, blue jeans, and white socks, no shoes. He looked tan in the weather-beaten way that said he hadn't got it on vacation.

"You remember Ms. Sterling, my associate," I said with a nod toward Velda.

He found a smile for her. He may have been grumpy but he wasn't dead, and this timelessly good-looking older woman in a khaki jumpsuit got his attention. He even gave her an additional nod, as he gestured us into his apartment, which was one large single room.

There had been improvements and additions since we met with him last year. The place had received some fresh coats of pale institutional green, a step up from peeling yellow. A decent second-hand sofa that no doubt folded into his bed replaced the military-style cot. The stove was new and the refrigerator, too, or anyway newer than the appliances whose places they'd taken. A fake-leather recliner was arranged before a big-screen projection TV as if the latter were an altar. The rest was as before: a scuffed chest of drawers, a few odd pieces of Goodwill furnishings, and an old Formica kitchen table with several wooden chairs.

And as before, the most striking aspect of this generous cell of an apartment was its neatness—no scattered dirty clothes, no dishes in the sink waiting to be washed, no layers of dust. On our previous visit, Marvin had explained he'd picked that habit up in the navy.

He asked us if we'd like beers and we declined. He didn't get himself one, just invited us to sit on the couch. We did, and he pulled over one of the kitchen chairs and sat facing us.

"I suppose I owe you a debt of thanks," he said with obvious reluctance. His voice was the only thing about him reminiscent of his father, and that gave me a slightly spooky feeling.

I said, "Why's that, Marvin?"

"You tracked down my father's killer. That Ugo Ponti son-of-a-bitch. Thank you for that. But I figure you might be... unhappy with me."

"Not at all. What makes you think so?"

He raised his eyebrows in tandem with a shrug. "I suppose I must have led him to you. Ugo, I mean. That night, he came by waving a gun, demanding to know what I'd told you. I cooperated and told him about my pop's boat and that urn with the numbers on it, the works. I thought I might still get a bullet, but instead he gave me a C-note."

"Classy guy, Ugo."

His face went tight with controlled anger. "Why didn't you *kill* him, Mr. Hammer? That's what you usually do, isn't it? That Jack Williams, who was in the service with you and Dad, you killed *his* killer."

I sighed. "That was a long time ago, Marvin. I hurt Ugo bad and turned him over to the cops. If he ever gets into the general prison population, he'll be dead in a couple of hours."

"But right now he's on Riker's Island, waiting for trial. I hope he gets lethal injection."

"Bet on it. Anyway, Marvin, I don't blame you for talking your way out of Ugo killing you. Good for you, man. Above ground is the place to be."

He was sitting with his shoulders hunched, his legs apart, the interlaced fingers of both hands hanging between, like a prayer that gave up on itself. "I appreciate that, Mr. Hammer."

Velda said, "You spruced the place up."

"It's still a hole, Ms. Sterling. But I inherited my father's house in Brooklyn, sold it, and that gave me a little something to supplement my income."

I asked, "What are you doing these days, Marvin?"

"Still following in my father's footsteps. You know,

after I got out of the navy and found out that Dad had gone out of business, I started up my own lawn service. Just mowing and trimming. Just me, nobody working for me—not a big outfit like Dad had going for a while."

"That was in Brooklyn," Velda said.

"Yeah. Then things slowed down, some heavyweight competition pushed me out, and I moved up here not quite a year ago. Partly to be near a woman I was dating."

Her smile was sympathetic. "You aren't any longer?"

"No." He returned the smile, rather shyly. "But I got a new girl. Life goes on, you know."

I asked, "Is your love life why you didn't just move into your father's house?"

He gestured around him, still smiling. "What, and leave all this behind, you mean? No, I couldn't live there, Mr. Hammer. Not in the house where that bastard killed Dad, just waltzed in and blew his guts out." He shuddered. "Anyway, it was no better a neighborhood than this. He took decent care of that house, but I got a hell of a lot less than I would've in a decent neighborhood."

I shrugged. "This is a nice pad."

"It'll do till I move in with Heather."

Velda smirked cutely. "She wouldn't be younger than you by any chance?"

He laughed once, first I'd ever heard from him. "Yeah, not a hell of a lot of Heathers my age."

I said, "You and your dad weren't close in recent years, were you?"

"No. No we weren't. I worked for him and Mom in the yard work business from junior high through high school. I was always tighter with Mom than Dad, which I hear is typical with only children. Then I went in the navy, and while I was stationed overseas, Mom died. I found out she'd... fallen off the wagon. Friends back here told me Dad had dropped her when she started drinking again. I confronted him about it, and it got ugly, and after that... well, we saw each other a handful of times. Kind of patched things up in recent years, but it was... strained."

"I'm sorry," Velda said.

"You know, now that I have a few miles on me," he said, and his eyes looked moist, "I can understand why Dad had to walk away from Mom. He was a lush, too, you know, or anyway a reformed one. An old AA guy from way back. If she was drinking, he just *couldn't* be around her. Not without risking... joining her."

Velda glanced at me. Her expression seemed bland but her eyes told me her heart was breaking for this forty-something "kid."

He sat with his head down for a few seconds, then straightened and gave me a nervous smile, asking, "So, what can I do for you, Mr. Hammer?"

"Well, first of all, I'm giving you a heads up. Do you own a gun?"

He nodded. "I have a Beretta M9 I brought back from the service."

"Good. Last year I told you that certain people may think your father entrusted information to you, and might come around wanting it."

"Ugo *did* come around," he reminded me.

"Right. But the hunt seems to be on again."

"Hunt for what?"

I felt Velda's eyes on me. "Marvin, your father did a sub rosa job for Don Lorenzo Ponti. A real cloak of secrecy deal. He was entrusted with some valuables and he hid them away."

He frowned in confusion. "What kind of valuables?"

"I need to keep it vague. Less you know, the safer you are. Just know that you should stay alert, and keep one in the chamber, got it?"

"Got it. So who's looking for whatever-this-is?"

"Mob. Feds. Them for sure. But maybe some interlopers as well. That's why I'm here. Did your father have any friends, particularly any one *close* friend, who he might trust to help him on a dangerous job? Somebody who could keep his mouth shut?"

Marvin was already shaking his head. "Mr. Hammer, I can count on one hand the times I saw my old man in the last twenty years. I knew he was working for Ponti as a groundskeeper and glorified handyman. That's partly why I steered clear of him. I didn't want anything to do with mob types. Still don't."

Velda said, "They may want something to do with you."

He nodded. "Understood." Then to me he said: "Mr. Hammer, I'm afraid I'm no help to you here."

"What about friends from back in the Brooklyn days? Back when your Mom and Pop's yard service business was thriving? Maybe somebody who worked with him?"

"No. He was a loner, my pop. He didn't let anybody in, except maybe Mom. He had a low tolerance level for stupidity and incompetence, and he would fire guys after three or four months. No second-in-command for him."

Velda asked, "What about old friends? From the war, or even before?"

The dark blue eyes narrowed. "Well, Dad grew up on the Lower East Side, you know. My grandfather owned a drug store, so they weren't as poor as a lot of people around there. I don't know much else about those years. I do know Dad went to some vocational high school."

I asked, "Metropolitan Vocational High School?"

"That could be it. He never said much about it, other than joke about being the toughest chess club president on the Bowery."

The Bowery again. Chess again. Coincidences?

"You know," Marvin was saying, "that was a kind of bone of contention between my pop and me. He loved chess. He and Mom used to play, and they were about equally good at it. But me, I'm strictly a checkers type."

"You and me both," I admitted. "So, did he have

anybody he enjoyed playing chess with, back in Brooklyn?"

"Other than Mom, I couldn't say. Sometimes he'd be gone on Sundays and Mom would joke that he was off beating Bobby Fischer in the Chess Nationals."

"Then he may have had a chess buddy or two in the city."

"It's possible." He shrugged. "Maybe dating back to before the war, in high school. Who knows? Listen, I got some boxes of Dad's stuff in a storage facility. Some of it goes back a long, long way. You want me to sort through it for you?"

"I'd rather do it myself," I said. I was on the edge of the couch.

"Let me gather it up," he said. "I'll give you a call."

On the way out, he finally shook my hand. "There *were* two guys who were really tight with my pop. He didn't see 'em much, but those two he talked about often."

"Yeah?" I asked, half-way out into the hall where the crying kiddies and battling parents fought their muffled wars.

"*You*, Mr. Hammer," he said. "You and Pat Chambers. That was his one regret—that you guys didn't stay in closer touch."

Hearing those words spoken in a voice that might have been Marcus Dooley's was like taking two more slugs to the heart.

I managed, "And I bet you know the feeling, right, Marvin?"

"That, Mr. Hammer, I do." He smiled at Velda. "Nice seeing you, Ms. Sterling."

And he closed the door on us.

CHAPTER EIGHT

I stood near my side of the bed and opened my belt, unhooking the clasp on my pants and pulling my shirt out. In the muted glow of a nightstand lamp, everything in Velda's bedroom seemed feminine but not overstated, nothing frilly or frou-frou, just soft colors and soft fabric and a few framed tasteful modernistic pieces dating back to the sixties by a starving Village artist who was worth dough now.

I draped my clothes over a nearby chair. Usually I only spent a weekend night or two here. Despite our decades-old relationship, Velda and I both knew I was a crusty old bachelor set in my ways, and liked living alone. This would change one day soon, but that wasn't the reason we were shacking it. I was still a target for parties unknown, making her a candidate for collateral damage. Steering clear of my apartment made sense, and it put Velda where I could protect her. And where she could protect me.

Standing there in my boxers, I looked down at the damage done me by bullets, old and new. Plenty of faded scars, of course, including souvenirs from the Pacific. And the blossom on my chest from the recent double-tap was taking on shades of purple and pink and yellow that rivaled any of the framed abstractions around me.

But it was the scarred area on my side that I wanted a closer look at—I had landed on it hard in that parking garage this morning, stirring up the old ache. It had been over a year since Azi Ponti's slugs had ripped those holes in me, outlets that would have drained the life out of me like rain from a sewer pipe if the weather hadn't been below zero and a drunken doctor hadn't been on the spot.

The healing had been slow but successful. Now the area around the scar tissue had taken on a pinkish glow where the skin had tightened over swelling flesh. The pain was minimal, but only in contrast to what it used to be.

Velda came in from the adjoining bathroom, toweling off all that hair, bundled in a white shortie terrycloth robe that showed off the muscular perfection of long legs still pearled with water from her shower.

Her dark eyes flashed with concern. "Mike… are you all right?"

"I'm swell, even if I'm as achy and stiff as an old whore working overtime."

She grinned and plopped herself on the bed, still drying her hair with the towel. "You do have a gift for the romantic turn of phrase."

I crawled up next to her, propped a fat pillow against the headboard and sat there, breathing slow. She paused in her toweling and had a look at the old wounded area.

"No fresh bruising. Hurting?"

"Some."

"How'd you antagonize it?"

"When I hit the deck this morning, the cement didn't do me any favors. Plus twisting away from those shots the other day didn't help either... At least nothing tore apart."

Her voice was gentle. "Maybe it's time, Mike."

"For what?"

"For hanging it up."

"Well, I admit I'm not gonna be running any foot races for a while."

She said nothing more on the subject, but everything was written right there on her face, framed by the mass of damp, dark gypsy curls that the shower had made out of her smooth pageboy.

Those lovely features were telling me the game was too rough to play it like I used to. Since that waterfront rumble, the odds had changed, the enemies younger and faster, and there were so many of them now. And I was just an aging P.I. hauling an anchor around by way of those sealed-over holes in my side.

I said, "I'll guess I'll just have to be smarter, doll."

She let out a short chuckle. "Little late in the game for that, isn't it?"

"I might surprise you."

"Okay, surprise me. What will your first smart move be?"

"Finding out who Dooley's chess partner was."

She dropped the towel in her lap and goggled at me, a friendly Medusa with that curly head of dark hair. "You're kidding, right?"

"Not at all. But I need to take you back before we ever met, for you to make sense of it. Back to the war."

Velda knew I rarely spoke of what had happened over there, so her response was a cautious nod.

"You can imagine what leave means to a guy who's been in combat, and who faces more. Pat and I did a lot of wild-ass things to keep our minds off the carnage. We thought we were having some good dumb fun, but in reality we were escaping the madness of death and destruction, any way we could, for just a few days, a few hours."

She nodded, respecting what I was sharing.

"But, Velda, it's the damnedest thing—Dooley never went on leave with us. Not once."

She frowned, then asked, "What *did* he do?"

"He played chess," I said.

"He… played chess."

"Played it with anybody who knew the game at all. He had one of those miniature pocket boards, and if he couldn't find a partner, he'd play against himself. I always wondered how he kept managing to line up any worthy opponents to compete with."

"He was really that good?"

"Well, he always had more money in his pocket than he made in the army, that's for sure. There was this two-week period when we were assigned to back up another unit. One of their men was a lieutenant whose father in the States was a big-band leader, and this kid was *loaded* with loot. *And* he was a chess player. World class, or so he claimed. Somebody put him onto Dooley and the two of them spent every free minute over that pocket-sized chessboard. Two weeks later Dooley mailed a fat packet of dough back home."

"Who to?"

"No idea. His parents, his girl, who knows? Maybe his high-school chess pal, because Dooley was playing by *mail*, too—one game went on the whole time Pat and I were with him, and he never wrapped it up. Mail was too slow and sporadic."

"Men are strange animals."

"Oh yeah? How many shoes are in your closet?"

"Don't change the subject."

I let out a sigh. "You know, never occurred to me at the time, but Dooley was like a damn drug addict with that game. Couldn't stay away from that chessboard. Sure, he'd stow it to fight the war, including teaching survival tactics to Pat and me, but when the shitstorm stopped? That miniature chessboard came out."

"Must have been what he needed."

"Must be."

"So, Mike, how did you and Pat get tight with a brainy guy into chess?"

"Behind the lines, when Hell was raining down, you bet we got tight in a hurry. And barracks life, we had plenty of fun, horseplay and sometimes dice or cards. But when the rest of us would be reading or heading off into town or taking in a new movie at the rec hall, that's when Dooley would disappear with his little chessboard."

We sat quietly for a few seconds, both mulling what I'd just revealed.

Then she said, "So you think some high-school buddy of Dooley's may also be his mysterious missing helper? Mike, some nerd he used to play chess with doesn't exactly compare to you or Pat."

"The war was over, doll. The bond between guys like us is something that will always be there… but while Pat and I stayed close, Dooley stayed the loner."

Her eyes were narrow with thought. "Well, why would Dooley go to a chess buddy for something that was more like a military expedition? If not you or Pat, why not his son? Marvin was in the service."

"Remember, Marvin and his father weren't close. And Dooley knew Pat and me well enough to figure neither one would get involved with mob money, even if what he had in mind was a gigantic sting with Don Ponti as the mark. No, Velda—he had to go to somebody else."

She shook her head, still not buying it. "He was in combat with you and Pat, but he calls on a *chess buddy* from high school. Right."

"You don't get it, doll. Men with a common interest bond together. They become the tightest buddies there is, this side of a foxhole. Guys who collect stamps or funny books, guys who go to every Rangers hockey game together. They may not know anything about each other's background, they can have totally different desires, economically they can be worlds apart, but if they have a common interest... I guess it's just a *man* thing."

She shook her head and water droplets flicked me. "You are a relic, mister."

"But I'm not in the museum yet. Look, men have their goals. Winning a war. Catching a fish. Knocking a little ball into a cup. Pursuits they share with other men."

Her eyebrows were high but her eyes were half-lidded. "Israeli women fight wars. I bet I've caught more fish than you ever have. And a golf course is the last place you'd ever be seen, Mike Hammer... but if you were, plenty of lady golfers would be there to make you look sick."

"Honey, I'm just saying you'd be surprised who a guy might call on to help him out."

"Like a chess buddy."

"Like a chess buddy."

She drew in some breath and let it out. Her hair was almost dry now and nicely tousled, and her eyes had an impish look. "I know something that beats a chess buddy every time."

"Tell me."

"A chest buddy."

She slipped the robe to her waist and, with a wicked little grin, put her shoulders back to emphasize the thrust of her bosom, defeating time and gravity, the perfect conical breasts even larger now than when she'd been a sleek young thing, her well-toned muscular shape with that narrow waist as impossibly, agelessly beautiful as a Vargas girl on the nosecone of a B-17.

Then she did the *woman* thing and let her arms slide around me and her mouth went soft and wet against mine. It was like falling from a high place, hoping you were never going to land and dreading it when it happened, and I didn't realize I was squeezing her so hard until her head lolled back and she gasped for air.

For many months, it had been doctor's orders that I stay celibate ("One round under the sheets with that lovely lady of yours, Mike, and you'll be on a slab") and we had made a game of it. That we were engaged and would wait till we were married. But business and circumstance had pushed the wedding date forward, and when my side was healed, we picked up where we left off.

She was clutching me now with clawing desperation; death had been on our doorstep, and it was time to feel alive. "Mike... Mike... are you sure you're up to it?"

I was up to it, all right.

* * *

Velda had never been a smoker, but someone like me who smoked for decades, this was one of those rare times where the old nicotine urge would come up and boot me in the butt, more gently now than years ago, but still there. Call it a cliché, but a post-coital coffin nail was always a sleepy, dreamy delight.

She saw me drifting off and nudged me awake. "No way, buddy boy. No sleepytime for you or cuddling for me. You got my brain buzzing and you're going to pay."

So soon she was back in her little white robe and I was in my boxers and T-shirt and we were sitting at her kitchen table sipping coffee.

"Okay, Mike... *chess?*"

"Kitten, that damn game is turning up too often to suit me. Brogan and Olaf played chess on those weekly visits, remember? And Dooley grew up on the Lower East Side himself."

Her eyes widened. "And you think Brogan and Olaf might've been members of your old pal's high school *chess club?*" She laughed and shook her head. "Is that what got you going? Mike, a whole lot of people play that game, even on the Bowery. And the population of the area has to be over a hundred thousand."

"Call it a hunch."

"You and your hunches. These aren't even the same *cases!* The Bowery Bum slayings of forty years ago have *zilch* to do with your mob billions."

"I grant it's a long shot that Brogan is the chess buddy who got recruited to help Dooley move all that dough. But *whoever* the chess buddy is, he's a real candidate. And we should find him."

She smirked. "You think, after the war, Marcus Dooley went back to playing chess with a high-school buddy?"

"High-school buddy or somebody else in the neighborhood, yeah. In or out of war, Dooley was still a chess player."

"And a very good one," she reminded me. "So why go back to the Lower East Side to find a regular opponent? There must be plenty of chess clubs in Brooklyn, and there are probably hundreds in Manhattan."

"Possible, but Dooley was a working-class guy on his best days, and a rummy bum on his worst. Those clubs are usually on the exclusive side, hardly the kind of atmosphere he'd feel comfortable in, much less be welcome at. No, his chess pal would have to be the same kind of unwashed genius as Dooley."

The dark eyes were half-lidded again. "So we go looking for chess clubs on the Bowery."

I sipped, shrugged. "If there is such an animal. More likely parks or other public places where low-class chess buffs like Dooley go to get their fix."

"And this is *whose* job to track down?"

I sipped and shrugged again, stirring in a grin.

Her chin was tight but there was humor in her dark eyes. "There's going to be a reorganization of this company, buddy boy, after the ceremony. Payback is a bitch."

"Don't threaten me, doll, I'm bigger."

Very seductively, with that soft, deep voice, she said, "You're not bigger, Mike. You're just taller."

The next morning at the office, around nine, the intercom blipped and Velda's voice told me, "A young-sounding woman for you, Mr. Hammer. Very musical, very nice. Anything you'd like to tell me?"

"What's her name?"

"She said to tell you it's Alma."

"Ha. Honey, you got nothing to worry about. She's just a bag lady I ran into the other day."

"I bet."

"Put her through, kitten, put her through."

Undercover policewoman Rita Callaghan said, "Don't tell my captain that I'm moonlighting for you now."

"Is that what you're doing?"

"Well, I'm reporting in, aren't I? Listen, friend, you have attracted some high-end attention. Surveillance of a most impressive kind. Not your local Crown Vics—very nice cars, Chrysler New Yorker, Buick Regal, Pontiac Grand Am. But then these are federal boys, and they have the budget for it. Also the right suits and haircuts."

"I'm not surprised I'm popular. The government called on me yesterday."

"Well, you're being baby-sat and baby-sat hard. They're pretty good at it—they move the cars as often as the parking in this town allows. Two teams, one watching the front, the other around the corner where your parking garage empties out. They were here when I went to work, and I went on at five."

"Much appreciated. Anybody else interested in me?"

"Isn't that enough?"

"Rita, there may be some mob talent, equally high-end. The guy who tried to kill me a few days ago was from overseas, I've learned. French Mafia."

"Classy killers they send after you, Mike."

"Nothing's too good for Mrs. Hammer's little boy."

"And you killed his French ass yesterday, I understand."

"I did. Well, his Corsican ass."

"His point of origin didn't make the little write-up I saw in the *News*. The reporter played it up like a robbery gone wrong. Somebody picked the wrong victim, that kind of thing. Any TV coverage? Plenty in your past to rate it."

"Naw, nobody remembers who I am any more. Not that I mind. Listen, 'Alma'—stay alert in your travels and keep me posted. Maybe I can do you a favor sometime."

"Judging by the liquid smoke of your secretary's voice, I doubt there's much else I can do for you."

"Not just my secretary. My partner. Also fiancée."

Some warm laughter came over the line. "You heartbreaker. And I do so love older men."

"And I dig older gals like you, Alma. Where are you

calling from? Can't imagine bag ladies are welcome to use the phone anywhere around here, even a public one."

"I'm in the alley across the way. On my cellphone."

"A shopping cart hag with a cellular phone. Times *are* changing."

Then, in her Alma voice, she said, "You don't know what you're *missin'*, ya big dumb bastard. This is one hag who could take you to all kinds of new places."

I bet she could, and she wouldn't even need the shopping cart.

I'd barely hung up when the intercom blipped again and Velda had Tim Darcy on the line. Pat and I had given him the exclusive on the parking-garage shooting, and he'd been good enough to keep his article low-key, as Rita had indicated. But right now he sounded high-energy.

"Mike, can you meet me over at the Cavern this morning? Around ten?"

"They don't even open till eleven."

"They'll let you in. I arranged it. Gives us some privacy. I got something good for you. Also, something bad, too, I'm afraid."

"And I get neither bad nor good over the phone, I suppose?"

"No. You gotta make the trip to get the skinny. Can you make it by ten?"

I was a minute early, the bartender unlocking the door to let me in with Tim just behind him, directing him. The bulky, florid-faced redheaded reporter was in shirtsleeves, loose tie, and jeans. He walked me to a rear booth, as if we needed the privacy in the bar area of a restaurant that was empty of everybody but that bartender and a waitress vacuuming the adjacent room. The lights were on, which was always disconcerting in a joint like this. It was like waking up in daylight next to the pick-up you settled on at last call the night before.

Cups of coffee were waiting for us in the booth, and also a rail-thin, pale character with short but shaggy blond hair that would one day turn white without anybody noticing, and the kind of red-edged, dark-circled eyes that spoke of lack of sleep or too many drugs. Hollow-cheeked, he had sharp, bird-like features and the jerky mannerisms to go with them. He was maybe forty and he wore a long-sleeve pale yellow shirt and tan chinos, both of which he swam in.

Tim slid in beside this creature and I got in across from them. My skepticism must have shown because Tim hurriedly said, "Mike, this is Danny Dixon. He's a recent Sing Sing grad."

"I heard of you, Mr. Hammer," he said in a fairly high-pitched, breathy, ragged voice. "You're a topic of conversation up there, sometimes."

"Should I be complimented?"

He smiled. His teeth were gray. "In a way. Anybody you put in there *needed* to be jugged. It's guys like me who coulda used a break." He shook his bony head. "These Rockefeller drug laws have ruined a lot of lives."

I thought it would be ungracious to comment that those breaking the laws had played their own role in that process.

Tim said, "Danny just did a dime and a half for selling a pound of cocaine in a police sting. He was twenty-two, just out of college, and it was his first conviction."

"I wasn't even a big user," Dixon said. "I was just helping a friend out who was trying to get out of a gambling debt with a one-time score. One mistake, Mr. Hammer, and my life went down the shitter."

"No offense, Danny, but it looks like you're using now."

His shrug was accompanied by a gash of a smile. "Let's just say I'm still in the state's care where my health is concerned. They owe me that much, don't you think?"

I figured he meant rehab.

He was saying, "Anyway, I got my real habit inside, and it wasn't coke."

"Horse?"

He nodded. "Easier to get inside than on the street."

"I thought Warden Ladd was pretty tough."

"He can be, but mostly he just wants to keep the lid on the pressure cooker. Anyway, Vlad the Impaler doesn't run that place. Or anyway, he didn't up until lately. I don't know *who* took over from the King."

"The King?"

Tim had been smiling almost maniacally through all this. He said to me, "Listen to this, Mike. This is why I called you... Danny, tell Mike who ran that place while you were inside."

He shrugged bony shoulders. "Like I said, the King. Ol' King of the Weeds."

I frowned. "Who?"

That gray smile was ghastly. Christ, this guy looked like he would float off in a high wind. "The con artist who just wormed his way out of stir after half a lifetime—Mr. Darcy says you're acquainted with him. You know who I mean."

"Rudy Olaf," I said.

Tim was grinning and nodding, but Danny's nod was sad-eyed and somber.

I frowned at the junkie. My gut feeling was that this was a load of bullshit. "How the hell does a guy running the library run a prison?"

His smile went from somber to jubilant. "Are you kidding? What better place for it? They do inter-library loans out of there, not just with other prisons but straight libraries, and it's a system infiltrated like a fucking spy network. As long as I was in there, Olaf was bringing in messages for all the mob boys, a regular underground mail service."

"Okay," I admitted, "I can see how that would work."

"But that's nothing compared to the smuggling. Olaf brought in every *kind* of contraband you can think of, from booze to H, but mostly cigarettes. Prisons run on cigarettes. That's why they call him the King of the Weeds, besides being King Shit of the bunch of losers we all were. Weeds is an old slang term for smokes, but I guess you're old enough to know that, aren't you, Mr. Hammer?"

"I guess I am."

His sigh had a rasp in it. "Rudy sure lived like a king in there. A king with a queen—there was this campy girlish guy who shared a cell with him for lots of years. Died not so long ago, of lung cancer. Not surprising considering how much smoking went on in that cell. If I sound prejudiced against homosexuals, Mr. Hammer, I'm really not. Most of the male-on-male sex in prisons is homosexual only by definition—it's just like... if you're a vegetarian but there's only meat to eat, you learn to settle."

"You say this went on with the blessing of the warden? And his guards, too, I suppose?"

"Blessing is the wrong word. What's the term? Benign neglect. That's it. Benign neglect. You see, Mr. Hammer, not every guard in that place is bent. Most aren't. But Rudy had every bad one in his pocket. Cash flowed through that library, too, you know. He could do what he wanted. He fucking ruled. I learned that from day one."

"How so?"

"First week I got there, I was assigned to help out in the library. It was easy work. Olaf was there. Smooth, nice, easy-going. Friendly on the surface. But the way he looked at you was like... like a *snake* studying you. A cobra looking for just the right second to strike."

"And he struck at you, Danny?"

He frowned. "Yes, but not how you might think. He was sizing me up. See, he sold me as a cellmate to one of the worst mob ice men in the joint. Well, 'sold,' that's not right—more like, rented out. I believe I went for ten cartons of smokes a month. I was young and I was pretty. I was also straight, but that didn't matter. I was the bitch of Bruno Garsi till somebody cut his throat in the prison yard."

"Was it you, Danny?"

His smile was razor thin. "Must not have been, 'cause nobody got caught, and the ruling was 'person or persons unknown.' I was sold or rented or what-have-you to five other inmates over the years, but then I got hooked and got older and less pretty and finally Rudy left me alone. But back while I was a valuable commodity, Mr. Hammer, that was when I got my H habit, which Rudy gladly supplied. When I became disposable, and couldn't get the stuff anymore, I got sick. I kicked it, though, in the infirmary. Old Vlad made sure I got weaned off—it wasn't easy, but it wasn't cold turkey."

"Why the compassion from the warden?"

"Do you think Vlad would like it getting out just how much he puts up with in that place, for the sake of keeping that place chilled?" He nodded toward Tim. "I came to Mr. Darcy here with my story, and he thought there was some value in it. Yes, he's paying me for it, but I currently got no other source of income, Mr. Hammer, I'm not exactly an employer's dream hire, you know… so I hope you will keep that part of this to yourself. Some people might think Mr. Darcy is compromising his journalistic integrity, but people like that aren't schooled in what the world is really like."

"Danny," I said, "you said you kicked inside. What got you back on the needle?"

"Oh, I'm not back on the needle, Mr. Hammer. I can see how you might think that. No, no, it's nothing like that." He gave me that awful gray smile. "I've got AIDS. That's something else I can thank the King of the Weeds for."

We spoke another five minutes and Tim slipped him a handful of twenties. I caught the guy's arm as he was leaving; it felt like a twig. I passed him a C-note and he gave me a nod and one last gray smile.

Tim's smile was yellowish and he reminded me of a greedy kid. "What do you think of *that*, Mike?"

"You won't get the Pulitzer paying off sources."

"I've got three more recent graduates of Sing Sing who sing a similar song. Danny's is the saddest, though. He'll be the star of my piece."

"And Rudy Olaf's the villain?"

"You bet. Start to see a different picture getting painted now, don't you, Mike? Rudy's been King Shit inside for forty damn years… but now his honeybunch is deceased and he's decided to retire to the outside world with a bundle of cash courtesy of the City So Nice he screwed it over twice."

A different picture indeed than the one Warden

Ladd had provided of a low-key, well-adjusted model prisoner who all but ran the library.

I finally tried the coffee and it was cold; I pushed it aside. "You need to go to Pat with this, Tim. You need somebody honest in the system to expose this corruption."

Tim waved that off. "Mike, I'm still investigating. My sources are credible by my standards, but a former-junkie-slash-dying-AIDS-patient like Danny would be simple enough to impeach. I'm probably three months away from publication, and, of course, that'll put Pat out of the picture, anyway."

"What do you mean?"

The upbeat attitude of a reporter with a scoop faded. His expression went cloudy and his voice became hushed, no enthusiasm in it at all.

"Mike, that's the other reason I wanted to see you. The bad news I mentioned on the phone. My sources at One Police Plaza and City Hall say Pat is out."

"What do you mean out?"

"It's apparently part of the deal with Olaf's lawyer."

Rufus Tomlin.

Tim was saying, "Seems Olaf does hold at least *some* grudge. The NYPD gets not to be embarrassed, and Captain Pat Chambers gets a forced early retirement."

CHAPTER NINE

When I got back to the office, Velda handed me a phone memo with a name on it I didn't recognize. "Who's Frank Hellman?"

Her eyebrows and shoulders went up and down. "New one on me, too. Mr. Hellman has a not inexpensive Wall Street address. I made a few calls and learned he's a very successful, very discreet 'financial advisor.'"

"A broker?"

"I don't believe so. He sits on several boards of privately held companies. That's as far as I got."

I went into my inner office, sat down and punched in the number off Velda's slip of paper, got a receptionist and asked for Hellman. She wanted my name, but that's all it took.

In a few seconds a pleasant, well-modulated voice said, "Good afternoon, Mr. Hammer."

"Same to you Mr. Hellman," I said. "You called my office earlier…?"

"Yes, and thank you very much for returning my call. I would imagine my name doesn't mean much if anything to you. But I can assure you I represent powerful people whose names you *would* recognize."

"Okay," I said, noticing he didn't share any of them with me.

Cheerfully, he said, "I would like to see you as soon as possible if I may. Do you have time yet today?"

"Rest of my afternoon is clear. You want to come by the office, or maybe meet for a drink somewhere?"

Hellman paused for a moment, then suggested, "Do you know where the Canterbury Club is?"

"Sure do."

"Would three o'clock be too soon?"

"No, I can make that."

"See you then, Mr. Hammer. I appreciate this."

Curiouser and curiouser, as the little blonde in the Disney picture put it. The Canterbury was a British-themed gentlemen's sporting club where I'd been a guest several times, though not recently.

The members owned handcrafted, gold-inlaid, decoratively engraved shotguns that cost as much as a new car. These highfalutin weapons remained in pristine condition, never to be shot, strictly collector's pieces serving as a membership requisite for the club. In the basement was a target range where the old Webleys came out—and late-model automatics and fine European pieces, too—for the venerable members to pop at targets for bragging rights, before re-boxing and storing them away.

I tugged the new .45 from under my arm, checked it over, pocketed two extra clips from a desk drawer, and checked my watch.

Moving through the outer office, I told Velda where I was headed and she jotted it down on her desk calendar.

Before I went out, I asked, "Anything on those Bowery chess clubs?"

"I have a call in to a woman researching a book on the cultural history of the Lower East Side. She's a friend of a friend, who should be able to give us some preliminary answers, or at least lead me to somebody who can."

"Good. I'll be back before we close up for the day. Then we'll catch a bite somewhere."

Out the window the gray sky continued to hover like a damp blanket waiting to get wrung out.

Looking in that direction, Velda said, "For some reason this dreary weather makes me long for the old Blue Ribbon and that wonderful German food."

"Live to be my age, doll," I said, going out, "and you get to see all your favorite restaurants disappear... and your best friends, too."

Here and there around New York City are reminders of a time going back before even the Good Old Days—

nineteenth-century structures with brass plaques attached to their corners that attest to the stimulating history of the building and/or its occupants.

The Canterbury Club was in a stately old mansion whose original owner signed the Declaration of Independence; somehow this city father had managed to keep his home out of the hands of developers or anybody else intent on spoiling this piece of the city's inherited past. The imposing edifice was protected enough by stalwart masonry and its original granite structure to withstand the years, aided and abetted by the city's Historical Preservation Society.

No doorman guarded the exterior, but once inside I was greeted by a sturdy-looking guy in his late twenties in a carefully tailored suit. He apparently rewarded any unscheduled visitors with a frigid smile that asked what the hell you were doing here if you weren't a member.

He made a question out of "Good afternoon, sir" and held his hand out for an invitation, because that was the only way a non-member might be admitted. I flipped open my wallet and showed him my P.I. ticket and my permit to carry a concealed weapon.

The smile on his lips did not thaw. He projected that peculiar combination of brawn and condescension usually reserved for trendy niteries.

"That's a private badge, sir," he said, "and even if it weren't, you would need a warrant."

I just looked at him, letting him suck eggs for a

couple of seconds before saying, "Mike Hammer to see Mr. Hellman. He's expecting me." I didn't take my eyes off his.

"Mr. Hammer, I've heard of you. Frankly, I didn't know you were still alive."

"Well, that's the rumor."

"Mr. Hellman *is* here. But I'm afraid he did not leave word to admit you."

"Then check with Mr. Hellman."

"If he were expecting a guest, he would have informed me."

"You've got a phone there. Make a call."

He thought about that. "I'll do that, but you'll have to wait outside."

Those cold eyes were telling me that I had had my day and this wasn't one of them. I was from a generation grown old and tired. We were slower and weaker and ready to fall, now that the new ones had come out of the shell.

"I'm going in," I told him, and started by.

He gripped my shoulder. "No you're not."

The greeter needed a lesson in civility, so I gave him one by way of a hard fist under his ribs and left him there, closed up like a jackknife as he gasped for air.

I was about to go through the ornate portals and into the foyer of the club when an old fireman in a new suit pushed through. His hair was salt-and-pepper and his face still bore a few scars from that Fourteenth Street blaze ten years ago.

His voice was as rough as freshly sawed timber. "How's it going, Mike?"

I said, "What's a nice guy like you doing in a place like this, Darrell?"

He brushed an imaginary crumb from his tailored suitcoat. "Good bucks, buddy, and damn easy duty. I was just on my way to let our watchdog know you were expected."

"You were a little slow off the starting block."

He was looking past me at the doubled-up kid, who was still struggling for his breath as he tried not to puke.

I said, "Tell that kid to be careful who he lays hands on in future."

"Oh, I'd imagine he just picked up on that."

"A lot of guards at the gates, Darrell. Why all the security?"

He took my hat and trenchcoat. "Old men who play with guns are a paranoid breed, Mike. Particularly rich ones."

Then the ex-fireman opened a fancy door and gestured toward an ornate single elevator.

"Mr. Hellman is waiting for you. You know where the shooting room is?"

I nodded, gave him a nice-to-see-you smile, got on the elevator, and pressed the bottom floor button.

A gentleman's gun club like this had a real attitude, even in the basement. The walls were decorated with hunting club paintings and royal infantry photos. No nudes—nothing so tasteless. Not even a trophy case— far too tacky. Furnishings were upholstered in old-style maroon plush like my grandmother had in her parlor. Unlike the latter, though, smoking was allowed here, everything from fancy cigars to lowly cigarettes in an atmosphere where tobacco and cordite mingled.

The shooters were appropriately dressed—no shirt sleeves showing, no blue jeans, just fine woolens with accessories to match, and each pair of shooting booths had an attendant at hand, although with no apparent score-keeping. Maybe that was considered tacky, too.

Most of the members shooting this afternoon were older men, probably retired, certainly wealthy. A number were British expatriates, as had been the founders of the Canterbury.

But one very American-looking, impeccably tailored gent was tall and graceful and thin, though the kind of thinness that carried muscle and sinew. The way he held the Glock automatic and triggered off a half dozen fast ones, as if science had never invented recoil, meant that nobody need retrieve the target to confirm his shots were tightly bunched.

I walked up to him and said, "You shoot like a real gangster, Frank."

He flipped the clip out of the Glock and said, "Well, that's what they call Wall Street types like me nowadays, isn't it?"

"You and lawyers," I said.

He turned and gave me a boyish grin. He had to

be in his early forties with a bare touch of gray in his temples that spoke of experience, while youthfulness, whether contrived or for real, was in there, too. He let it all flash at me for a brief second, courtesy of teeth that God or a great dentist had done a fine job on.

He said, "If you're going to call me 'Frank,' I'll have to call you 'Mike.'"

"It's a deal."

Something in his manner conveyed a silent animal message: *I'm big, I'm strong, I'm fast, and I enjoy deadly engagements.*

"How did you know me, Mike?" he asked, reloading. "No one is on duty down here that you might ask."

"I just didn't see anybody else who could be you."

He flashed the teeth again, pleased by my remark. "I guess you've had the time to hone your detective skills, at that."

"Which is a very polite way to call me an old fart, Frank."

His expression turned serious, though some amusement remained in the dark green eyes. "You carrying, Mike?"

"Certainly. You don't visit a nudist colony unless you're ready to strip down."

That got a smile from him, but more sly than amused. He hit the button that returned his target, then removed it, angling it to let me see his tight cluster before slipping a fresh sheet into the hangers.

When he rolled the fresh target back to the twenty-five-foot mark, where it had been when he fired off his rounds, he seemed about to shoot, but thought better of it. He stepped aside and nodded to me. "Be my guest, Mike."

Idiotic challenges like that amuse me. They are all show, and grown people should know better. Nothing was on the line except pride and since Frank Hellman had already racked up a perfect score, nobody could beat him.

I unbuttoned my suitcoat and gave him a smile and a shrug.

He never saw the .45 come out from under my left arm as the roar of the seven slugs seemed to be one big sound that was over as fast as it started. The fusillade was still echoing, despite all the sound baffling, as I hit the return button to bring the target back so Hellman could see the one fist-size hole smack in the center of the bull's-eye.

"Good shooting," Hellman said with a slightly glazed smile.

"No."

"No?"

"Good *target* shooting. Shooting and aiming a .45 automatic on a range is only a matter of practice. Doesn't really count."

"Why not?"

"Nobody's shooting back at you."

He considered that for a moment, then asked, "Do you always carry a round in the chamber?"

Now I let him have a grin. The one that showed off *my* teeth. "You'd better believe it, buddy. I'm not going to waste time jacking one in the chamber when the shit's flying."

I reloaded and eased the gun back into the holster. A little Cagney shoulder move got it settled where it should be. He didn't need to know that firing off those rounds had both my side and chest aching.

Down the row, a pair of old gentlemen waited until we had moved away, then walked to our booth to inspect our respective targets with their impressive groupings. The old gents turned and looked at us and murmured something I didn't catch, but they were obviously impressed. Like Nigel Bruce when Basil Rathbone made a monkey out of him.

I said, "Now that show-and-tell is over, Frank, shouldn't we sit down and talk? Maybe some place less noisy?"

"I agree, Mike. Time to head upstairs."

A small under-lit area off the main dining room provided a place for members to discuss business with just the faintest piped-in classical-music backdrop. The tables were arranged for groups of four or two, discreetly separated to keep conversations private. We chose the smaller seating and gave a drink order to a quiet waiter who, despite an age rivaling the old boys downstairs, was quick to bring two highballs, several napkins, and a bowl of peanuts.

I settled back in the comfortable leather chair, with its shell-like button-tufted back, and waited for

Frank Hellman to break the ice.

He made a silent toast that I ignored, sipped at his glass, then said, "Mike, may I assume you never heard of me before today?"

I nodded.

"There's a reason for that. I provide a very high level of… insulation… for certain men of business who have unique needs. I serve on a number of boards of directors… this you will be easily able to confirm, as there's nothing secret about the firms in question… and recently I was appointed CEO of one."

So I'd made it up a rung.

I smiled, chuckled, and said, "You're Rufus Tomlin's client."

He drew in air, seemed to think about what to do with it, then let it out and said, "I am."

"And *you* have a client. The man or men behind the company over which you have recently been promoted CEO."

"Very good, Mike. Very astute."

"No, about average." I tossed some peanuts in my mouth and chewed as I spoke. "You're the high-end money-laundering guy. You are the final step up a ladder of turning dirty money into something clean enough to pay taxes on."

He didn't deny it, but he said, "That would have been a more accurate statement had you made it ten or fifteen or even twenty years ago. So very many of the business interests I represent are entirely legitimate now."

"Sure. But money still comes in from new foreign partners handling the old moneymakers—Asians, Russians, Colombians. You're a guy in a thousand-dollar suit, Frank, in a very fancy old gentleman's club, so respectable you squeak. That doesn't mean you don't get some oil when nobody's looking."

He shifted in his chair. "Beyond the associations you refer to…"

"The Five Families, you mean."

"…I am aligned with persons in high positions, quite influential and very active in civic affairs. Nothing illegal in the backgrounds or practices of any of these respectable individuals. If you go looking for dirt, Mike, maybe you'll find, oh… a traffic ticket."

"Fixed?"

He shook his head, smiled. "Paid for."

I picked up my drink and tasted it. Good whiskey. Great mix. I swirled the ice around and took another sip. Off-handedly, I said, "I've already spoken to Mr. Tomlin about those supposed eighty-nine billion bucks that rumor has me sitting on. What's left to discuss?"

Hellman shrugged rather elaborately. "The terms of our negotiation."

"Is that what we're doing?"

He leaned back in his chair and took another sip of his drink and tasted it a while before swallowing. "This rumor you refer to has inspired wild tabloid yarns, bandied about in the media as if it were the contemporary equivalent of the lost Dutchman's mine."

"Maybe it is."

A hand painted a lazy picture in the air. "Think of it, Mike, a fabulous treasure that belongs to whomever finds it, since nobody can prove ownership... hidden where even the finest tracker dogs in the land can't sniff it out... a location known only to one rather eccentric private investigator, who as it happens couldn't care less about the big bucks."

"That's a new one, Frank—eccentric. Not sure I like that."

"All right, then—we'll call him a *remarkable* private investigator..."

"Better."

"...who, should he allow that site to be examined, could name his own finder's fee, and it would even be arranged in such a way that it could be legitimized. That means that he and any family or friends he might designate could enjoy that fortune, for many, many years to come. Because, you see, Mike... Mr. Hammer—the cash is a secondary concern."

So something among that vast pile of currency was even greater than the money itself.

I asked, "What exactly is a pile of cash that size 'secondary' to, Frank? Stocks? Bonds?"

"Indeed yes, Mike." His eyes tightened and took on a gleam. "But also deeds to some of the most valuable properties in Manhattan. Eighty-nine billion? Think *twice* that, and more. As for the cash, those large denominations are problematic. But we have a way of dealing with them."

"By paying off Uncle Sam?"

"Perhaps. But certainly by paying off the person who leads us to this modern-day Eldorado."

I took a nice big final sip. "Make up your mind. A minute ago it was the Lost Dutchman's Mine."

"Either way, Mike, it's a fortune."

He handed me a card with several numbers on it, one of which was circled. "That's my cellular phone. When you are ready to take these negotiations to the next level, Mr. Hammer, call me there, and only there. But I would suggest sooner rather than later."

He walked me out and offered to call a cab for me, but I told him I preferred to walk back. My fireman friend Darrell returned my trenchcoat and hat and opened the door onto the foyer for us as Hellman accompanied me. On the way to the street, the greeter opened the door and gave us both a sickly smile. Maybe the younger man *had* learned his lesson.

Out under the gloomy sky, Hellman offered his hand and I shook it.

"One perk of our negotiation," he said, "might include a membership here at the Canterbury."

Well, it was for paranoid old men with guns, wasn't it? Maybe I qualified.

Hellman was saying, "You'd be a great member, Mike. You are one *hell* of a shot."

I could have been gracious about it, but that just wasn't me.

I said, "I draw fast as hell, too, Frank. And keep one in the chamber, remember."

"I won't forget," he told me with a smile.

And I wasn't about to forget him, either. He wasn't a bad shot himself, for a fancy-ass mob front man.

Before I could report the details of my meeting to Velda, she had news for me.

"Sit down," she instructed me like a strict school teacher, indicating the client chair in front of her desk. She lacked only the ruler.

I sat.

She said, "You and your damn hunches. Could you please be wrong once in a while?"

"I'll work on that. What is it?"

She frowned, just a little. "First, my contact writing the book about the Lower East Side knew of no formal chess clubs, but plenty of chess and even an occasional tourney, back in the fifties and sixties."

"Where?"

"Various defunct coffee houses. Spillover into the Bowery from the Village—Beat Generation days. Plenty of similar coffee houses in the Village itself, where chess players were welcome to hang out, through that same period. And of course, a lot of the game was played in Washington Square Park and others, and still is."

I shifted in the chair. "Doesn't help us much. Sounds like a lot of leg work against terrible odds."

"Doesn't it."

"Those coffee houses are long gone, and talking to old-timers playing chess in a park, in hopes of linking Dooley to Brogan or Olaf? That's the worst kind of fishing expedition."

But now her lush lips formed a smile both teasing and triumphant. She had been sandbagging me. "Oh, we don't have to go fishing to do that, Mike."

"Yeah?"

She put a hand on her phone. "Five minutes after you left, Marvin Dooley called. He sorted through half a dozen boxes of his father's things, as he promised us, but said it was mostly a waste of time. Clothing, old family pictures, and the accumulated junk of a lifetime."

I gestured to myself with a thumb. "I still want to go through that stuff myself."

"Take it easy, Tarzan. Seems Marvin *did* find one item of interest…" She smiled devilishly, making me wait for it. "…a 1941 yearbook from Metropolitan Vocational."

The Bowery high school Dooley attended.

She slid a crisp new manila folder toward me. I opened it and saw two black-and-white slick-paper print-outs, first the cover of the yearbook (METROPOLIS 1942), then an activities page that included faded photos of the debate team, Quill and Scroll, and the chess club.

Pleased with herself, Velda was saying, "I had Marvin go to a copy center and fax us those."

There were five members of the 1942 Metropolitan High School chess team, all of them wearing sweaters and ties and embarrassed grins, several in glasses. These were the dorks and twerps and nerds of my high-school years, and I would have known them well without ever having met them at all.

But three of them I knew, all right: Henry Brogan, Marcus Dooley and Rudolph Olaf.

"The creepy thing," I said, "is that Olaf doesn't look all that different. Even his damn hair's the same."

"So you were right, Mike," she said, acknowledging me with an open hand. "Brogan was Dooley's chess buddy."

I tossed the fax sheets back on her desk. "Olaf may have been, too. We can't know *who* Dooley was trading chess moves with by mail during the war."

"No," she said, "but what's important is *after* the war. His regular, drive-into-the-city chess pal couldn't be Olaf, not unless Dooley was visiting Sing Sing."

She was half-kidding I knew, but just the same I said, "Impossible. Brogan was the only visitor Olaf had for forty years."

Tapping the faxed photo, she said, "You're right, Mike. Brogan's the chess pal. But what does it mean?"

"I'll be damned if I know," I admitted.

"If Brogan is the old buddy enlisted by Dooley as helper in hiding the mob money, where is Rudy Olaf in that equation? If at all?"

I asked my own question: "What does Brogan coming forward to take the rap for Olaf after all those years have to do with the billions?"

She shook her head and the raven locks came apart in sections, then reformed themselves perfectly. "Does it have to have *anything* to do with the billions? You're the detective who believes in coincidences, remember."

"Not this blatant, doll. Somebody sends a hitman to kill me—twice. At the same time that Olaf is getting sprung by his old Bowery buddy Brogan, *and* just as I'm getting it right and left by parties with renewed interest in the billions."

I told her about the meeting with Hellman.

"So our Wall Street biggie is a mob shill," she said. "But *which* mob?"

"You mean which family? Probably the Pontis— they've been leaderless and in disarray since Don Lorenzo bought it and Ugo went to stir."

Velda sat forward, her hands folded, as if she were saying grace at a meal. "Mike, whatever's going on, one thing seems clear. Marcus Dooley had something in mind for all that cash. He risked his life hiding it for a *reason.*"

I shrugged. "But he died before he could tell me."

She tapped the fax sheet again. "But isn't it clear? Dooley wanted you to *find* it, right?"

"Right. That's what he asked me to do, right before he kicked."

"His dying wish, right? Why? So *you* could have it, the old war buddy he'd barely seen since? No. It was for his *son,* Mike. They'd had a strained relationship from the start, and after Marvin's mother died, you might even say they were estranged. Isn't it natural Dooley would want to make it up to his boy somehow?"

I said nothing.

She pressed: "You don't take the kind of risk that your friend Dooley did just to put one over on Don Ponti. Just to tweak a very dangerous damn man. What, for a horse laugh?"

I still said nothing.

She got up and came around the desk. She put a hand on my shoulder, and her voice was gentle but firm. "Mike, last year, when we were on the hunt for that money, you weren't thinking clear. You weren't yourself. How many times during that case did your friend Dr. Morgan have to sedate you and take you off the front lines to recover?"

"Once."

"No. Three times. Shot you up and sat you down."

"More like laid me out." I shrugged. "Okay, kitten. So you're right. I was off my game and not thinking straight."

"Thank you."

"It's obvious, now. Dooley wanted me to take care of his son with that dough. What do you suggest we do?"

She sat on my lap and put her arms around my neck. This was hardly fair. She said, almost cooing, "I think you should take the government's offer. You're not about to get in bed with the mob. We know that much."

"Yeah."

"So get in touch with that Treasury guy—Buckley.

Take the finder's fee. Split it with Marvin, or if you're too high and mighty, give Marvin all of it."

"But you'd rather I hang on to half."

She settled herself a little bit in my lap in what was perhaps her most convincing argument. But what she said made sense as well: "Is it wrong for us to have some cushy years together, after all we've been through? Did you do it all, over all these years, just to build a collection of bullet scars?"

I said nothing. She slid off my lap, straightened her skirt, smoothed her silk blouse, and took her place behind her desk again.

I picked up the chess-club fax sheet again and studied it. "I'll take it under advisement."

"What do you think *I'm* doing? I'm advising."

My eyes went from the youthful Dooley's smiling face to Brogan's to Olaf's. Olaf's smile was slighter, but even the fax image from an ancient yearbook gave a hint of a glimmer in his eyes. He was a snake, Rudy Olaf. A fucking snake. I knew one when I saw one.

"I'm not doing anything until I figure out what the hell is going on," I said. "Fair enough?"

She nodded, then her eyes flashed. "Oh, Pat called. He wants you to meet him at Pete's Chophouse at seven. I said you'd be there."

"Are you coming?"

"He didn't invite me. Mike, he doesn't know that *you* know he's being forced out. He probably wants to tell you. One on one."

"All right. Then we'll wrap it up for the day." I got up. "Can you fend for yourself tonight, doll?"

"Are you kidding?"

CHAPTER TEN

The blast came out of the window of the parked car, a fiery red finger that put a sudden crimson glow in the night air and hit Pat right in the belly. The sudden force was enough to knock him into a fetal position before he even hit the sidewalk with a sickening-sounding *thud*.

When the driver hit the gas pedal, wheels shrieked against pavement, then took hold in a leap forward that scattered traffic and in that one second as the open window went past me, I got a good look at the grinning idiot who still had the gun in his fist and in that same second he saw the .45 in mine as I squeezed the trigger and that copper-covered slug got him in the right upper shoulder, slamming him into the driver with such a jolt that the latter wrenched the wheel too far, couldn't recover, and the big eight-wheeler truck coming down the street mashed both of them into instant remains.

Pat was lying there, his knees drawn up, both hands grabbing his belly, red squirting between his fingers, his breath coming in short wheezes. He could barely talk, but I could still make out what he was saying: "It hurts, Mike, damn... it *hurts*... it *burns*..."

A dozen people were already crowded around and somebody was calling 911 on a cellphone, a young woman standing with the instrument still in her fist, and I yelled, "Tell them an officer is down!"

She got the message, and added the information, then asked, "Who?"

"Captain Pat Chambers!" I called out his shield number; I knew it by heart. Almost instantly I heard sirens open up, heading our way.

I was kneeling beside him. His face was pale and contorted as he lay with his knees up, helpless as a turtle on its back. Gently I pushed his hands away and opened his trenchcoat and suitcoat to where blood soaked what had been a white shirt. I applied pressure.

He gurgled a cry of pain.

"Stay with me, Pat."

Now blood was squirting through my fingers.

"Mike... Mike..." He was looking skyward, past me, like he was looking for that shaft of white light to take him away. But every word was for me: "We... *know* who... who *did* this... don't we?"

"I'll get him, buddy."

He nodded his approval.

Once, long ago, Jack Williams had died, a guy who'd given an arm for me in combat and over whose gut-shot corpse I had made a youthful self-righteous speech about the lousy court system and how the only jury that would judge Jack's killer would be me. Pat had been there, and had tried to calm me, had tried to convince his hot-headed friend to let the wheels of justice turn, but I had done it my way, and the killer had died.

So many years later, and here we were full-circle, Pat and me. But this time *he* was down and gut-shot.

And this time I had his permission.

Pat was half-gasping, spitting up blood, but he was hanging on. Sirens were coming in from Broadway even though this was a one-way street in the wrong direction. That helped them cut off escaping traffic more effectively.

"Hang on, pal," I said. "Hang on."

He was half-awake when I helped him on the gurney and up into the ambulance, and I thought about accompanying him but knew I needed to stay at the scene. I went over and guarded the puddle of red, and I didn't have long to wait. I dealt with the uniforms and then the plainclothes, going through the preliminary details. *Yes, I got a good look at the shooter. No, I didn't know him. He was white with spiky hair and teardrop tattoos trailing down his cheek—a gangbanger, probably the Red Commando bunch.*

Mandy Clark, the lovely redheaded assistant D.A. who had joined us after supper, found her way to my side about half-way through the proceedings. When the questions were over, she asked me how I was doing.

"Better than Pat," I said.

"Can you make any sense of this, Mike?"

It had always been "Mr. Hammer" before—tragedy breeds familiarity.

I gave her a hard sideways gaze. "I think it fits in with what we discussed, don't you?"

Her eyes were tight and she nodded. "I do. You've got me convinced, all right. But it's *still* all theoretical. That limits us."

"It limits you."

She didn't know what to say to that. Then she shivered, hugged herself; she wore a lightweight raincoat. "Where did this cold snap come from, anyway?"

"I don't know."

"We're lucky it isn't snowing. Mike, someone from Pat's office will be in touch, and I'll be in touch, too."

I nodded.

"You should wash your hands," she said.

Pat's blood was all over them, sticky going dark and dry. The coppery smell of the stuff was in the air. I would wash my hands, but not of what happened here tonight. Until this was over, I would look at my palms and see them scarlet.

Time slowed and sped up and then finally the last of the squad cars was ready to go. The forensics team was still working, flash cameras strobing the night, but everyone else had gone. Behind me, the lights of the restaurant suddenly cut off and the chill wind picked up. I pulled the trenchcoat around me, buttoned it and made a mental note to put the winter liner in. Maybe I needed something heavier. Trenchcoats were as out of style as the Old School detectives who wore them.

Detectives like Pat and me.

And for one second, no more, just one second the wind got colder than made sense for this time of year. It had a cutting, icy edge to it and it came straight at me, a howling, shrieking, bitter thing with razor-sharp claws curved to kill.

Pat's coat was almost a duplicate of mine. A little cleaner, a little newer, but in the same dim light of night you couldn't tell the difference. We were roughly the same height and weight, and were among the few men in this city who still wore hats. I hadn't had mine on when I stepped outside, lagging behind Pat a few steps having picked up the check. He might have been me.

Would Pat be the latest "accidental" cop fatality?

Had the killer thought he was shooting at me?

An hour ago, we had been in a back booth of Pete's Chophouse. I'd finished off my center-cut pork chop and Pat had eaten most of a bone-in rib-eye, rare. We'd shared an order of Pete's signature hash browns with onions, a mammoth plate no one man could handle, and were passing on dessert in favor of highballs. No business had been discussed.

"Man," Pat said, after the bus boy had cleared our table, "even after all these years, I crave a smoke after that kind of meal."

"Not me. But I admit I may miss the second-hand smoke when New York gets around to banning smoking in bars."

He shook his head. "That'll never happen. That's California-thinking, Mike, not New York."

"Well, if it *does* go through, at least you won't have to make the arrests."

He gave me a look. "Then you know?"

I nodded. "Tim Darcy told me. Give me a list of guests and I'll organize the retirement party."

He sipped his drink. "Won't be for a while yet. No paperwork has gone through. End of the year and I'm out, though."

"Why are they letting you hang around that long?"

His smile was rueful. "They don't want some reporter as smart and shifty as Tim telling the public that I was the sacrificial lamb who made the Rudy Olaf settlement possible."

I gave him half a grin. "So are you going to dog it, these last few months?"

"What do you think?"

"I think you're going to try to hang Rudy Olaf up with piano wire. And I'll be glad to help."

He gave me the other half of the grin. "You already are... *Ah!* Here's Mandy Clark. I asked her to join us after supper."

"Why her?"

"She's an ally, Mike. Really. Truly."

The good-looking redhead was picking up a martini

at the bar. Then she came over, with a fluid feminine walk that was worth taking in, her hair up, her nice figure downplayed in a trim black-and-brown business suit. She shook hands with me, by way of paying respect, and slid in on Pat's side of the booth.

She asked him, "Have you brought Mr. Hammer up to speed?"

"No. Be my guest, Ms. Clark."

She gave me a direct stare and a tight smile. "You suggested to Captain Chambers that we might want to explore the original case file of the so-called Bowery Bum slayings, and beyond that, dig into records for the year or so previous to the first victim, to look for precursor crimes."

I started nodding half-way through that. "That's right, Ms. Clark. Have you come up with something?"

"Well, *Captain Chambers* has, or at any rate his staff, who should be commended. We found reports of similar robberies on that particular block, on that same side of the street that was a notorious section of gay bars at the time."

"Did these reports involve two assailants or one?"

She smiled, glanced at Chambers, who smiled and shrugged, as if to say, *I told you so*. "Two, Mr. Hammer," she said.

I had to grin. "They were a *team*, weren't they? One of them, my guess is Olaf, lured a victim into an alley for some quick pants-around-the-ankles fun, then Brogan came around with a gun and robbed the guy instead. Before the killings, was there any violence?"

She nodded. "Yes, they roughed their victims up and intimidated them."

"Do you think that just escalated into killing?"

"Actually, no. But we think we know at what point the modus operandi shifted. One of the victims fought back, took the gun away from Brogan, or at least we *assume* it was Brogan, and pistol-whipped him."

I looked at her over the edge of my highball glass. "You can prove this?"

"The victim is alive and well, Mr. Hammer, and willing to testify."

"Forty years later?"

"Forty years later. There were half a dozen earlier incidents where we had complainants who later declined to aid investigators in their work. But we hope we might track them down and find them alive and willing to help."

Pat said, "Like you say, Mike, this is forty years ago. Being identified as gay meant a man's life was over, professionally and even personally. Many of these men were successful businessmen, with wives and children."

"And when they travelled for business, they sometimes indulged a secret side of themselves. I get that."

"Mike, if it hadn't been for their sexual interests, many of these men would never have set foot in a Bowery bar. So after they'd been robbed and roughed up, they came in initially, indignant about the experience, but then in the light of day decided not to cooperate any further."

"That was Olaf's genius," I said.

Mandy Clark frowned. "How so?"

"Well, I assume he was the brains. They are both smart men, Brogan and Olaf. But whichever of them chose that area as their hunting ground took a page out of Jack the Ripper's book—the Bowery, Skid Row, who cared what became of its denizens? Add to that victims who were homosexual, and you've paved the way for a psychotic killer's fun and profit."

She gave me a very pretty smile. "Well, we caught a break with our witness—the one who fought back? He's in his eighties, sharp as a tack. His wife is dead, and their two children are grown with their own families, and he says he doesn't 'give a diddly damn what anybody thinks' about his 'sexual recreational inclinations.' Interesting phrase from an interesting man."

Pat said, "But one witness isn't enough. Even that sharp, a guy in his eighties might be impeached by a lawyer with the skills of Rufus Tomlin."

I asked, "What are you going to do about it, Pat?"

"We're looking at the other incidents in the same time frame. Mike, you sent us in the right direction. Thanks."

The assistant D.A. said, "Yes, Mr. Hammer. We're grateful."

"No problem. I love it when other people do my work for me. So what's the plan?"

She said, "The plan... and this is as confidential as it gets, Mr. Hammer... is to prove that Henry Brogan and Rudy Olaf entered into a conspiracy to defraud the city of New York of… a considerable amount. That figure is one even *I* am not privy to."

I gestured with an open palm. "Why not just throw Rudy's ass back in the slam on the old murder charge?"

Pat said, "Part of the terms of his release was a full pardon from the governor. It was the only way to avoid a new trial and a lot of embarrassment."

"Shit," I said. "And he can't be tried on the Bowery Bum slayings again because it would constitute double jeopardy."

That got glum nods from both of them.

"We could go after Brogan," she said, "but he wouldn't live to reach trial. Our only real option, Mr. Hammer, is proving conspiracy between Olaf and Brogan to defraud the city. That accomplishes two things—it gets the city its money back, and it redeems the reputation of a fine public servant."

"That would be me," Pat said with a quiet smile.

I grunted a humorless laugh. "It's sort of like putting Capone away on income tax evasion… but it's better than nothing."

Our waiter came over and asked if we'd like another round. We said yes.

Pat said, "Do you mind, Ms. Clark, if I fill Mike in on that other matter?"

She frowned in momentary thought, but then said, "I have no objection. I don't believe there's a tie-in to the Olaf case, but be my guest."

Pat took a breath, let it out, and said, "These

'coincidental, accidental' cop fatalities that have been hanging over our head—that cop who was wounded interrupting a burglary died in the hospital this morning, Mike. That makes ten."

I smiled mirthlessly at the assistant D.A. "And the city's statistician doesn't like those odds… right, Ms. Clark?"

"No, he doesn't," she said. "But Captain Chambers may have evidence that somebody is fixing the game."

Pat said, "As I told you earlier, Mike, I have two top homicide teams working these deaths. We have three so far that look suspicious. This stays here, Mike, got it?"

"Got it."

"The driver of the delivery van that blew a tire and rammed a squad car, killing the driver, has a record that includes drug dealing and assault with a deadly weapon. The robbery where the two cops were shot down with rifles from the getaway car may have been timed for those officers to be in the wrong place at a designated right time. And that young cop whose funeral we went to, who was caught in the gangbanger crossfire? He was on his way home on a route he always took at a time he always travelled."

"That," I said, "would be easy to put in motion, as well."

He nodded. "And we're exploring the other deaths. The old mob guy who went to that restaurant to commit suicide may have been on a kamikaze mission—we're looking at whether his family is being particularly well looked after. Of course, some of these deaths may really be purely coincidental, feeding the notion of a rash of fatalities—like an officer off-duty, out jogging, who dies of a heart attack. But the majority of these deaths may have been… arranged."

The assistant D.A. said, "I am pleased that Captain Chambers is delving into these tragedies, but I have to admit that I am not as sanguine about the possibility that they are linked somehow. That they might be part of a… master plan by some criminal genius out of Sherlock Holmes. Frankly, it's ridiculous on the face of it."

Pat shrugged. "I admit, it sounds wild. But somebody who hated cops might take real pride and pleasure in sitting back and pulling off something like this."

She was shaking her head. "But who could manage it? Who could reach out to enough disparate criminals… from gangbangers to armed robbers to outright thugs… in such a sophisticated, complicated manner?"

"The King of the Weeds," I said.

They both looked at me like I was out of my mind. Not the first time I'd been looked at that way. Likely not the last.

In any case, I told them what I had learned from Tim Darcy and his source Danny Dixon. I didn't provide names, though I said I would do so when I felt it wasn't a compromise of trust. A P.I. has to protect his sources the same way a journalist does.

I said, "Rudy Olaf is a chess master, Ms. Clark, both literally and figuratively. And if my source isn't just yanking my chain, then Sing Sing's answer to Professor Moriarty has been running the criminal power structure within the most famous prison in America for decades. From his post as de facto head librarian, he can communicate with anyone on the inside or outside he wishes, and he has money to burn—just like the cigarettes his kingdom uses for currency."

Pat looked like he'd been slapped. "If what you've heard is *true*, Mike, then Rudy Olaf is just the man to put something this complicated in play."

The assistant D.A. still wasn't sold. "But why in hell would he *do* it, Mr. Hammer?"

"For fun, Ms. Clark." She had a right to see the nasty grin, so I showed it to her. "To exercise his power. Maybe in anticipation of getting out of stir after four decades, he saw this as his crowning touch, the final achievement of the King of the Weeds."

She was shaking her head, though I could tell she was getting on board. "How would we ever prove it?"

Pat said, "You'd only need to prove one murder and link it to him. We have four Red Commando punks in custody right now, from that young officer's killing, and if you swung a deal with one, Ms. Clark, maybe...?"

"I'll think about it," she said. Her expression had gone unreadable. "I'll think about it."

We had another drink, and I asked Ms. Clark a few questions about her background. She answered them in an affable manner, and I was starting to wonder if after all these years I finally had a friend in the D.A.'s office.

"Let me get this, Mike," Pat said, reaching for the check.

I snagged it. "Nope. You're about to be fired, old buddy, and need to save your shekels. You got a rocking chair to save up for."

"Screw you, pal," he said with a grin.

And we headed out of the place, with Pat in the lead.

Velda found me at Bellevue. She came running down the corridor in her black raincoat, dodging nurses and orderlies who gave her irritated looks, and finally flung herself into my arms. We were in a waiting area at the end of the hall down from Pat's room in Intensive Care.

"Oh, Mike," she said, hugging me desperately. "Tell me. Tell me."

I held her away from me. Tears streaked her face. She already knew what had gone down, from when I called her at home; what she wanted was the medical update. She hadn't bothered with make-up and her hair was an uncombed tumble, and she had never looked better to me.

"He's in surgery," I said. "The medic I talked to said the bullet went straight in and out, which is good. Didn't go bouncing around inside him like a pinball. Did *not* knick his spinal cord."

She nodded, arms loose around my waist now. "Then no danger of paralysis…?"

"No. But a lot got torn up on that slug's way out."

Anger tightened my gut. "If he makes it, he could be shitting in a bag for the rest of his life."

"*Mike!* Don't talk that way."

"I'm not going to pull any punches, kitten. This is bad. He lost a lot of blood… but it could have been worse—the ambulance boys got there in a hurry, anyway. The docs give him about a one in three chance."

We sat down on a metal-frame couch with thin cushions, a big window at our backs. Matching chairs were at right and left separated by metal tables with last year's magazines. This was a designated smoking area—the tobacco stench hung like death.

She said, "You have blood all over your coat."

"It was on my hands and face, too. I looked like I stepped out of a war zone."

Her dark eyes flashed. "Well, didn't you? Mike, why *Pat* this time? Why was *he* the target?"

"He wasn't," I said, and explained why I thought as much.

"If you're right," she said, and her eyes were clear now, emotion replaced by professionalism, "then something doesn't track. You have both the feds and the mob very much wanting you alive, *needing* you alive—you are the keeper of the keys, Mike, the only one who can lead them to those billions."

I squeezed her hand. "*You* could."

She shook her head. "They don't know that. And I think you were right before, when you said most people would assume an old-fashioned hard-ass like

Mike Hammer would never share that kind of secret with a woman. No, I'm sure I'm safe."

"*I'm* not so sure. Doll, we're going to get you fitted for a vest first thing tomorrow."

She didn't object. "Then the question is the same one we were asking after that dictionary saved your life—who wants you dead?"

As if in answer to that question, a tall skeletal figure moved down the hall toward us, in no hurry, like a wraith floating through fog. At first I didn't make him out and then when I did, I wondered if I was hallucinating. In my mind he was still in prison, even though I knew he'd been recently released.

But there he was, Rudy Olaf, the King of the Weeds himself, in a gray off-the-rack suit a little big for him, the narrow oval of his blue-eyed face damn near as gray as the suit, white shirt buttoned up to the throat but no tie, his cheekbones sharp and high, adding to his walking-skeleton appearance. He was getting something out of his suitcoat's breast pocket, and my hand drifted near the .45 under my arm.

But Rudy didn't seem to see us. His expression was distant, distracted, oblivious to doctors and nurses and the intercom announcements and dings of bells and rattle of carts and the two people seated in the waiting area, too. From that breast pocket, he withdrew a pack of cigarettes, and removed a book of matches from where it was tucked in the cellophane wrapper.

He was two-thirds of the way to us when the sky did

a tympani number and that wet gray blanket hanging over the city finally let go. Thunder shook the blinds behind us like a disobedient child and for a moment I wondered if the power would go and a generator kick in. Hospitals had damn good ones. The rain was immediate and hard, unrelenting, not quite torrential, just insistent, like the drumming of a drum-and-bugle corps preceding invading troops.

Then just a few yards from us, he stopped. He said through the slash in his face that was his smile, *"Well, Mr. Hammer... imagine running into you here."*

It had just been "Hammer" at Sing Sing. Now I was "Mr. Hammer." Now he was polite, a friendly but respectful old acquaintance.

I got to my feet. "I'm visiting a sick friend."

"We have that in common. Henry Brogan is one floor down. I suppose you know that."

Actually I had known that, planning to go downstairs and slip in for a little private talk with Brogan, while I waited for Pat to get out of surgery. But I sure as hell didn't want Olaf around when I did.

I asked, "What are you doing on this floor, Rudy?"

He shrugged knobby shoulders. "This is one of the few smoking areas left in this facility. They make the doctors and nurses smoke outside now, you know. Barbaric. What do they do in rain like this?"

He lighted up a cigarette and drew smoke in, held it a long time, then politely blew it out to one side. The gray-blue smoke went well with his suit and his skin.

He re-pocketed the deck of smokes with the tucked-away matches.

Through a grin that was half-hidden by my upper lip, I said, "Paying respects to your old pal Brogan, huh?"

"Yes. You may find that difficult to fathom, Mr. Hammer, since one might think I would resent Henry for letting me serve so many years for the crimes he committed. But I understand his behavior. He had a sick wife he was caring for, and then later, a family. His daughter was no great shakes, just a junkie really, but she gave him those two grandkids, who became the lights of his life."

I shook my head, still grinning. "So you expect me to believe you willingly served forty years so your pal could enjoy his *grandkids*."

"Oh, I didn't know that's what was going on. For all those years when Henry would visit me each week, I just thought he was a good friend. We were old chess opponents, you know."

"I know."

Olaf shrugged again. "I had no idea he was the real Bowery slayer." He pulled in smoke, held it, then let it out dreamily. "Perhaps I would have a different attitude if my stay at Ossining had been more... trying. But I am an adaptable type, Mr. Hammer. I make the best of whatever situation I find myself in... What's that on your coat? My, is that *blood*?"

"That's what it is."

His smile was a ghastly thing as gray as his suit and

his skin and his cigarette smoke. "Surely not yours, Mr. Hammer. You look healthy as a horse."

"Some drive-by punk shot Pat Chambers tonight, outside a restaurant. Or do you know about that already, Rudy?"

He frowned and did a passable imitation of someone hearing sad news and responding sympathetically. "Is that why you're here? Oh dear. How badly was he hurt?"

"Fighting for his life in an operating room right now, Rudy."

Smoke came out his nostrils and his eyes were half-hooded, cobra-like. "Well, I'll send up a special prayer for him... Is *this* lovely woman your fiancée, Mr. Hammer? Sorry to be rude, my dear, I didn't mean to ignore you—I'm Rudolph Olaf."

The King of the Weeds held a bony gray hand out to her, but Velda ignored it, looking right through him.

He shrugged to himself, withdrew the hand, then turned icy blue eyes on me. "Ironic, isn't it?"

"What?"

"That we would both be here on this dreadful night, visiting friends in Intensive Care. I just hope *your* luck is better than mine."

"Yeah?"

"Yes. Henry Brogan lapsed into a coma this morning, and died fifteen minutes ago."

Olaf gave me a patronizing smile and took several long drags on his cigarette, exhaled smoke grandly, stuffed the butt into the sand of a canister nearby, and strode off.

I said nothing and neither did Velda. And the sky's only comment was a muffled grumble.

CHAPTER ELEVEN

By three in the morning, we knew that Pat had made it through surgery and that his odds had improved to fifty fifty. He was in an induced coma and would stay there for several days… *if* he made it that long.

The doctor in charge didn't reveal such information lightly—I had to convince him that I was as close to next-of-kin as Pat Chambers had. Over the years Pat had been engaged three times but had never married any of the women, since each came to understand that he was already wedded to his job. His only brother had died in Korea and his folks were long gone.

"Doctor," I asked him, "were you in the service?"

"Vietnam. Medical Corps."

"Pat and I were in combat together in the Pacific. That brother enough for you?"

It was.

Velda and I somehow made our way back to her apartment and were so exhausted, we slept in till eight. She made us a bacon-and-eggs breakfast while I stood at a window with a cup of coffee, looking out on another cold gray day, the rain taking an intermission for now. People died on all kinds of days, but this one seemed made for it.

Later I sat sipping my second cup of joe and said, "I'm not sure what's coming up in the hours ahead, doll. Why don't you dress for the country."

She knew what I meant, and when she returned from the bedroom she was in an olive jumpsuit with running shoes.

"How's this?" she asked, holding her hands out presentation style. "I'm afraid I look like a commando."

"If that's what commandos looked like," I said, "I would have stayed in the army."

Instead of going to the office, I hustled Velda into a cab that we took over to Thirty-Fourth Street, then got quickly out and grabbed another cab and headed to a nondescript Midtown building and a very private office where Velda had never visited. She knew something was up without asking, seeing me go through the routine of fouling up anybody following us with that two-cab shuffle.

Bud Langston ran a strictly one-man operation. There was not even a receptionist to greet us as we entered a small office dominated by computers and monitors sitting on counters that surrounded a central area given over to a file-cabinet book-ended desk with neatly arranged paperwork, several phones, and no computer station at all. A high-backed wheeled stool made each counter's work area accessible, while an adjacent room was a laboratory set-up, where Bud had his real fun.

Bud's computer programming business was more than just a cover, but he made his real money from a secret D.C. bureau. He was a world-class inventor and the research that went on in that modest lab had saved lives around the globe... and ended some.

There was nothing special about the way he looked. He was one of those medium guys—medium height, weight, build, his round face made rounder by the echo of dark round-framed glasses. His mousy-brown hair was cut short and balding on top, where it was coming in spottily like grass trying to grow on fallow soil. He wore a white smock, which meant he planned to be working more in the lab today than on the computer side.

"Thanks for seeing me at short notice," I said to him, shaking his hand.

"No problem, Mike," he said. His voice was medium, too, somewhere between a second tenor and a baritone. He beamed at the lovely woman at my side. "You're Velda. I've heard a lot about you."

Her forehead frowned as her mouth smiled. "Haven't we met...?"

"Good memory," he said to her with a boyish grin.

"I sat next to you and Mike at Lincoln Center when they performed the Ring Cycle, oh… must have been ten years ago."

She said, "*That's* not Wagner," referring to the classical music playing at a low, soothing volume in the background.

"Can't work to Wagner," he said with a shy smile and shrug.

"That's Liszt, you uncouth type," I told her. "Listen, Bud—we're on the firing line. Both of us. That high-tech lightweight body armor you loaned me, last year—you still got that handy?"

He frowned, nodded. "I do. Need it again?"

"Yeah. Pat Chambers got clipped last night."

His frown deepened and he shook his head. "I heard that coming in today on the radio. Terrible." His eyes narrowed. "That's right, you two are tight, aren't you? Sorry, Mike. Never met the man, but what a reputation he has."

I pressed on: "Bud, is there any way we can get Velda one of those special vests, too?"

He looked her up and down but not in the way most men did. "I think I have just the thing. Come with me."

We followed him into the lab.

The material in question was not one of Bud's own creations, though it was as amazing as anything he'd ever come up with. The very lightweight mesh was a modern-day take on chain mail, and made Kevlar feel like a suit of armor. The light, flexible fabric was an offshoot of research into metal mesh designed for scuba divers as shark protection.

The inventor went to a closet and came back with what might have been a long-sleeved T-shirt on a hanger. He held it before me and said to Velda, "The surprising lightness of this metal fabric isn't its *only* benefit. Most body armor leaves your arms open to bullet wounds. This gives you protection to the wrist and below the waist. I arranged this one for Mike last year, so that this flap comes up between the legs and fastens with Velcro. Slick, huh?"

"Very," she said. "You can do the same for me?"

"Don't have to. The first one I made came out too small for Mike. It's all I have left of the material, but I can make some alterations if need be."

"Now he's a tailor," I said. "What kind of needle are you going to use, a laser beam?"

"Nothing so high-tech," he said, and nodded to a workbench across the lab. "Acetylene torch."

I said, "Not while *she's* in it you aren't."

"No worries, Mike. We'll just take measurements."

Velda asked, "Is the material difficult to produce?"

Bud turned to her. "Right now, I don't know *how* to produce it. The young inventor responsible died under somewhat suspicious circumstances, and several of his suppliers did as well. It's expensive stuff to contrive and he only made a few sample swatches for demonstration purposes."

I asked, "Didn't the government balk at the price?"

Bud nodded. "And he went back to the drawing board to try to bring down the cost, but in the meantime I think somebody may have spent money keeping this miracle product off the market. Or perhaps he *did* die accidentally—he was working with very critical materials when the blast took out his lab. But that doesn't explain the several related 'accidental' deaths."

Velda asked, "How did you end up with even a limited amount of the stuff?"

Bud's smile was bittersweet. "The young genius and I were members of the same diving club. Our lockers were next to each other, and he'd been trying the material out in the club pool. After he died, I admit I helped myself to it. He'd told me all about it, and I was obviously interested."

She felt the mesh-armor shirt he was holding out, as if she were in a boutique, testing the feel of fabric. "I remember this stuff from when Mike used it last year. Such a satin-like texture. Bud, you could make a fortune."

"If those deaths were due to industrial espionage," Bud said, "I don't need to get myself killed picking up where my late peer left off. Maybe one of these days I'll hire Mike to look into it. But not now."

He handed me the mesh shirt on its hanger and went back to the closet and came back with a second, smaller-looking long-sleeved affair also on a hanger. He presented the shimmering garment to Velda and pointed her to the rest room. Several minutes later, she returned, smoothing out her jumpsuit, giving us a smile and a shrug.

"Fits fine," she said.

"I'm pleased," Bud said.

I said, "Don't lie, pal. You're disappointed you don't get to measure her for the alterations."

His smile crinkled his chin and his glasses bobbled on his nose. "Would have been a first for me, got to admit. I don't do a lot of fittings in this place. Mike, you're a little heavier than you were last year. You came here straight from a doctor's care, if I remember right. Get into yours, too, would you? I might need to let it out with that torch."

And he pointed to the rest room.

I did as I was told, and it fit fine.

"We'll leave these on," I said, "and bring them back when we're out of the woods."

"Maybe I should let you have them," Bud said with a frustrated smirk. "That way I won't be tempted to get myself killed by developing that stuff, and taking it to market."

I leaned against a counter. "Something else I wanted to ask you about, Bud. Nothing to do with this body armor, really. It's related to this rash of cop fatalities."

Bud frowned and nodded. "Awful thing. You may think I'm a kook for saying so, but I suspect something nastier than coincidence is going on there. Call me a sap for going along with the tabloid alarmists if you like, but I think a serial killer is at work."

"So do I," I said. "But why do *you* think so?"

"Well, I've dealt with a lot of spook types, Mike. I've designed some fairly nasty things for the C.I.A. I can't be more specific, but it's put me in contact with some deadly people. These espionage types are brilliant and damn tricky and as manipulative as hell. There's a word nobody uses anymore—diabolical. That's what they are, Mike—diabolical."

I frowned at him. "A spy isn't behind these deaths, Bud."

"No, but someone with that kind of mentality is. I don't believe it would be difficult to arrange accidents by knowing the habits, the patterns, of intended victims. Those officers killed both on duty and off duty were likely driving home on a regular route or walking beats that were entirely predictable, based on their normal behavior. Assassins working for the government use that kind of intel routinely."

I nodded and tried another angle. "What about causing coronaries or other deaths by apparent *natural* causes?"

I had in mind the jogger who'd had a heart attack.

He waved that off. "Child's play. That's been around forever, Mike. You know some of the ways the C.I.A. tried to whack Castro, don't you? Poisoned wetsuit, exploding conch shell, bacteria-laced hanky, exploding cigar, you name it."

Velda said, "Sounds like slapstick comedy."

"Slapstick tragedy is more like it," Bud said. He

frowned, raised a finger. "Here—let me show you something from my archives. These don't date back to Castro days—these are currently in-use tools of spy tradecraft. Just don't ask me whether or not *I* developed any of them…"

He went to a drawer and unlocked it. From there he began displaying items in sealed plastic bags. "This ballpoint pen has a hypodermic needle with a point so fine, the victim receives a dose of deadly poison without even knowing it."

"Mightier than the sword," I muttered.

Bud withdrew another plastic bag. "This contaminated cigar… not the exploding one they tried on Castro… has a poison that provides instant death when heated and introduced into the lungs. Ten minutes after death, there's no trace. Autopsy says heart attack, any examination of the remainder of the cigar shows nothing. Pack of Luckies here, same deal, and no surgeon general warning covers it. How about this innocent bottle of aspirin? These are the new improved variety with a secret ingredient—an explosive that detonates when triggered by stomach acid. If you take two, you won't be calling the doctor in the morning. Here's a new model of an oldie but goodie—this fake folded-up umbrella has a trigger that doesn't spread itself but instead fires a small poisoned and very fatal dart. And this tube of lipstick… perfect for you, Velda… is a 4.5 millimeter single-shot weapon."

"But does it come in Drop Dead Red?" Velda asked,

tugging at her jumpsuit unconsciously.

Bud glanced at her with a frown. "That thing's riding up on you, isn't it? Bunching up. Let's have a look."

So he got to take her measurements, after all, though we stayed well across the lab while Bud in his goggles used the small acetylene torch at his work counter to make the minor alterations.

We were in the office by ten-thirty. I sat behind my desk and studied the card that Roger Buckley had given me that included his number at the local Treasury Department office but had his cellular phone circled.

He answered on the second ring. "Buckley," he said.

"Hammer," I said.

"Well, good morning, Mr. Hammer. Have you made a decision about Uncle Sam's offer?"

"I have."

"What's the verdict then?"

"Pick me up in front of the Hackard Building at two o'clock. Come alone."

"Are we going somewhere?"

"Like they used to say in the gangster pictures, we're going for a ride."

"That sounds rather ominous, Mr. Hammer."

"Then come armed if you like. I will be."

I hung up.

Moments later, Velda slipped in sporting a curious arched eyebrow. Half-closing the inner-office door, she said quietly, "We've got an intriguing pair of walk-ins."

"Too busy today, doll. No time for new clients. Give them a time next week."

But she was already shaking her head, raven arcs swinging like lovely scythes. "You'll want to see *these* two. Interesting-looking couple of kids."

"Velda…"

"Amy and Nick Brogan."

"…*Brogan*?"

"Yup. Henry Brogan's grandkids, or so they claim."

I waved for her to let them in, then said, "You better sit in on this. Hit the recorder out there, so you don't have to take notes."

She nodded, and then moments later ushered them in. Willowy but shapely, Amy Brogan was in a crisp white blouse with black slacks that would have said she was a waitress even if she hadn't absent-mindedly left the little AMY name-badge on her breast pocket. Her black hair was short and curly and her lipstick was almost black, too. Skinny Nick Brogan was in a black CBGB's T-shirt, frayed jeans and tennies. He had curly black hair about as long as his sister's, which gave them the unnerving look of twins, though they clearly weren't. Both were slender and attractive in a ragged way, with not a trace of rat-eyed Henry Brogan evident in their faces. Both were in their early twenties.

They were nervous, even anxious, and came right to me before I'd even had a chance to rise. They thrust slender hands at me simultaneously and I shook them one at a time—gentleman that I am, I went with Amy first.

"Have a seat, kids," I said, gesturing. I was half-way up and on my way back down. "Please. What can I do for you?"

Velda guided them into the two client chairs, and then got herself the spare from against a wall. She angled herself so that her attention was on our visitors, her pleasant, even bland expression hiding the microscope-like scrutiny she was giving them.

They were both energetic and clearly upset. They started talking at the same time, then Nick put his hands up as if in surrender and let his sister have the floor.

"Mr. Hammer," Amy said, in a husky second soprano that carried considerable appeal, "I apologize for barging in on you. It's just that… everything's been so *sudden*. And I'm supposed to go in for work at *eleven*, and—"

"Take a breath," I said, and did so myself. "I assume this has to do with your grandfather's death."

They both nodded.

Nick picked up. "We have no illusions about what kind of person our grandfather was. Our mother died when I was six and Amy was eight. He owned that building he was living in, and it was an even bigger shithole then, but that's where we grew up."

"Your mother had an apartment there?"

Nick nodded, but this time Amy went on: "Henry… I'm afraid we never called him 'Grandpa' or 'Gramps' or anything warm and fuzzy like that… Henry put us into the foster home system. We both bounced around there. Nick and I didn't see each other again until after he graduated high school."

Nick said, "Despite dumping us, Henry wasn't all bad. He stayed in touch, and he provided money to our various foster parents, and directly to us, on holidays and birthdays. He even put Amy through college. He would've done the same for me, but I dropped out to play my music."

"You're a musician."

He nodded. "Yeah. I work steady. I have a band that's doing okay. We may get a record deal, if… but it's always touch-and-go in that business."

"And I'm an actress," Amy said. Her smile was embarrassed. "Yes, we're both in the arts, Mr. Hammer, which isn't the smartest thing, we know. But when we moved back to the city… Nick, you tell this part."

Nick nodded and took the ball. "We went to see Henry at his building in the Bowery. We thanked him for all he did for us over the years, and he got weepy saying he wished he could have done more, wished he could've raised us himself, but he just couldn't do it, an old man alone."

Amy, with a smirk, said, "He wasn't *that* old when we were growing up."

Nick continued: "But you have to give him credit for trying, anyway. An apartment had opened up in that building of his, and he offered it to us. Amy and I still are rooming there right now. It was the pits, but we cleaned it up and—"

"Never mind that, Nick," Amy said. "Mr. Hammer, our grandfather made it clear to us that we were going to inherit that building. And you know, dump that it is, it's gonna go for big bucks one of these days. That whole area is getting refurbished, you know."

Nick said, "It's worth money *now*, but we would probably sit on it. Couple of years, who knows?"

She sat forward. "But there's more to it than that. Henry said… and this is the exact phrase he used… 'After I'm gone, you and your brother are never going to have to worry again. You can be an actress and your brother can be a rock and roller and you'll have all the cushion anybody would ever need.'"

"But he wasn't specific about it," I said.

Nick said, "Well, he said we'd get a 'windfall.' He used that word a bunch of times. He was happy about being able to do that for us."

Velda asked, "When was this?"

Amy shrugged and said, "Starting maybe… six months ago?"

I said, "When he found out he had cancer."

She shrugged again, bigger this time. "I don't know about that. Henry never told us he had cancer."

I looked from her face to his. "And now you figure that *'windfall'* was the settlement that the city made with Rudy Olaf. That your grandfather made a deal with Olaf. That if Henry came forward and confessed to being the

Bowery Bum slayer, then the cleared Olaf would share any settlement proceeds with you two kids."

They nodded slowly.

"It's also possible," I said, "that *Olaf* did the murders, and your dying grandfather stepped forward to take the blame—after Olaf told him where that murder gun had been hidden away all these years. And assuring Henry that, again, you two would share in the settlement."

Another mutual slow nod.

I went on: "But that wasn't the kind of deal you can put in writing. Your grandfather had to trust Olaf. Trust him not to betray him… and you."

Amy sighed in frustration and Nick frowned the same way.

I shifted in my chair. "Listen, kids… you do know who I am? What role I played in your grandfather's life?"

Amy said, "You and that Captain Chambers put Rudy Olaf away for the crimes our grandfather committed."

I said, "You really think your grandfather murdered those men?"

Nick said, "*I* don't. Olaf was his best bud going back to high school, and I figure when Henry knew he was going to die, he made the deal with Olaf that you outlined, Mr. Hammer."

Amy shook her head. "That's where Nick and I disagree. I think Henry did those crimes. I mean, our grandfather was *always* a guilt-ridden old goat. He was depressed and he drank a lot and felt sorry for himself.

He couldn't go to sleep without drinking himself that way. Yes, you bet your *ass* I think Henry framed his friend, and then made a penance out of visiting him in prison. Playing speed chess with him weekly, if you can imagine."

I asked, "Did your grandfather play chess with anyone else?"

Shaking his head, Nick said, "Not that I know of. Just Rudy Olaf. When he was a kid, I think Henry was really into chess. But he lost interest a long time ago."

"Except for the ongoing game with Olaf."

"Right."

Amy was shaking her head. "No, that's not right. There *was* that one guy from Brooklyn, Nickie... when we were kids, remember? He'd come in and play with old Henry now and then."

I exchanged glances with Velda: *Marcus Dooley.*

"I don't remember that," Nick said with a shrug.

I asked Amy, "Do you remember his name? What he looked like?"

"No," she said. "I was a kid, he was a grown-up. That's it."

But that felt like enough: Brogan was Dooley's chess buddy, all right. Had he been Dooley's helper, too?

I looked from young face to young face again. "So why did you come to *me*, Amy? Nick? The last time I saw your grandfather was in his hospital room, and our meeting was less than cordial."

Nick said, "I don't know anything about that. What

I do know is that Henry said to come to *you* if anybody tried to… this is what he said, *exactly*… 'screw you and your sister out of what's rightfully yours.'"

I shrugged. "Well, he just passed away, last night. Don't tell me there's already been a reading of the will and you were left out on the curb."

"Worse," Amy said, bleakly bitter. Nick was nodding forcefully. She went on: "That slimeball attorney Rufus Tomlin called this morning to inform us that there would be a reading of the will in his office tomorrow afternoon, and that we were welcome to come… but needn't bother."

Velda sat forward. "Needn't *bother?*"

Nick said, "That's right. He said we 'needn't bother' because we weren't *in* our grandfather's will. The sole beneficiary is—"

"Rudy Olaf," I said.

"*Yes!*" they both said.

I sighed, rocked back. "There's a possibility that your grandfather had an arrangement with Olaf to provide for you. Apart from whatever was in the will. Nothing in writing, but maybe Olaf will honor it."

Veins were standing out in Amy's forehead as she sat forward, but Nick beat her to the punch: "Oh, we talked to that old bastard this morning! He's living in Henry's *apartment*, you know! Same building we live in."

Amy said, "We asked if our grandfather had made any provisions with him to make us a part of his estate."

I asked, "And what did he say?"

"In a word," Amy said, "he said, 'No.'"

"And that's it?"

Nick said, "Well, he said we were welcome to stay on in our apartment, but that we weren't *his* grandchildren, so we should expect to pay rent, like anybody else."

Amy was sitting with clenched fists, trembling all over, her dark eyes flashing. "It's *obvious* Olaf is bitter about spending all those years in jail for what our grandfather did. I mean, who could blame him? Obviously Olaf encouraged Henry to come forward in that scheme to squeeze money out of the city. That way Olaf could benefit, and our grandfather could leave us well-off. But that sneaky old bastard *bamboozled* our grandfather. *Clearly.* Mr. Hammer, is there *anything* you can do?"

Nick said, "I know we must sound terrible to you, a couple of greedy kids who've been dreaming about the windfall they'll get when their grandfather dies... but Henry *did* say we should come to you for help."

Something in what the kid said made a puzzle piece slide into place with a click that reverberated through my brain. Something that had not made sense before suddenly did. And it was nothing to do with why these kids were here. And yet it was.

Velda, sensing I had drifted, said, "Mike?"

"Yeah?"

"You should tell them. Tell them what can be done. What is *being* done."

I nodded. They were on the edge of their seats, the hope in their eyes so desperate it was almost funny. And pitiful.

"I think you're going to come out of this all right," I said. "I'm certainly going to do my part. But before I fill you in, you need to understand something. You need to understand who your grandfather was."

They frowned.

"Don't ask me to go on," I said, "unless you're prepared to hear the worst."

They swallowed, exchanged glances, then nodded in tandem.

"The most likely scenario," I said, "and one that newly uncovered facts support, is that Rudy Olaf and Henry Brogan were accomplices—they were, together, the Bowery Bum slayer. They trolled gay bars on the Bowery looking for victims to lure into alleys promising sex but delivering robbery and murder. My guess is that Olaf did the luring and your grandfather did the killing, granted at Olaf's direction. Olaf took the fall, and your grandfather owed him, and stayed his friend... his chess partner... all those years. And then Henry Brogan got cancer. Your gramps stepped up to take the blame and absolve his partner, freeing the latter while taking the city for a ride... to provide for the two grandchildren he loved."

They said nothing. Their mutual expression might well have been Henry Brogan's the moment after the doctor's fatal diagnosis.

Nick grunted a kind of weary laugh. "I guess our grandfather shouldn't have trusted a sociopath to do the right thing."

"Probably not," I said. "But here's the deal—and this is confidential, kids—the D.A.'s office is looking into both the original murders *and* the conspiracy to defraud the city that your grandfather and Rudy Olaf entered into."

"That means," Amy said, eyes tensed, "that the settlement money would be returned to the city."

"If the investigation is successful," I said, nodding, "and I believe it will be."

Nick smiled a little. "So much for the windfall."

"True," I said. "But the rest of your estate—that tenement apartment building that is going up in value even as we speak—will go to you two, once the dust settles."

Amy frowned. "Why is that?"

"Any inheritance received as a result of the commission of a crime—in this case conspiracy—is revoked… and goes to the next-in-line to inherit. Which is you two."

"Well, that would be wonderful," the girl said.

"It'd be *great*," Nick said, grinning. "And Rudy Olaf will go back to prison?"

Sending the King of the Weeds back to Sing Sing was like tossing Br'er Rabbit into the Briar Patch.

"Or something," I said.

CHAPTER TWELVE

The sky remained as gray as the city it draped itself over, but there was no overt threat of rain, and I didn't mind the chill. Wearing my blood-spattered trenchcoat might have made an interesting fashion statement on an afternoon trip with a Treasury agent. But Velda had already sent it off to the dry cleaners. She was both female and private investigator, after all, so her desire to make things right ran deep.

She would not be making the trip to the Adirondacks with Roger Buckley and me—I had another assignment for her. Right after the Brogan grandkids left the office, I'd had a call from faux bag lady Rita Callaghan about the surveillance efforts outside the Hackard Building. It appeared the government guys were gone—Buckley had apparently called them off after we set up our day trip—but two other vehicles *might* be stalking our building. Each had a single party who remained in a parked car—sometimes on the rider's side or in the back seat—which was periodically moved. Basic surveillance technique. And from Rita's descriptions I thought I made them both.

I was down on the street at two o'clock when Buckley pulled up promptly in a dark blue Buick Regal. I was in suit and tie and looked like any other businessman, or at least an Old School one in a porkpie fedora. That I was a .45-packing P.I. was not at all apparent, thanks to the cut of my suit—certainly not one wearing body armor, however lightweight.

Buckley, too, looked like any other businessman, or anyway executive. He might have been my boss. His dark gray vested suit was beautifully tailored. He looked like the guys in magazine ads in the '60s gone just slightly to seed, his chiseled good looks compromised by pouchiness and paunch.

Nothing about us said we were off to visit a treasure hoard in the Hall of the Mountain Kings.

We established right away that Buckley would drive and I would navigate. A major part of the deal was for me to provide the location of a hideaway filled with mob loot. He might as well learn his way there today.

I directed him to cross the George Washington Bridge and head up 9W, taking the scenic route along the Hudson River. I didn't need a map—I'd made the trip only a few times, but the pathway to billions isn't something you forget.

For the first leg of the trip, we just rode. Maybe each of us was waiting for the other to make the first move. Just outside Newburgh, Buckley glanced my way, his gray eyes tight.

"You know," the Treasury agent said, "I'm aware we're headed to the Adirondacks."

I grinned. "Well, if you have it narrowed down that much, what do you need me for?"

"We do have a deal, right, Mr. Hammer?"

"Isn't that understood?"

"Let's spell it out—the finder's fee we discussed in exchange for taking me to this secret location."

"That's it."

At least a full minute passed before he said: "Why don't I tell you what *I* know, Mr. Hammer? And then you fill in the rest."

"Sure. It's a long drive."

"Is it?"

I nodded. "Like you said—you go first."

He knew that the New York state police and the federal government had both gone to two suspected locations for the stored money and other valuables. First, a cavern on the property of Don Lorenzo Ponti, which turned out to be in use for mushroom farming. Second, a cavern in a mountain roughly in the same area that had been used by a bootlegger named Slipped Disk Harris both during Prohibition and after.

Nothing had been found in either.

That seemed to be the extent of his knowledge.

So I told him what I knew. That the old dons of the Five Families had distrusted the next generation and taken the remarkable step of turning assets into cash and commodities. That Marcus Dooley had been a trusted non-mobbed-up worker of Don Ponti's who had been recruited by the capo to help him move all that money. That Dooley had double-crossed the don by hiding it elsewhere other than the cavern on Ponti's own property. That on his deathbed Dooley had given me the clues that had led me to the treasure. And that I had come to believe that Dooley meant for his son Marvin to benefit when the billions were either turned back over to the mob or handed in to the government.

Buckley, behind the wheel, said, "Your friend Dooley must have known that any finder's fee would be substantial. That there'd be plenty to go around, for you and his kid."

"Maybe. Anyway, I'm really not that interested."

That made him smile and his gaze went from the highway to me and back again. "You really aren't, are you, Mr. Hammer?"

"Oh, I'll take that finder's fee you're offering. This isn't a hobby, it's a business, and I don't mind plumping up my retirement funds. But how does any one man spend a billion bucks, anyway?"

He let out something half-way between a sigh and a laugh. "Many a man would relish the opportunity to try, Mr. Hammer. Tell me, do you expect us to provide Marvin Dooley with a separate finder's fee?"

"Naw. I'll take care of him."

Outside Albany, I had Buckley stop at a farm equipment store, where I picked up two mag flashlights and some batteries. Soon we were headed into the North Country, the real New York, where you could smell pine cones, not exhaust fumes, where trees and mountains towered, not buildings.

When the state roads ran out, county ones took over, but these were inconsistently maintained, depending on whether the townships in question wanted to bother. But finally, without a single wrong turn, we came to the single narrow lane that corkscrewed through the trees toward the majestic rise of the Adirondacks. We passed a landmark that had become familiar to Velda and me—a ditch where lay the twisted, rusted wreckage of an old truck held by two stout pine trees preventing its further downward slide.

Buckley, eyes wide, asked, "You suppose that relic was hauling slate when it skidded off the road?"

"More likely booze, a lifetime ago. A legit business would have salvaged the thing."

Then the Buick swung around a turn and the forest fell away, replaced by a vast empty field on the edge of a mountain that worked hard at blotting out the gray sky. Here and there around the property, hillocks of gray slag rose like ugly oversize anthills, wearing thistles that stubbornly insisted on growing.

When Velda and I had first seen what was left of the old estate of Slipped Disk Harris, three weather-beaten buildings had lurked in the mountain's shadows. Now they were gone. The mighty power of the federal government had swept them away, tearing apart anything that might provide a clue to those missing billions. Little piles of what discoveries metal detectors *had* made— rusty cans, truck chains, and assorted other debris— served as ironic reminders of a search that failed.

We stopped at the point where the lane branched out in five ways, only one of which was passable.

Buckley shot me an irritated look. "What's the idea, Hammer? This is the *Harris* property. This site was ruled out by all the experts. It's been gone over with a fine-tooth comb."

"I didn't use a fine-tooth comb," I said. "I used a backhoe." I pointed. "Drive."

Frowning, the Treasury man did as he was told, not stopping till the path ran out and we faced a high ridge of bushes.

"Pull around them," I said.

"There's no road."

"That shrubbery was planted by bootleggers to hide the entrance to their cave. It's a little overgrown, but you can still see the ruts of other vehicles in the grass. Drive."

He drove, and as we came around the ridge of bushes, the ground veered steeply up, its green merging into the rocky side of the mountain proper, as if a volcano had burst through a hillside. The quietness here was almost startling, the only noise wind whistling through the trees. This is what it would sound like when the infestation that was man was finally purged from the planet. And it didn't strike me as all that bad.

Buckley was hesitating. "Should we get *out* here? I don't see anything."

"Look there. Look closer." I pointed again. "See that cleft in the hillside? The angle from here makes it look narrow but it's fairly wide. They used to have a big wooden barn door there, to drive their booze trucks in and out."

The T-man frowned, but hunkered over the wheel and crept up the hillside, *bump bump bump*. He paused at the clutch of bushes that partially concealed the cleft and I said, "Push on through the brush. We can use the headlights in there."

"This *is* the Harris cave."

"It is. Now ease on through."

He scowled but followed orders, and barely inside the mouth of the cave, he put it in park. I told him to drive a little deeper, because we could use the visibility, and he somewhat reluctantly obeyed. The surface under the wheels was surprisingly smooth.

Finally I told him to stop but leave the headlights on, and we got out into the cool, dry atmosphere. Somehow you could sense the size of it all around you, and if you ever wondered how silence could be deafening, you understood now. I handed him one of the big heavy flashlights and kept the other for myself. We both clicked them on and their beams immediately picked up dust motes the car had kicked up from the hard-packed dirt floor.

There was just enough incline for the headlight beams to have an upward angle, and that provided an immediate sense of the actual size of the big natural cave, of its impressive width, depth and height. Even so, we could only make out one rough wall of this almost chilly cavern that had made such a perfect warehouse for a bootlegger.

I asked him, "Would you like a tour?"

Buckley nodded, frowning, uneasy. "Are we going to run into any bats?"

Our voices echoed, just a little.

"Not in this chamber," I said. "Anyway, they have built-in radar. They won't touch us."

"Then there *is* another chamber?"

"Oh yeah. But let's get a sense of this one first."

Following the irregular curve of the walls, I led him around the perimeter. Our flashlights poked at the dirt floor to reveal the scattered ghosts of bootlegging days—wooden boxes, an old truck seat, vintage tools, broken bottles—and in fifteen minutes or so we were back where we had started, near the Buick's headlights. We'd stirred more dust and the stuff swam in the beams like amoeba under a microscope.

I asked, "Notice anything the experts might have missed?"

"No."

"Let's get in the car and drive deeper. I'll point you in the right direction."

Buckley got behind the wheel again and I climbed into the passenger seat. The headlights could not yet find the far wall of the cave, not by a long shot, but did pick up the scattered refuse here and there on the floor.

"Hammer, there are broken bottles... the tires..."

"Just go slow and careful. *This* way..."

He inched through the vast empty dome. It took a while, but finally the high beams hit that far wall beyond a scattering of boulders—a high, wide, hard-packed pile of stony rubble.

Buckley asked, "What happened here?"

"When I got my first look at this place, the old caretaker said there'd been a minor cave-in years ago, and everything that fell from the ceiling got pushed up against the wall. To accommodate the bootleggers using this space."

He looked at me carefully. "Are you implying something else is going on?"

"I'm not implying anything."

I got out. So did he. He shut the motor off but of course left on the headlights. I ran the mag light up at the ceiling, where the stone showed scarring. "That's minimal damage compared to this wall of rubble and stones."

Buckley began running his flashlight's beam around and across the cave's back wall.

"Do you hear something?" he asked, giving me an alarmed look. "Something's back there. What's *back* there?"

Chirring and flapping.

"There's your bats," I said with a grin. "We've woken them up. Thousands of them guarding billions."

He looked at me sharply, with a very unprofessional wildness in his eyes. "The other chamber's beyond this wall of stones. Enclosed?"

"Not entirely. Somewhere up high, those bats've got a way in and out. It might be possible to get in that way, if you had a real spelunker in charge. When you bring in workers to move these cartons of money, better make it a no smoking zone."

"What? Why?"

I shone the flash on the wall with its near pebble-stone look. "There's as much bat guano in there as money."

"So what?"

"So the stuff is flammable. They make explosives out of it. Unless you got money to burn, Agent Buckley, keep the smoking lamp out."

Buckley was studying that rocky wall as if maybe he could say, *Open Sesame*, and a door would open in it.

"You've been behind here," he said softly, pointing the flash in one hand and gesturing with the other.

"Actually, I built that wall, or re-made it, after I broke through with a backhoe and took a little look around the chamber beyond. Which is, by the way, larger than this one."

Buckley sucked in air—it was damn near a gasp. Then he frowned at me. "You closed it back up again?"

I nodded. "Yeah. Partly with the backhoe. Also used

a little square of plastic explosive that somebody had generously left attached to the starter in my car. I hung on to it in case of emergency."

That made him blink, but he asked for no further details.

I shone the flash toward him, not in his eyes, but still putting him in the spotlight. "So are we done here, Agent Buckley? Have you seen enough?"

He frowned at me. "You have to be kidding. I haven't seen *anything* except a pile of rubble against the back wall of this cave."

"You heard the bats, didn't you?"

"I don't know what I heard, or what I believe."

I shrugged. "Well, I don't expect payment until you've excavated this site and recovered the money and other goodies. I'll take your word. If you can't trust Uncle Sugar, who can you trust?"

He was shaking his head. "No. No, no, no. We've come this far. I need to *see* it. *Now*, Mr. Hammer."

That desperate gleam in his eyes spoke volumes.

"Buckley, why would I make this long trip in the company of a fed if I was trying to pull something?"

I sensed something was wrong, and I admit having suspicions about this guy from the start—a Treasury agent working as a lone wolf, wanting me to contact him only by way of a cell number, with a willingness to offer a civilian a billion-dollar finder's fee the way a dentist promises a kid a lolly-pop before the drilling.

But I didn't *know* he was dirty until he went for the

.38 in the cross-draw holster, only my .45 was out and on him before he could jerk the gun free. His eyes were wide and so was his open mouth and his nostrils flared, like a rearing horse reacting to a rattler. He thought he was looking at death as I trained the .45 on him with one hand and the beam of the big flash with the other, purposely blinding him.

"You're lucky you're a fed," I said. "Putting a bullet in you isn't worth the red tape… Let's have those hands up."

Blinking at the brightness, he said, "Hammer, be reasonable. You can still have that finder's fee. We can just forget this little bump in the road between us."

"Agent Buckley, you never intended to pay me that finder's fee. You were going to leave me dead somewhere, weren't you? You've spent a career chasing tax offenders, at government pay rates. Now you've located the hidden funds to end all hidden funds, and the boodle is right here near your grasp… but as a fed yourself, you can't even claim a finder's fee."

I caught something flash out of the corner of my eye and felt the burning sensation cut across the upper edge of my wrist before the echoing thunder of the gun caught up with it, and that searing pain popped my fingers open and the .45 thudded to the hard dirt floor. A wide red welt of torn flesh right at the join of hand and wrist was the end result of some very fancy shooting.

I hadn't heard him come in. He must not have

driven his vehicle inside the cave. He had followed the voices and walked quietly through the darkness to where those high-beam headlights pinpointed us. My flash, still gripped in my left hand, swung over to catch the lanky frame of Frank Hellman approaching in a charcoal suit better than mine or even Buckley's, Savile Row perhaps, a Glock in his right fist pointed my way as he flashed that confident smile I'd seen at the Canterbury Club where he had first shown off his marksmanship skills.

The tall, thin, youthfully handsome financial advisor with those touches of gray at his temples stopped five or six feet from me. "Mr. Hammer, I've proven you wrong. You said shooting only counts when someone else is firing at you. But it also counts if you shoot somebody *before* they can fire at you."

"Point taken," I said. I felt the blood dripping around either side of my right wrist, but no serious flow was going.

Buckley had put his hands down. He came over to Hellman, saying, "*Jesus,* I thought I'd lost you outside of Albany. You worried the hell out of me, Frank. This maniac might have *shot* me!"

I ignored this piss-ant display, preferring to speak to Hellman, in whose direction my flash beam stayed. "The feds can't pay an employee a finder's fee, but your people sure can… right, Frank?" My laugh was loud enough to rate an echo. "You two have been in on this from the start, playing me from either side."

Hellman shrugged. "That's right. It's not very complicated, really. A finder's fee of a billion is nothing when it leaves another eighty-eight... not to mention all those deeds and stocks and bonds. An ideal way to infuse new capital into an old but profitable business."

"So we're back at the Pontis," I said, wiping the blood from my wrist onto my suitcoat; it burned but not bad. "Fitting. That's enough money to make you the new don, or whatever it's called in this brave new era."

"CEO will do. There's a crisis of leadership among the Pontis and *somebody* strong has to step forward."

"But somebody else strong was planning to, right, Frank? *Rudy Olaf.* That evil old man has dreams of taking over a criminal empire himself... he wants to be CEO of Ponti Enterprises, too, right? So you had to beat him to it. You got your chance when Rufus Tomlin put you in touch with Sing Sing's favorite librarian, before his release. Your job was to get things ready for Olaf to step in and take over the Ponti throne. Olaf knew all about the billions, thanks to his pal Brogan, who helped Marcus Dooley fill this cave with mob goodies and seal it up after. Only Olaf didn't share with you *where* those goodies were hidden, did he?"

Hellman seemed impressed and maybe a little surprised. "You really aren't stupid as you look, Hammer."

Buckley muttered, "How *could* he be?"

I went on: "So while your client was tied up with getting out of stir and dealing with the city government and other fun and games, you figured to snag it away from him, before he got the chance. And *I* was your way in—the hard-ass private eye rumored to know where the billions were storehoused."

The smile on Hellman's smug face had faded. He was thrown off balance by me knowing as much as I did.

"I won't confirm or deny any of that, Hammer. It's all moot now. All that's left is to make sure you haven't led us on a snipe hunt. We're going to *see* what's on the other side of that wall."

I swung the flash from Hellman to the pebble-and-rock wall. "I can save you the trouble, Frank. It's the Lost Dutchman's Mine. It's Eldorado." Then I brought the beam back in his direction. "But I'm afraid I left my backhoe in my other pants."

The smug smile was back. "I was prepared for this contingency, Mr. Hammer... Roger, my car keys are here in my right-hand suitcoat pocket. Get them, would you?"

Buckley did, having to juggle his own flash to do so.

Then Hellman said, "Go get me the duffel bag in the trunk."

With a nod, Buckley disappeared quickly into the darkness, footsteps echoing and diminishing.

"Explosives?" I asked.

Hellman nodded, the smug smile widening but not showing those impressive teeth. "An educated guess. I knew the theory had the hoard stashed somewhere in these mountains, and that these two caves had been the chief candidates. I figured you might wall it up in a side shaft or something."

The echo and increasing volume of footsteps announced Buckley's return. Hellman handed the T-man the Glock and took the duffel bag from him, walking it over to the solid wall of smashed-together rubble. From the bag he took a pliable square of yellow putty-like material that I took to be plastic explosive. He molded five such squares, each set several feet apart on the wall, roughly making a connect-the-dots circle. I could just make out the blasting caps stuck into the blobs. From the duffel bag he also removed a spool of yellow plastic detonator cord that he used to daisy-chain the charges.

"Mr. Hammer," Hellman said as he came over, "you'll want to accompany us."

This suggestion was amplified by Buckley jamming the nose of the Glock in my back. Hellman and I got in the back seat of Buckley's Buick Regal, which he backed up until we reached the shaft of daylight near the cave's opening. Then I was instructed to get out, and prodded with the gun again until we all three were just outside the cave in daylight thinning to dusk. Not far away a silver Mercedes, obviously Hellman's ride, was parked off to one side on the steep grassy slope.

I was directed to stand away and to one side of the opening with Buckley putting that rod in my neck now and Hellman likewise avoiding the opening when he used a hand-held detonator to set off the charges.

The explosion sounded farther away than reality, and the boom echoed big but died away fast. I expected smoke to billow out the opening, but none came. The cavern was just too deep and large and, if that wall had given way, the smoke would follow the bats up and out through some high crevice.

You could hear them escaping, the flapping of wings en masse and the chilling scree *of their song.*

Buckley had an anxious expression while Hellman's smugness had been replaced by satisfaction. The latter was clearly in command, the Treasury agent with the big bad rep turning servile around the would-be mob CEO.

Hellman said, "Roger, get back in your car and drive inside and park perhaps six feet from that wall, with your high beams on, so we can see what we've uncovered. May take a little while for that smoke to clear... But first, give me my car keys and my gun."

Buckley nodded, handed his partner the items, and slipped back inside the cave. Glock in hand, Hellman marched me over and directed me to get behind the wheel of the Mercedes, then came around and got in on the rider's side. He looked over at me warily, handing me the keys.

"No hero stuff, Hammer. Drive on in there and help put some light on the subject. You go faster than a crawl, and I'll put one through your head. You are fast outliving your usefulness, after all."

I drove through the narrow entry, almost scraping one side of the vehicle. The windows were up and the air conditioning on low, and I smelled only the faintest trace of smoke. The headlights cut through the darkness and smoky wisps floated like yolk in egg-drop soup, nothing substantially limiting visibility, certainly not the fog-like conditions I might have expected after that explosion.

"You're doing fine," Hellman said, and I floored it while throwing an elbow into his throat and he was too busy gurgling and choking to fire his weapon. The Mercedes made a purring roar as I gave him another elbow in the side of the head and that made him groggy, and seconds from crashing into what was left of the wall, I opened the car door and threw myself out, rolling into the darkness as the vehicle's nose smashed into the wall and Hellman crunched a spider's web into the windshield.

The Mercedes shut itself off, the engine crumpling like a paper cup, but it didn't explode—cars aren't the fire bombs movies make them out to be. The headlights were out. But I was off in the relative safety of the darkness, and with the echo of the crash dying away, I could hear Buckley's desperate yells: "*Frank!* Frank! My God, *Frank! Jesus!*"

Somewhere in this darkness, on this dirt floor, was the wedding-gift .45. But the odds of me finding it in all this darkness, all this vastness, sucked to hell. And I hadn't bothered with a hideout gun, figuring they'd frisk me, which they hadn't.

Maybe I was *just as dumb as I looked...*

Over by the wreckage, Hellman was stumbling out, staggering out, having to crawl down from the smashed upraised vehicle, helped by Buckley. If I'd been closer, I could have jumped them. Hellman was like a drunk, the whites of his eyes stark against the smeared and dripping red of his face, giving him a crazed look.

But I'll give him this much: he still had the Glock in hand. And once Buckley seemed certain his partner could stand on those two shaky legs, the T-man pulled his own weapon, that .38 on his hip, and then they both went fishing for me in the dark, sending their flashlight beams crisscrossing.

Quietly I crawled behind a boulder. I was hurting. When I jumped from the car, I'd landed on my bad side, and rolling had aggravated where the two .22s had punched me in the chest. I was breathing hard and every intake felt like a kick. I slowed my breathing, tried to keep it quiet. Tried to be the quietest thing in this vast cool cave.

Buckley said, "Maybe he hurt himself!"

"Jumping from the car, yeah," Hellman managed. He sounded out of breath. He was hurting, too.

"Prick doesn't have a gun. He's no threat."

"Roger, take a goddamn look at me. Hammer's *always* a threat."

"I say fuck him. I say we take a look. It's what we came for, isn't it?"

"Okay. Okay. But stay alert. That guy is batshit."

My breathing was slowing to normal. I hurt but I

wasn't in pain. Quietly, carefully, staying so low I was almost crawling, I moved out into the darkness.

I wanted a look myself.

In Xanadu did Kubla Khan, a stately pleasure-dome decree...

The Buick was parked at an angle and its headlights revealed a hole wider and taller than the one my backhoe had made, which had been just wide enough for Velda and me to enter side by side. This was a portal, a big ragged window onto the adjacent chamber where all those over-size cartons were stacked six high, making a fortress whose front wall was fifty feet wide while the massive rest of it yawned into the darkness like the Great Wall of China—eighty thousand cartons worth. That warehouse where they burned Charles Foster Kane's sled had nothing on this place. Smoke from the plastique explosion drifted like lazy fog, giving the bizarre tableau a haunting, unreal look.

I risked moving closer, and other aspects of the chamber presented themselves. There were piles of black pellets everywhere, on the floor, massed on top of the cartons, heaps of the stuff as high as a man's waist, elsewhere just scatterings. Hellman said I was batshit, but that's just an expression. This was the real thing, created over years and years of the grotesque flying vermin making a home out of this crypt of cash.

And off to one side were the discarded skeletons of butchered mob soldiers draped in shrouds of black bat droppings.

They were in there, Hellman and Buckley, their

flashlight beams stroking the cartons as if those cardboard vessels were the soft inner thigh of a beautiful woman. They had guns in hand, but their backs were to me. They had forgotten me. They didn't even notice the crap piles they were all but wallowing in. Maybe that was because they could see, on the nearest carton—where I'd slit it open last year to collect a modest fee for my trouble—fat stacks of green were waiting.

This one I heard coming.

He was moving quickly but quietly, and he was all in black, black sweatshirt and black jeans and black tennies, blending nicely in the darkness and staying low. The two men in the treasure chamber did not notice his approach, but I did. I moved quickly toward him and when he sensed me, he swung the .357 magnum my way and I held up my hand in *stop* fashion.

Marvin Dooley had never resembled his father particularly, other than his general build, but I would swear at that moment I saw my old buddy in the clenched features of his son. I had figured Marvin would follow us here, just as I knew Hellman would, thanks to the descriptions of them Rita Callaghan had shared with me.

I whispered, "I'm unarmed. Can you take them?"

He nodded. Moving low like a commando, like the soldier his father had been, utilizing the military training his own navy service had provided him, Marvin crept quickly, soundlessly, toward the portal torn in that wall of rocks.

I followed him, but kept a decent distance, and I did not go with him when he bolted up the mini-slope threshold of the treasure chamber and stopped there to say, "*Put the guns* down, *gentlemen!* Slow and easy and *down.* Don't turn around! Just *do* it."

Still paused at that first carton, Hellman and Buckley glanced over their shoulders stricken, then bent at the knees and deposited their weapons on the hard earthen floor.

"*Now* you can turn around," Marvin said. "Slowly."

The two respectable-looking men in the expensive suits turned and faced Marvin, disappointment and surprise commingled in their expressions, and rage was in there, too. The blood mask of Hellman's face had a streakier look now, but the whites of his eyes still made them pop crazily.

From the darkness I called out: "*Allow me to introduce Marvin Dooley! He's the son of the man who stored this money away.*"

Buckley said, "Hammer told me about you. You have a right to a share of this. We can talk."

Hellman was nodding.

Marvin stood on the hillock of stones at the entry, like he was about to plant the flag at Iwo Jima. "I have a right to *all* of it!"

His voice echoed in both halls, filled with indignation and frustration and so much more.

I called out again: "There's a case to be made for Marvin taking the whole magilla, fellas! After all, he killed his own father for it."

Marvin sort of hung there in midair for a moment. Then he looked over his shoulder at me and just smiled. No denials. But it was an awful goddamn smile. I almost couldn't hear him say quietly: "Took you long enough to figure it, didn't it, Hammer?"

Too long. Ugo Ponti had blustered to me that he had killed Marcus, but that had just been to twist the knife. I'd have known the truth from the start, if I hadn't been half-crazed by pain and sedatives last year, after almost dying on the waterfront.

There had been no sign of forced entry. The killer had unlocked the door with a key given to him by Marcus, or perhaps he just knew where Marcus kept it—under a mat or a flowerpot, maybe. Or was that door just unlocked because his son was dropping by? And the killer had stood in the doorway and fired his .357 as the seated Marcus had turned toward him. That was as close as the killer could bear to stand to Marcus Dooley.

They were father and son, after all. Which was why Dooley hadn't fingered his killer to Pat or me, blaming a shadowy figure in the doorway. And why he'd wanted me to take that urn of his ashes to his son. The urn with a clue to the whereabouts of the treasure. Even in death, the father had wanted to make it up to the son.

The billions were rightly his.

In a way.

"He promised you a windfall, didn't he, Marvin?" I called out. "But you waited and waited, year after year, and it never came. You didn't realize your old man had to wait out Don Ponti—nobody thought that old boy would survive deep into his eighties. You got understandably impatient. You figured your pop would have to *die* if you were ever to inherit whatever-it-was, and finally you struck preemptively. But then the shit hit the fan—I came around, Ugo Ponti and other hoods came calling, and the shooting started, and you backed away, forced into a waiting game again. Well, Marvin—the time has come. It's here. *There's* your windfall. All eighty-nine billion of it."

That froze him at the gateway to that fortune, but his eyes were still focused on the darkness from which my voice emanated. Then he turned his gaze on the treasure chamber, walking carefully down the piled stones into the big carton-filled cavern where he approached the two men already in there, skirting piles of rodent pellets to do it.

Hellman and Buckley spoke quietly with Marvin, all of them glancing my way, into the darkness. A new partnership was being formed. This became particularly apparent when Marvin allowed them to pick up their guns, and they stood together quietly discussing how exactly they would manage my removal. It was as if the blackness of the first cavern had become home to some bloodthirsty beast that required a hunting party to seek it out and slay it.

They weren't wrong.

Then she was at my side in the darkness, pressing my spare .45 into my right fist. She had a .38 in hers, crouching there in her olive commando jumpsuit, smiling at me, though I sensed that more than saw it.

I whispered, "Beautiful timing, kitten."

"Marvin led me here like you said he would," Velda whispered back.

"Go right. I'm heading straight in."

Then I was running, and my first thunderous shot caught Marvin in the left shoulder, thrusting him back into the nearest carton. The other two yelped with fright and surprise and ran with their handguns deeper into the chamber, cutting down a corridor between stacked cartons, throwing shots at me around the corner, gunfire echoing and booming above us as if promising a quenching rain that would never come.

They didn't concern me. I stayed low, knowing I didn't need to see them to take them out, just like I knew I didn't need to hit Marvin when he took cover behind a high pile of black pellets. I could shoot damn near anywhere and take all of them out, though whether it was my rain of .45s or Velda's shower of .38s that started the fire, I couldn't say.

But suddenly that first carton was wearing flames like a festive hat, leaping orange and blue, and sparks were spitting, and when the hill of guano he was hiding behind exploded, Marvin stood screaming, his whole body ablaze. He ran and danced and shook his arms and tumbled and tripped and landed in another pile of guano that exploded in a smoke puff like a genie might appear and ended his dance in a cracking, crackling percussive display. The other two came running out from the corridor between piled burning cartons, and they were on fire, too, screaming and shooting randomly, their shots coming nowhere near us.

I didn't waste any ammunition on them. They could die on their own steam in with the billions they coveted, cash and deeds and stocks and bonds that were going up in flames that spread row to row, swaying like the upraised arms of exotic dancing girls, sending billowing smoke upward to seek the exit the bats had used, foul-smelling smoke as dirty as the money that made it. One of the screaming flaming men fell and twitched and stopped screaming and died. Impossible to tell which. Not that I gave a damn. The other shot himself in the head and cut off his scream and went down on a scattering of droppings that popped like corn all around him.

The heat was incredible, the entire chamber an enormous furnace, the corpses on the floor flickering with orange and blue flames but already charred black, hints of green in those cartons turning dark and crispy, until one huge tongue of flame seemed to travel with a roar racing down the endless row of piled cartons, turning cavernous darkness into a hellish glowing thing whose teeth gnashed and ate and ripped and consumed.

The heat and light sent a pulsing glow through our adjacent chamber and we had no trouble seeing where we were going now. We left the Buick and the Mercedes to be devoured by the flames that had taken their owners. I spotted the wedding-gift gun and retrieved it on the way out. Nice piece of luck. We were coughing some as we exited into a dusk that was damn near night, and made our way to where Velda had left the Ford, half-way up the grassy slope.

Heading down the lane as we drove away, we saw black smoke climbing from a high crevice on the mountainside, as if the aftermath of an erupting volcano.

"So much for our cushy retirement," she said.

"You know me, baby," I said. "Money always did burn a hole in my pocket."

CHAPTER THIRTEEN

Any New Yorker who thought the Tombs was an underground catacomb of jail cells flunked history. Back in the first half of the nineteenth century, the original structure had been built on an Egyptian mausoleum motif that inspired the familiar grim nickname. The original structure and several others over the years had been torn down or remodeled, while the current version was two towers joined by the pedestrian walkway known as the Bridge of Sighs. The South Tower, where Rudy Olaf currently resided, was twelve stone-and-steel stories on the corner of White and Centre Streets on a plot of land no bigger than that of a suburban home.

Just two days after Velda and I returned from our upstate day trip, Assistant District Attorney Mandy Clark brought multiple charges against Rudolph Olaf, including conspiracy, attempted murder, and first-degree murder. Olaf had been arraigned, denied bail due to the extent and seriousness of the charges, and was currently in a one-man holding cell on the sixth floor of the Tombs, awaiting transfer to Riker's Island.

After going in under an art-deco archway dating back to the 1941 version of the building, I had to stand for a frisk, a sign telling me what the guard was looking for:

POSSESSION
OF
CONTRABAND
(WEAPONS)
RAZORS KNIVES SHANKS SHIVS
BULLETS
And any other weapon capable of causing
injury and/or
otherwise endangering the safety of the
institution
WILL RESULT IN YOUR IMMEDIATE
ARREST

I'd been through the drill before and had left my .45 at the office. Why go through the hassle of checking it? The guard said other prohibitions included chewing gum, electronic devices, camera, mirrors, aluminum foil, pencil sharpeners, glass, and mace. Though there was NO SMOKING IN THIS FACILITY, visitors were not being relieved of their cigarettes. A correctional officer walked me through several gated, guarded areas to the sixth-floor holding-cell area.

This was a rarity in the Tombs—an under populated mini-cell block, though it had the same stale locker-room smell of the full-size variety. Of these eight cells, only four were in use. Assistant D.A. Clark had arranged a brief visit for me, but not in a visitation area or an interrogation cell. I would just stand on my side of the bars and Olaf would stay on his. We did not inform him I was coming.

The six-by-seven cell was concrete block painted cream-color, which went swell with the cream-colored bars. Bars were on the narrow vertical window, too, with mesh beyond that—Rudy Olaf was one of the privileged prisoners with a view on the street. He also had a cot and a stainless steel crapper and not much else. A book was folded open on the cot—*Karpov on Karpov*—but it apparently hadn't held his attention.

The tall, nearly skeletal prisoner was pacing as best he could in the limited space, and his longish gray hair had an unkempt look. He looked even grayer than usual, in part because he had swapped Sing Sing green for Tombs orange. His arms hung loose and he was wiggling his fingers and there was a twitch in his shoulders.

I'd just planted myself at the bars when he turned in his pacing and the washed-out blue eyes, bloodshot now, flared. "*Hammer!* What the hell are *you* doing here?"

I glanced at the big black guard who'd delivered me and nodded. "I'll be all right, officer. Thank you."

He nodded back and returned in no hurry to his post, a desk at the end of the corridor.

I folded my arms and smiled affably. "I arranged for us to have a little talk, Rudy. Thought we should catch up. Compare notes."

He scowled. "Go *fuck* yourself, Hammer."

"Disappointing repartee from a literate fella such as yourself, former librarian and all."

He clutched a bar. His narrow oval of a face had been deeply lined before, but his grimace emphasized the grooves. "You wouldn't have a goddamn *smoke*, would you, Hammer?"

"I told you I don't smoke anymore."

He let go of the bar and walked to his window and back again, saying, "It's bullshit! What kind of jail doesn't let you *smoke*? How do they do *business* in this hellhole? The unfair thing, the unconstitutional travesty, is that they let the *guards* smoke. What the hell!"

"How many days without a smoke, Rudy?"

"...three."

I beamed at him. "You know when *I* quit, I just quit. Didn't have one tough day or night. But I hear it can be rough—headaches, constipation, nausea. You can feel tired as hell yet not be able to sleep. Anxiety can set in. Depression. They say it can be a rough damn ride, Rudy."

"You're a sadist."

I unfolded my arms. "Coming from you, that's saying something. Why don't we chat, just for a few moments? I can fill in some blanks for you, you can do the same for me."

Now both bony, vein-streaked hands clutched the bars, like in the old prison pictures. "Why should I talk to *you*?"

I shrugged. "Maybe I can get a carton of smokes smuggled in to you."

He swallowed thickly. He blinked his eyes repeatedly. Then he said, "You're an officer of the court, aren't you?"

"That's right. Goes with the P.I. ticket."

"So if I ask you if you're *wired*..."

"Rudy, I'm not wired. I'm in more of a laid-back mood."

"...if I ask you if you're wired *electronically*, smart-ass, you have to *say* so. Otherwise it's not admissible."

I waved that off. "I'm not wired for sound, Rudy. Lighten up. How about these new digs of yours? Have you checked it for bugs?"

That rip of a mouth in the gray face formed a sneer. "I've checked for bugs, all right. I've got more varieties of cockroach in here than Carter has pills. But no *eavesdropping* type bugs."

"Good." And I almost whispered now. "Because I need to share a few things with you. Since you've been inside, you haven't heard from your man Hellman, have you?"

That seemed to startle him almost as much as my showing up had. He frowned, and his eyes focused on me, tight. "*My* man?"

"Let's not waste time here, Rudy. They're giving me about five minutes. Frank Hellman was *your* man. He was setting things up so that when you got your hands on that eighty-nine billion, plus those deeds and stocks and all, you could buy your way in as the leader of the floundering Ponti family."

He tried for an innocent expression and it was pitiful. "What eighty-nine billion?"

"That's not how you get smokes for Christmas, Rudy." I grinned at him. "Marcus Dooley, the guy who hid the money for those aging capos, was an old army buddy of mine. But your pal Brogan was an old high school buddy of *his*—and so were you, Rudy. Chess club champs, the three of you. Wow, you must have been big men on campus in those days. Bet you got loads of tail."

"If you only have five minutes, Hammer, maybe you want to skip the comedy."

"Dooley got Brogan's help in moving that money, and promised him a cut when Don Ponti died, when that hoard would be all Dooley's. Likely they'd have to peddle it back to the mob or maybe to Uncle Sam, but that would mean a finder's fee of a billion or so. Couple of middle-aged guys could probably scrape by on that. Only they got old, waiting."

He said nothing, but his expression was foul.

I went on: "I'm guessing Brogan didn't tell you about this until his cancer came into the picture. How was a sick old man going to access that much money? And what the hell would he do with it, if he got it? So he came to you, Rudy, and the whole scheme came together in your grand chess master fashion. Dying as he was, all Brogan wanted from you was to cut his beloved grandkids in for his share. Of course, that's just not your way, is it, Rudy?"

He was frowning again, and the grooves were deep and plentiful. "What *about* Hellman, Hammer? Why haven't I seen or heard from him?"

I gave him half a smile. "Well, Rudy, I've got bad news and I've got bad news. Hellman was trying to double-cross you, scrambling to get that hoard of dough for himself in the small window of time that it would take you to get out of prison, settle up with the city, and set yourself up as a player in the Ponti power grab. Three days ago, Hellman and a crooked T-man he was partnered with were killed."

"*Killed?*"

I nodded. "Burned to death."

The washed-out blue eyes went wild. "How the hell did *that* happen?"

"Well, it was an offshoot of me setting those cartons of money on fire. All those billions of yours, Rudy, that new life you were planning? Nothing so shabby as king of Sing Sing, but as the head of the Ponti organization... what can I say? Burn, baby, burn."

He was shaking his head as if he weren't hearing right, and looked like he was having one of those nicotine nausea attacks. "Hammer... why the hell would you take such a destructive, insane, *idiotic* course of action?"

"Seemed like the thing to do at the time. You see, Hellman and his buddy were shooting at me and I was shooting back. The boxed-up dough was in a cave up in the Adirondacks, but you probably heard that rumor. Bats live in caves, you know. Thousands of them were living back there with all that money, sealed in for decades. Oh the bats could get in and out, but the money couldn't. Still, it made a nice comfy home for those critters. For years and years. So..."

The de facto head librarian of Sing Sing was a reader. A smart man, maybe a brilliant one. *He knew.* "My God," he said, his gray face turning even more ashen. "Sodium nitrate..."

"But why does it matter, Rudy? You're facing charges that will put you away for the rest of your life. What are a few little money woes at a time like this?"

The sneer formed again in that rip of a mouth, but it curled into a terrible smile. "I'm *not* worried. So a few old faggots came out of the woodwork to identify me. So a drug-addled gangbanger is making crazy accusations to get himself a plea bargain. Crimes from forty years ago? Tough to prove, Hammer. Conspiracy with Henry Brogan? He's dead, you fucking dope. And if maybe I do go back to Sing Sing for another stay? I'll be King Shit all over again. That place is probably *chaos* by now, without me around to run things."

"Wouldn't count on it, Rudy. A reporter pal of mine is doing the kind of investigative digging that snags Pulitzers. When this is over, you may be sharing a cell with old Warden Vlad the Impaler himself."

That made him momentarily blanch, but he forced a smile and said, "You're as naive as you are imbecilic, Hammer. Warden Ladd has friends in all the right high places. Politics trumps reform efforts every time."

"Maybe. My guess is, because of your history at Sing Sing? They'll send you somewhere else. We got dozens of slams in this state. Maybe you'll get Adirondack Correctional—that would be a sweet irony."

That thin upper lip curled back and the light blue eyes were hooded in disdain. "I doubt you know the *meaning* of the word 'irony.'"

"Don't count on it. Anyway, Rudy—you don't *really* want to get off on those charges, not *now*. Without the billions, and minus that settlement with the city… wouldn't you *want* to get back into the prison system?"

His chin went up and pride came into his tone. "If that's what it comes to… Wherever they might send me, I'd soon be in charge."

I grinned, shook my head. "The ol' King of the Weeds himself. Only now the King of the Weeds has the nicotine jim jams, 'cause he can't lay hands on a single damn weed. See, *that's* irony, Rudy."

His face seemed to freeze. "Cheap irony, maybe… Are we about over?"

"Just one more thing I'm curious about."

"Which is?"

My grin was long gone. "The cop fatalities, Rudy. Were any of them really accidents? Or did you arrange them all?"

Now the rip in his face turned up at both corners and amusement brightened up his expression. "What do *you* think, Hammer?"

"I think in a long and bloody and, as somebody said, storied career… I have never met up with anybody more evil than Rudolph Olaf. I think you were responsible for *every one* of those deaths, in part because you hate cops and what better prey could a serial killer want?"

He seemed genuinely offended by that. "Serial killer? Why, I've never killed *anyone*, Hammer."

"Not yourself. You just move the chess pieces. Everybody else is a pawn to you."

His eyebrows went up. "Not at all. There are rooks, bishops, knights…"

"Kings. Queens. Oh, I know *that* much about the game. You never killed any of those gay men, either— you had Brogan do them for you. What were the gay victims about, Rudy? Killing yourself by proxy? Is there some kind of twisted conscience in there somewhere that had you punish yourself through others? Or were the victims just the fish who happened to be in the Bowery waters you were swimming in at the time?" I batted the air. "What the hell's the difference? Who cares why? What matters is *you* did it. You arranged the Bowery slayings. Just like you arranged those cops to die… in part to cloud the eventual kill that was the one kill you *really* wanted to see go down—Captain Pat Chambers. The cop who caught you."

A smile flashed showing teeth almost as gray as his complexion. Gray like Danny Dixon's, the AIDS victim who'd been one of the King's Sing Sing subjects.

"Hammer, we're back to irony. Your friend was shot, all right, and by one of my charges… but he was *not* the intended target."

"Oh, I know that. *I* was the target. You hadn't got around to Pat yet… but you would have. You would have. He was the cop of all those cops who you *most* wanted to kill—the rest were for fun. Pat would be for revenge. *He made the arrest that sent you away.* But that night outside Pete's, *I* was your target… of course, I'd been your target before, hadn't I? *You* sicced that Corsican hitman on me."

He seemed amused. "And why would I do that? Simply because you were there when Chambers arrested me?"

I shook my head. "I was Pat's friend and potentially trouble. You planned to murder Pat, which meant I would come looking for the killer. You didn't need that grief, did you, Rudy? That was why the Corsican was set in motion."

Now he did not look so amused.

I went on: "So that night outside Pete's Chophouse, when Pat took the hit, *I* was the target again. You wanted me out of the game. Why? Because an evil son of a bitch like you knows when another evil son of a bitch is on to him."

He was projecting boredom, or anyway trying to. He seemed calmer now, as if the conversation with me had distracted him enough to momentarily forget about his nicotine pangs, and perhaps it had. His hands were on his hips and his chin was up and the washed-out blue eyes gazed at me patronizingly.

"We are done here," Olaf said. Then he raised an eyebrow. "But I'll expect that carton of cigarettes."

I shook my head. "Not going to happen."

He chuckled, sighed. "Hammer, Hammer... you're such an anthropoid. Such a Neanderthal throwback to simpler, more terrible times."

"I may be simple, but I promise you... I understand irony."

He pointed a bony finger, like a cruel parent banishing a ruined daughter. "Leave. Go. Get the fuck out. We have nothing more to discuss, and besides... I prefer my own company."

"Sure thing, Rudy. It's been real."

I gave him a nod, started off, and then after a few steps stopped short. Eyes on the floor, I knelt with a laugh. "Well hell, Rudy! It's your lucky day."

He leaned his gray face out between the bars as far as he could.

I stood and pointed down to the crumpled, almost empty pack of cigarettes on the floor near the toe of my shoe. One smoke stuck itself out barely, and a book of matches was tucked in the mostly crushed cellophane. "Will you just look what one of the guards must've dropped."

"*Give* it to me, Hammer."

"Why don't you work for it?"

I watched him get on his hands and knees and stretch his hand desperately out, his long skeleton's arm reaching, reaching, reaching, until his fingers found the crumpled pack and he pulled it back into the cell with him. He sat on the floor with the thing in his hands, like a prospector panning for gold who had just come up with one hell of a nugget.

"I'm happy for you, Rudy," I said. "But it's a little undignified, isn't it?"

"Go to hell, Hammer! Go to hell..."

I was back out on the street within two minutes, where Velda was waiting. We were planning to catch a bite in nearby Chinatown. After that, we would drive over to Bellevue and see how Pat was doing.

"Well?" she asked, as we started across to where the Ford was parked. "You boys have a good talk?"

I snugged up the collar of my freshly dry-cleaned trenchcoat. "Ol' Rudy copped to everything. And, baby, let me tell you—we've never been up against a nastier son of a bitch than the King of the Weeds."

We paused for traffic. She smiled at me wickedly. "Maybe. But *Olaf's* not the King of the Weeds, Mike."

"Oh? Then who is?"

"You are."

"Oh, so now I'm a weed?"

"What's wrong with that? A weed grows anyplace it wants to. It's tenacious as hell and stronger than everything around it. When everything else dies, it stays alive and keeps breathing. Almost impossible to kill, too."

"There I disagree. You *can* kill a weed. Even a king weed."

Across the street now, I stopped and turned to look over and up at the sixth-floor window where I could see the gray face gazing down on me, sneering in contempt and condescension. He blew out a cloud of smoke and held up a middle finger.

"Checkmate, asshole," I muttered.

Velda said, "What?"

Even at this distance, through the bars and mesh, I could see those washed-out eyes go suddenly dead, and then Rudy Olaf was gone from the window, slipping down out of sight. Bud Langston's trick cigarette had done its work.

End game.

Hugging my arm, Velda was giving me a questioning look.

I shrugged. "I told him that shit would kill him."

ABOUT THE AUTHORS

Mickey Spillane and **Max Allan Collins** collaborated on numerous projects, including twelve anthologies, three films and the *Mike Danger* comic book series.

Spillane was the bestselling American mystery writer of the twentieth century. He introduced Mike Hammer in *I, the Jury* (1947), which sold in the millions, as did the six tough mysteries that soon followed. The controversial P.I. has been the subject of a radio show, comic strip, and several television series (starring Darren McGavin in the 1950s and Stacy Keach in the 1980s and '90s). Numerous gritty movies have been made from Spillane novels, notably director Robert Aldrich's seminal film noir, *Kiss Me Deadly* (1955), and *The Girl Hunters* (1963), in which the writer played his famous hero.

Collins has earned an unprecedented twenty-one Private Eye Writers of America "Shamus" nominations, winning for *True Detective* (1983) and *Stolen Away* (1993) in his Nathan Heller series, which includes the recent *Ask Not*. His graphic novel *Road to Perdition* is the basis of the Academy Award-winning film. As a filmmaker in the Midwest, he has had half a dozen feature screenplays produced, including *The Last Lullaby* (2008), based on his innovative Quarry series. His documentary *Mike Hammer's Mickey Spillane* (1999) appears on the Criterion Collection edition of the film *Kiss Me Deadly*. As "Barbara Allan," he and his wife Barbara write the "Trash 'n' Treasures" mystery series (recently *Antiques Swap*).

Both Spillane (who died in 2006) and Collins received the Private Eye Writers life achievement award, The Eye.

LADY, GO DIE!

MICKEY SPILLANE & MAX ALLAN COLLINS

THE SEQUEL TO *I, THE JURY*

Hammer and Velda go on vacation to a small beach town on Long Island after wrapping up the Williams case (*I, the Jury*). Walking romantically along the boardwalk, they witness a brutal beating at the hands of some vicious local cops—Hammer wades in to defend the victim.

When a woman turns up naked—and dead—astride the statue of a horse in the small-town city park, how she wound up this unlikely Lady Godiva is just one of the mysteries Hammer feels compelled to solve…

"Collins knows the pistol-packing PI inside and out, and Hammer's vigilante rage (and gruff way with the ladies) reads authentically." *Booklist*

"A fun read that rings true to the way the character was originally written by Spillane." *Crimespree Magazine*

ALSO AVAILABLE FROM TITAN BOOKS

HARD CASE CRIME THRILLERS

FROM MICKEY SPILLANE & MAX ALLAN COLLINS

THE CONSUMMATA
DEAD STREET

FROM MAX ALLAN COLLINS

TWO FOR THE MONEY
DEADLY BELOVED
SEDUCTION OF THE INNOCENT
THE LAST QUARRY
THE FIRST QUARRY
QUARRY IN THE MIDDLE
QUARRY'S EX
THE WRONG QUARRY
QUARRY'S CHOICE

TITANBOOKS.COM